# ALL
# THE
# LITTLE
# THINGS

## SARAH LAWTON

**CANELO**

First published in the United Kingdom in 2021 by

Canelo
31 Helen Road
Oxford OX2 0DF
United Kingdom

A CIP catalogue record for this book is available from the British Library.

Print ISBN 978 1 80032 299 8
Ebook ISBN 978 1 80032 168 7

Look for more great books at www.canelo.co

Printed and bound in Great Britain by Clays Ltd, Elcograf S.p.A.

*For Josie, always my first reader.*

# Prologue

I watched my daughter die.

The days leading up to her death are seared into my memory like one of those old clicking reels of film, snapshot images flickering behind my eyelids. There, Vivian, looking up at me. There, Alex, wild-eyed and frantic.

I'd made the mistake of trusting the wrong person, again.

Never trust anyone.

Never trust yourself.

# Rachel

On the night I first saw Alex the air was so hot it was almost fetid. It choked my throat and groped at me with damp fingers, slipping under my hair and arms, wrapping my legs, making my skin prickle and itch. I was late for my class.

By the time I got to the village hall most of my sign-ups had arrived: the usual suspects, a motley bunch, probably just there for the company and free biscuits. Geoff was already present, resplendent in his greying towelling robe. He always liked to strut around whipping up his crowd of admirers. Not that there was much to admire exactly, except perhaps his bravado.

He clambered onto the stage and dropped his robe with a flourish, lying back on the chaise. I noticed he had a new varicose vein on his leg, a violent burst of bulbous purple, hot against the milky white of his skin. I filed the observation away for later; the contrast of colour, for use in a painting, maybe. I did not care to look further up to where he was arranging himself to his liking.

A new name had appeared on the list I had pinned up on the village noticeboard in the hall for that week's class. Alex. I had entertained the thought that he might be a woman, as most of my class were female, but something about the firm and determined cursive told me the hand was male. Whoever it was, they were late, and would have to take the last easel, which was directly in the line of sight of Geoff's now spreadeagled legs.

The room settled into a hive of subdued activity. Drinks made, biscuits crunched, gossip caught up on. The hissing sound of scratching charcoal moving across parchment. I made my first round, saying nothing, merely observing how shapes were being pulled together, the creamy paper taking the gift of shade, throwing light against dark. I will never tire of watching people create.

Mrs Baxter had positioned herself away from Geoff's business end and was sketching the great bulk of his shoulders, shading the gingery hair that covered them with sharp strokes, making them bristle in a porcine manner. Poor Geoff was an easy target for her tendency to veer into caricature. She caught my attention and nodded towards the other end of the hall. 'Not what that one expected, I'll bet.' Following her gaze, I saw that the last easel had been occupied by a teenage boy who had slipped in while I wasn't watching. 'Do you think he was hoping for some nubile young goddess, throwing her clothes off with abandon?'

'Probably,' I answered with a grin, trying not to laugh. 'It wouldn't be the first time, would it?' I usually asked sniggering young people to leave, but there was a gravitas about him that gave me pause.

He seemed to be made entirely of angles, sharp and new. His shoulders looked as though they were broadening in front of me, a child-man. Dark slashes of eyebrows were heavy over startling eyes that glinted like sea glass. I knew they must be extraordinary if even a hint of their colour shocked me from the small distance between us. His hand skimmed back and forth on the paper with a deftness that spoke of talent. He had a precision and stillness about him that should not belong to the young.

His eyes flicked between Geoff and the sketch in front of him, and there was no embarrassment on his face. I imagined I could hear somehow the particular sound that the heel of his hand was making as it scuffed the paper above all the others in the room, and I thought that it might smudge his drawing and bother him, this boy who moved so succinctly.

As I moved closer I could see that his face was rescued from its hard lines by his mouth, which was full, although he pressed it flat now and then with concentration. Suddenly, the very tip of his tongue peeked through, and then sharp white teeth bit down on the edge of his lip. I didn't like the feeling that the flash of pink and those white teeth produced in me. There was something disconcerting about him. He reminded me of someone. It put me on edge so I turned away to talk to Mrs Hayward, who was struggling with perspective, as usual.

At the end of the class the dark-haired boy left as silently as he arrived. I readied the easels for the caretaker to store when he came in to lock up. No one worried that something might be stolen: a somewhat complacent mentality in a village where nothing bad ever happened.

The last easel was Alex's. He'd left his sketch. It was exceptional. Clever strokes had built up from feather-light shimmers to a crushing, nearly tearing force, giving Geoff an almost majestic appearance. He could have been Zeus, reigning from Olympus, strong limbed and fierce of face. And yet, here was Geoff, in his essence. Portly, no shame, jolly. How had he done this? I could never have captured him like this, not in an hour. Not ever, perhaps.

This boy was special.

I took the sketch and rolled it up carefully. Closing the door to the hall behind me, it was a thirty-second walk to the Goose and Lavender. As ever, Steve, the landlord, saw me come in and pointed to the table by the door, joining me there with a bottle of wine in an ice bucket, and two glasses. The night was still warm, and the windows were all open. The breeze brought in a smell of warm asphalt and cut grass from the verge; Bill had been out with his strimmer, tidying up the green.

He sat down with a huff and squeezed around to settle opposite me. He poured us each a large glass of straw-coloured liquid, condensation forming almost immediately on the sides.

'Thanks.'

We lifted our glasses to clink. 'Cheers.'

'Look at this,' I said to him, as he sipped his drink. 'An odd boy came into my class tonight. He's really talented.' I smoothed out the paper between us and he turned it around to face him, studying it for a long moment.

'Wow.' He traced the long line of a leg with a careful fingertip. 'Who knew I could almost bring myself to fancy Geoff?'

'Don't be mean!' I laughed.

'God, it's so unfair!' said Steve, as I pointed out some of the techniques he had used that were quite remarkable for someone his age. 'Why can't I draw like this? I never made it past stick men, or dogs with ten legs.'

'Maybe you should actually come to one of my classes, then,' I replied with a laugh, loosening up the further we got down the bottle, tensions of the day melting away.

'How old do you think he is?' asked Steve, leaning back in his chair and rolling his head, making his neck click revoltingly.

'Who, Geoff? Ancient.'

'Ha ha. No, not Geoff – your new mystery boy.'

'Oh, I don't know, it's hard to tell sometimes. He's probably a couple of years older than Vivian. Eighteen, maybe? Nineteen?'

'Old enough then!'

'Old enough for what?'

'You know. There's not a lot of choice in the village.' He winked slyly as he said it, a slow droop of one eyelid over a hazel eye.

'Urgh, Steve! I'm old enough to be his mother!'

'Who says I'm talking about you?' He leaned back and creased up with laughter. It echoed in the confines of the pub, and several people looked over and grinned themselves.

'Can we get another bottle?' I asked impulsively, still feeling a residue of the disquiet that Alex and his drawing had provoked in me. 'If you don't have to go on the bar? We haven't had a proper catch-up for ages.'

'Are you sure?' Steve replied, with a grin. 'Don't need to get back and make sure Vivian hasn't burnt the house down?' He was teasing me, but we both knew how long it had taken me to let Vivian stay at home alone or go out with friends in the evenings. It had mainly been Steve's persuasions that convinced me, but I still worried. She was getting to the age where 'sleepovers' were code for sitting in the park and drinking beer that they had purloined from their parents' stashes. Steve didn't have, or want, any children, but he was always interested in what my girl was up to.

It was strange, the friendship I had built with him. I generally kept people at arm's length, only had acquaintances locally, but I had found myself drawn to going into the bar when Vivian had started to spend more time with her friends, wanting to feel part of a crowd when the loneliness bit. Somehow, he had picked up on it, and we had become almost close.

We took the second bottle out into the garden, which had quietened down now that people had wandered off to get their dinners. I could feel the alcohol warming my stomach and giving me a buzz of well-being that was veering toward being outright pissed.

It was late, almost ten, although the sky was still light by the time I left. I hugged Steve at the door of the pub, thinking I shouldn't have stayed out so late. I was glad of the short walk home, my head spinning slightly. I got to the stile and pulled myself over it, muscle memory making it a smooth movement despite being tipsy. I cut across the field, breathing deeply. The air had cooled finally and smelt faintly of turned soil and honeysuckle from the hedgerow. I felt so lucky, relieved, to have found this life for us, in this safe place. Listening out for small creatures rustling in the long grass and keeping an eye out for the barn owl that roosted in the cowshed at the end of the field, I made my way across, resisting somehow the temptation to lie down and stare at the stars that were popping out against the velvet of the darkening sky.

Our cottage stood alone at the end of the path that cut through the field. It had belonged to a local farmer and he had sold it to me for a pittance. Maybe he could see I was as much a wreck as the house was, but I fixed us both up. It wasn't the first time I'd had to rebuild myself, but I felt I got shakier each time, lacking foundations.

I almost tripped walking up the path – I never did fix that stone – and I put my hands flat on the door of our home. The blue paint was smooth and still warm from the sun. I rested my forehead against it briefly, truly regretting suggesting the second bottle of wine. My stomach roiled and dipped, and I felt guilty again for staying out so late when I should have come home to check on Vivian.

I managed to get my key in the door without too much difficulty, though I knew that the marks of previously erratic attempts after nights out with Steve were there to see in the daylight. I pushed open the door to halfway – any further would make it creak loudly – and slipped round. The house was silent, and I assumed that my girl was already asleep. I stepped out of my sandals and padded through to the kitchen, trailing my fingers on the wall for balance.

As I'd expected, the detritus of Vi's dinner was scattered across the kitchen. The bread was open, a dirty plate abandoned by the sink. I spotted a tin of beans by the cooker and picked it up. She hadn't eaten them all and I decided that I would, cold, with a spoon. The savoury-sweet taste reminded me that the last time I had done this was as a first year art student, getting back to my room at dawn, heavy lidded and ravenous after a night of drinking, smoking, laughing. The flavour curdled on my tongue, saccharine, and I tore off a chunk of bread to clean it away, then twisted the packet closed and put it back in its place.

Feeling a little better for the carbs I crept up the stairs as quietly as I could, and paused outside Vivian's room. I couldn't hear anything and no light shone around the door which, as always, was ajar. I pushed it open and carefully poked my head in. She was lying on the bed with her arms raised above her head, a ballerina pose that made her collarbones look delicate and finely drawn, shadows like spilt ink across her body. She was tiny, bird-like, and her hair shone on the pillow like silk in the moonlight. I slipped into the room to tuck her in – even though she was fifteen, I still wanted to do that, keep her safe, always – and I dropped a light kiss on her forehead, promising her silently that I would spend some quality time with her over the weekend to make up for missing her tonight.

She was the most beautiful thing I ever made.

# Vivian

When I hear the door close I open my eyes and wipe away the kiss.

Mum is so weird. I hardly need tucking in when I'm nearly sixteen, and it's boiling. At least she didn't wake me up this time, all drunk and miserable and wanting to talk about the hospital and remembering to express our feelings, thinking I didn't realise that her hands smoothing along my arms were looking for razor slices. Like I'd ever do that to myself. She's the one with scars she won't tell me about.

My phone buzzes from under the pillow. It's Molly. She's wittering on about this new boy she's seen at the six-form college that's attached to our school, and how hot he is. I suppose he's okay-looking. I can't say I'm particularly interested. She wants to know if I think he would like her. Who doesn't like Molly? She could have anyone she wanted. Sounds like he's going to be getting some random messages from her anyway: she's managed to weasel his number off someone or other.

I lie awake for a while and listen to Mum stumbling around before collapsing into her creaky old bed. Then it all goes quiet, but I keep listening. Everyone says the countryside is so quiet compared to cities, especially to London, and I thought that too when we first moved here, but I wasn't right. The countryside night is full of all sorts of interesting sounds, my favourite being the owl who hunts the mice who rustle in our garden. I wonder what mice taste like. I don't hear him tonight. Instead I fall into dreams, red hands and white rooms, and I wake up late.

'Mum!' I yell, when I realise that it's already gone eight o'clock. 'Mum! You need to give me a lift!' I rush into the bathroom and jump in the shower.

'Mum!' I shout again on the way back into my room to dry my hair and get my uniform on. 'Mum, are you dead?'

'No,' comes a muffled voice. 'But I might be soon.'

She's obviously hungover after her boozeathon. Probably shouldn't drive me, now I think about it – I don't particularly want to die today.

'Okay, don't worry about the lift… I'll call Tilly and get her brother to swing by and pick me up!'

Tilly is lazy and pays her brother to take her to school from the money she gets doing shifts at her dad's chippy in the village. I wouldn't usually ask because her brother is creepy and stares at me in the car mirror, like he wants to lick me. He makes me feel sick. I'd rather walk, but I hate being late.

I quickly get my uniform on and stuff my homework in my rucksack. I haven't got time to make any lunch so I shout to Mum that I'm taking a fiver from the pot and I hear a muffled 'bleurgh' in reply, which is either a yes or a yakking up; either way, it's in my pocket as I hear Tristan's old banger pull up outside. I open the door before he beeps and run and jump in, pulling my skirt down so he can't ogle my legs. His piggy eyes watch me in the mirror all the way to school.

Tris drops me and Tilly off on his way to work and we stroll in chatting, eyes out for who is around. It's nearly time for registration and we're making our way to our classroom when Tilly nudges me and whispers, 'Look, .there's Newboy.'

Sure enough there he is, waiting outside the entrance to his part of the building, staring at his phone. He's doing a good job of being mysterious – he looks a bit like an eternally teenaged vampire from one of the young adult books my mum does the covers for, with thick black hair and cheekbones that Tilly would die for. His eyelashes are so long they cast a shadow.

'Don't stare!' I tell her, even though I am the one doing that. 'Molly will go mad, she's already bagsied him.'

Molly is the prettiest one in our group, which puts her in charge. Her hair is thick and sunny coloured, and nearly down to her arse. Boys all go mad over it, because they are disgusting, and she's always flicking it or pulling at it, or chewing on a bit, which is so gross, or twisting it around her fingers while she peeps up at them through it. Everyone loves her. She always makes an effort to be nice. I always thought to be popular you had to be cruel. Why would people want to be your friend if they weren't afraid of what you would do to them otherwise?

We've been best friends since I moved here and she took me under her wing. She wasn't so pretty then, but she is now, which suits me because being friends with the most popular girl in school means that I am too, by default, without having to put up with all the bullshit, which is good. I don't have time to deal with more idiots than I already do.

'Speaking of Molly...' Tilly points her out as she walks in. She's also spotted Newboy and she's doing her thing, walking slowly past him shaking her mane as she does, but he doesn't pay her any attention at all, much to Molly's disgust, as she walks over.

'He'll notice soon enough,' she says, supremely confident in her ability to snare any boys in the vicinity. We fall about laughing.

'Maybe he doesn't go for year ten girls, like us,' I tell her, with a comforting pat to her shoulder. 'I wonder why he's started at the sixth-form college at the end of the year.'

'Because he's a creepy old freak?' suggests Serena, who has also sauntered in half-late, uncaring as always. 'My sister says he's a right weirdo who just sits at the back of the class and stares at everyone. Apparently he lives on his own in some scuzzy bedsit miles away. He's here for some random mature-student course one of those crusty tutors in there offers, because he missed his A levels. He's nearly nineteen already.'

'I wish I lived on my own,' I say, wondering how Serena always seems to know so much about everyone. 'And anyway, I'm sure he'll warm up once Molly gets her hands on him!'

'I'm not going to some scuzzy bedsit, though,' she replies, running her hands through her long hair before picking up her bag. 'I don't want fleas.' This inspires more hysterical giggling and we walk into our class, arm in arm, a unit.

–

It takes me a long time to forget about Newboy and his disconcerting vampire-like eyelashes as we settle in to the day. We've got science to start with and, interestingly for once, we're getting to watch a dissection. The lab tech has brought in a shallow dish covered with a blue paper towel. A couple of the girls refuse to watch.

Chloe sneers at our teacher. 'I'm a *vegan*, sir.'

'I'm not asking you to eat it, Chloe,' he quips back, quick as always. 'Just understand how its systems fit together. No one has to stay who doesn't want to watch – that's absolutely fine. You can sit in the corridor and read chapter seventeen of your textbooks quietly.'

Chloe flounces out with Becky, who is unable to do anything independently, reliant as she is on the other girl for any sort of social life.

Mr Forsyth whips off the blue paper with a flourish. There is a fat rat in the dish, splayed out, crucified. Its fur is stained yellow with what I think is formaldehyde, and it doesn't look like it's ever been alive. Matthew Grey takes one look at it and walks out of the classroom, grabbing a textbook as he goes.

'Anyone else want to leave?' asks Mr F, picking up a delightfully shiny scalpel. Molly and I are sitting directly in front of the operation but we can handle it. Scientific minds. He uses the scalpel to make a bloodless slit in the rat's stomach and then picks up what looks like a pair of miniature scissors on long handles and uses them to cut through the small creature's rib cage with a crunchy little *snick* sound that makes me shiver. Another one of the boys walks out looking a bit pale, but Molly and I are fascinated, leaning forward and watching intently as the rat's skin and muscle is peeled away and its tiny bones bent back, revealing the lungs, liver, kidneys, stomach. It's all so small. It's all so dead. I'm aware of the buzzing bluebottle voice of Mr Forsyth as he talks through the pieces he's exposing with deft thrusts of the scalpel, but all I see are the colours of the rat's insides, like bruises but shiny and slippery. My skin feels tight. I think that I can smell the guts, meaty and thick. Raw.

'Would you like to see the eye socket?' he says suddenly, and before anyone can answer he slides the scalpel into the rat's cheek and twists it. The perfectly round casing of the rat's eyeball pops right out of its head and, next to me, Molly vomits.

—

'I can't believe I threw up,' Molly says, as she makes me hold her mass of hair back so she can rinse her mouth in the bathroom. It feels heavy and hot in my hands, almost alive. I don't know how she can bear it all over her in this weather. It's revolting.

'Have you got any chewing gum, Vivi?'

I let go of her hair with relief and scrabble around in my bag and find that I do have some – a scuffed and folded packet with one left in the bottom, the foil twisted and soft like the skin on an old lady's fingers.

'It might have gone off a bit,' I say apologetically as I hand it over, but I doubt Molly cares beyond getting the taste of sick out of her mouth.

'I can't believe he just sat there and did that,' she moans, resting her head against the cool mirror and staring into her own blue eyes. 'Its eye socket just popped out. It looked like one of those chocolate bits you get in a corner yogurt.'

Now I feel sick, too.

Molly recovers quickly enough and is more embarrassed than anything – it goes around our small school in a matter of minutes, passed gleefully from mouth to ear with a giggle and a 'No way!' People veer away from her good-naturedly and call her 'vom breath', but she is too well-liked for it to last for long and she takes it well, brushing it off and shrieking with laughter when people run up behind her squeaking like rodents. It's probably only the lab tech who had to clean up after Molly, as well as incinerate the cut-up rat, who is bothered. I briefly picture it burning, its little body curling and twisting and going black and grey and white, crumbling to ash and nothing.

The bell rings and we all bustle out of our chairs, buzzing with anticipation as we grab our bags and push our way through to the corridor, and then outside. I wait for the girls at our usual spot under the oak that spreads itself into the sky at the boundary of where our school field meets common ground, and a copse.

I'm always first on a Friday afternoon because Molly and Serena and Tilly all have pretentious drama, which is on the other side of the school from the art rooms. Their teacher is a failed actress turned teacher who faffs around and usually keeps the class over time because she wants them to watch her perform something they are supposed to be learning, so they are always late out. I don't mind, though; it's good to have a moment to unwind and the sounds of everyone leaving are already fading away as I lie back against the knotty trunk of the tree and close my eyes.

I'm almost dozing off when I hear a scraping noise above me and I open my eyes and look up into the tree to see that there is a boy – Newboy, actually – sitting in the bloody tree and just staring at me. I don't move; I look back, challenging him to speak first. He doesn't, he just laughs and then I'm cross, temper suddenly bubbling up in me, which makes me even more angry because I don't *like* to get angry; it doesn't agree with me.

'Pervert!' I shout up at him. 'Do you get off staring at girls when they don't know you're there? Why are you up there anyway, you weirdo? Aren't you a bit too old to be climbing trees?'

He lets his weight pull him out of the tree, leaning forward and falling feet first, landing so quietly that I briefly wonder if he is even real. He sits down next to me.

'I was there first,' he tells me, in an annoyingly sexy voice. 'I wasn't staring at you the whole time; anyway, I didn't realise you were even there until you started snoring.'

'I was not snoring!'

'Are those your friends?' he says, nodding in the direction of the school.

'Yes,' I reply, turning to look at them walking towards us through the warm hazy air. Molly is wearing her long socks pulled up over her knees, her skirt shorter now she's out of school and can hike it up without being told off. She looks curvy and touchable, and I'm suddenly bitter-jealous and all awkward elbows and scrawny hips.

Newboy is silent for a moment and then says: 'Right, I'm off. Nice to meet you…?' The word hangs in the air between us, it's a question for me to take.

'Vivian,' I say, willing myself not to blush like a twelve-year-old.

He doesn't repeat it back to me incredulously or laugh, like most people do at my stupid granny name. He looks pleased with himself instead, and for a heartbeat I get the impression that he's keeping it in his mouth and tasting it somehow, and I feel a bit light-headed, but then he grins at me, teeth flashing white.

'I'm Alex.' He looks at me for a long moment, searching my face like he's waiting for a reaction, but when I don't give him one he smiles again and pushes himself off the ground in one fluid movement, and he's gone.

Time seems to have slowed down while we were talking; I feel as if I were caught up in it, thick and hot, melting like tar, and I have to shake my head as the girls come up to me, to clear it. For a moment I think I see a dark look on Molly's perfect face but it's gone so quickly I must have imagined it. She's got no reason to be jealous of me, anyway. I put my hands out to her and she grabs them and pulls me to my feet. I make sure I don't wipe my hands off straight afterwards, even though hers were damp and horrid. I wait until she's not looking.

'What was that about?' she asks, casually. 'Were you getting chatted up by Newboy?' I can hear the undertone to her question. *You? Mousy, skinny, flat-chested Vivian – you, attracting the interest of someone that good-looking?*

'Of course not,' I say, pretending to laugh off the insult I feel – I know I'm not as pretty as her, she doesn't need to rub it in. 'He wanted to know what your name was.'

'He already knows my name,' she says, sharply. 'I told Ben to tell him when he got his number for me. I told you I was going to text him last night.'

'Maybe he wasn't sure which one you were,' I say, back-pedalling. 'You guys do all look a bit similar from a distance.'

It's true, they do all look the same at first. All of them are blonde, though Molly is the only one who doesn't need help from a packet at the chemist, and all of them dress in the same way, with anything that shows off their long and lean legs and tanned arms. They are all taller than me: I seemed to stop growing at a tiny 5'2" while they soared, stretching away from me, leaving me behind in the dirt.

Molly links my arm with hers as we begin to walk away from school. 'What are we doing tonight, then?' she says, our routine slotting back into place after the intrusion of Alex. I haven't shared his name, I realise, as we take the path through the trees; I'm not sure if they know it or just prefer to call him Newboy, but I decide to keep it to myself, anyway. Like it's mine, and a part of him belongs to me now.

The air feels cooler as we walk through the woods, gossiping about the day and what we are planning on doing later. Serena's sister turned eighteen last month and will buy us cider if we want it, and we do of course but we need somewhere to drink it and are discussing options when Molly tells us that her parents are going to be away for the night, reviewing some hotel in Devon, and we jump on it immediately.

'You kept that quiet!' squeals Serena. 'I'll definitely have to get Sasha to get us some booze! Party time!'

'I didn't know until they literally just texted me,' says Molly, looking pissed off. 'They always do this – they just fuck off whenever they feel like it and leave me on my own. I'm only fifteen. I could get raped and murdered or anything and they probably wouldn't even notice until my corpse started to go off and stink up their perfect house.'

We laugh at this, but it does have a ring of truth about it. Poor neglected Molly-wolly, all alone. I would give my right leg to be left alone by my mother.

'You always stay at mine when they go away,' I tell her, squeezing her arm against me, even though I don't like the feel of it; like it's just a lump of hot meat, thrumming arteries. 'I'm sure your mum called mine all ready and checked. Maybe we can hang out at yours and go back to mine later.'

'Well, we definitely have to have a party if your house is free,' says Serena, stubbornly. 'I have V plates I need to get rid of!'

'Serena!' Tilly shouts, before screaming with laughter. 'Why are you always so obsessed with sex?'

Probably because it's all we talk about. Chloe-the-vegan has been bragging for weeks about what she's been doing with her boyfriend Dan, even though she's only fifteen like the rest of us. I'm not sure if I believe her or not, but I'm not interested in going there just yet, even if anyone was interested in me. I can't ever stop thinking of the videos we all watched on Molly's laptop once, of the gross men and the women all shaved and slick and sweaty, screaming and grunting. Massive, thick cocks thrusting into them, every bit of them, while they whined and choked and got jizz in their eyes and all over their hair. It looked *awful*. I felt sick afterwards. I know all the stupid feminists say sex is nothing like porn, that it's nothing like that in real life, but that just makes me wonder, what *is* it like? Why would anyone want to do anything at all like that? It looks disgusting.

'Well, I'll have to wait for Mr Right,' says Tilly, in a huff. 'I have to work at the shop tonight because Mum and Dad are going to the Lav for their anniversary, and Tris doesn't have to do shifts now he's got the job at the chicken factory.'

We laugh at her calling the pub the Lav like we always do, and then ask her what Tristan is doing in the factory. Last week he was on one of the assembly lines shoving dead, plucked chickens onto silver trays and into plastic bags ready to go to supermarkets. He has to wear a hair net over his horrible greasy hair and we take the piss constantly when we see him.

'He has to stuff them!' she yells, forgetting her mood. 'He got moved off the packing line because someone got sacked for filming themselves drop-kicking the chickens and he's been promoted to shoving stuffing up their arses!'

We all have to stop and find trees to lean on because we are laughing so much.

'Stop!' gasps Serena, 'I'm going to wee myself!' But this just makes it worse and we are crying now and I can feel my ribs creaking because I cannot stop thinking of Tristan in his hair net sticking fistfuls of stuffing up naked chickens all day long.

Eventually we calm down but we nearly lose it again when Serena cruelly points out that it's probably the closest he's ever going to get to fingering something female, and I can feel trails of tears sticky on my face, which reminds me briefly of those horrid videos again and I stop laughing. We are at my house now anyway; the rest of the girls live over past the pub, so I say goodbye and tell them I will text them later about going to Molly's. I am already wondering what to wear.

Mum isn't in the house when I get in and call but that's not surprising. She told me she had a deadline today so she's probably in the garden studio working, and I sauntered past without noticing. I run upstairs to my room and look out of the window. I can see her at her desk, see the blur of her arm skimming across whatever it is she is working on.

I take off my uniform so I can put it in the wash basket and then I flop on the bed in just my bra and pants. It's so hot. I will need a shower or seven before I go to Molly's.

I get my phone out of my bag and see I already have forty-seven notifications from our group chat, even though I've only been home for ten minutes. I scan them quickly. Nothing particularly interesting. Serena wants Molly to invite Matthew Grey because she fancies him. Molly has decided she doesn't fancy Alex any more and that he's a weirdo but she might get Ben to invite him anyway. They are all just twittering about what to wear and ugh, sometimes it's just so boring trying to be a normal person.

I throw the phone down on my bed and stand up to look in my wardrobe, hoping vainly that something that will make me look awesome will have appeared in it. There hasn't, of course. I open the wardrobe door wide so I can look in the mirror on the inside of the door and critique myself for a bit. I realise that looking like an average person can be useful, but I think there might be even more benefits to being really attractive, like Molly. She could get anything or anyone she wanted, just with a look. That's power.

The wardrobe door shuts with a creak, my reflection banished, and I pull on a vest top and shorts from the drawers before going out to the garden to find Mum. I creep up on her quietly because it's funny making her jump.

'Hi, Vi,' she says, before I can even poke her.

'How did you know I was here?'

'The birds stopped singing,' she replies, freaking me out, 'and I saw your reflection in the glass.' She laughs. 'What do you think of these ones?' She puts her arm around my shoulders and I lean in for a second because I know she likes it and I need to keep her sweet, before wriggling away and looking through her pictures.

'Ooh, moody,' I say of a boy with bird wings sulking on a beach, ignoring the small poke of jealousy at how amazing she is at drawing. 'What's the book like?'

'I don't think you'd enjoy it,' she says, with a light laugh. 'You'd have to use your imagination – it's about love and fairies and magic.'

'Ugh!'

'You can give it a try, if you like. Though no blabbing about it online – it's not being published until next year.'

As if I would admit to reading online. I can't stand those sorts of books. I don't really like fiction at all: what's the point? Better to learn proper facts about things that might come in useful, like how to fix the car for when we break down *again* on the way to bloody Dorset, or anything but fairies. I'm going to have a swing in the hammock instead, try and get some colour on me for once.

–

I end up falling asleep in the hammock because it's so warm and I'm having a really weird dream about Newboy – we're in London for some reason – when Mum wakes me up on her way to make dinner.

'C'mon, sleepy,' she says, with a laugh. 'I assume you're all off out later to terrorise the wildlife?'

'Ha ha,' I reply, rubbing my eyes, feeling little balls of sweat and dirt pile up under my fingertips because it's so hot. 'We're going to go to Molly's and sit in her garden, but I need a shower first, yuck.'

I follow her down the paved path and into the house, where it is much cooler and breathing is distinctly easier. After I've had a quick shower and got changed into my skinny-jean shorts and a vest top I run downstairs and sit at the scruffy old kitchen table and watch Mum getting out bowls and chopping boards. I hurry her up mentally because if I say it out loud, she will be annoying and even slower on purpose.

'I thought a salad might be nice tonight.' She leans into the fridge. 'I can use this chicken up.'

I briefly think of Tristan fondling chickens and bite my lip. I hope it's not one of his. I don't think I'd like to eat a chicken that he had been fingering. She gets some jars out of the cupboard and whisks up a dressing with oil and mustard and vinegar, which has a sharp smell that I can feel in my nose.

'Sounds good. It's too hot for cooking.'

I eat quickly and I deliberately have an extra piece of bread because I want to line my stomach. Tilly spent all last Friday night with her head down the toilet after drinking on an empty stomach and I don't want that to be me. I can't not be in control of myself, but I don't want to be the weird non-drinker when everyone else does it.

'Abigail called me,' Mum says. 'I want you and Molly back here for twelve, please, and make sure you lock up properly. You aren't having a party, are you?'

'No, of course not,' I lie. 'Molly's garden is just the best because it's got all the furniture and stuff.'

'Mm. Well, best you don't — I doubt Abi and Gavin would be very pleased to get back to a trashed house.'

'As if we would.'

'Are there any boys going?'

'Mum!'

'Vivian, I mean it. You know we have to talk about these things, don't you? You know we agreed, when we moved here? You have to tell me what's going on with you.'

'Yes, Mother,' I sigh. 'And no, no stupid boys. Just us.'
She's so easy to lie to. Six years she's been banging on
about this; you'd think she'd have got bored of it but, alas,
no. 'Right, better be off – see you in the morning, don't
wait up!' I tell her this, even though I know that she will.
I steel myself to drop her a quick kiss on the cheek and
then I'm out of the door and running across the field, free.

# Rachel

Vivian bolted down her dinner and I wondered where she put it all. She looked like a little bird fluttering around, but her appetite was healthy enough. As soon as she finished she ran out of the door to Molly's; I remembered doing the exact same thing when I was her age. I only hoped she wasn't making the same mistakes that I had, or worse, of her own. When she left I made a mug of tea and went out into the garden to finish some work.

Although I fell in love with the cottage the moment I saw it, I knew it would never do for drawing. The low ceilings were cosy, and suited mine and Vi's hobbit stature, but there was not enough light. I can't work with any sort of light but natural, so I had a small studio built at the end of the garden which was glass on two sides and had two sky lights – nothing but light everywhere to suit my snobby eye. It was my happy place, to use a trite phrase. My only one.

The author of the book I was working on wanted ten images, one every other chapter, at my discretion. The only problem with illustrating for books was that I had to read a cumbersome proof print of the damned things first to get a true sense of character. Sometimes – most times, actually – I did like the books that I read. Young adult fiction is generally pretty easy going, if a bit predictable. It's either a dystopia where some people have magical powers, or it's sexy vampires or, currently, they all seem to be mad keen on faery worlds that sit alongside ours in parallel dimensions of magic and mayhem. I'm not sure why they all insist on writing it 'faery', but there you are. Some of those ones were quite dark and delicious, and it's a guilty pleasure to stay up and read all night, tucked up on the sofa.

I picked up the latest, which was tentatively titled *Prince of Dark Wings*, and flicked through to the end. I had rough-sketched eight of the ten plates already, so only had two to go.

> *His cold lips crush down upon hers, cruel fingers grip her waist, pulling her against his hard, angular body. Arabella can feel how much he wants her, this Dark Prince, this would-be king. She pushes him away, though it tears something vital inside her to do so.*
>
> *'I am not for you,' she whispers, the words choking her.*

I managed to not grimace at the purple prose as I pulled my sketchbook toward me. The usual thrill rose in me as I began to draw, pen scratching across the paper in a pleasing skitter as I quickly traced out the figures, standing waist pressed to waist, her pushing back from him, thick hair twined with small flowers and bells and braids flying wildly, looking up into his face with over-large eyes. His own slanted cats-eyes were brooding down at her, his black, feathered wings swept up high, wanting to fold and protectively curl around them both. Winter trees surrounded them, barren branches split the paper as I slashed black ink against the page. It felt strange drawing a cold landscape when my own was so warm.

I put down the pen – this would do for the bare bones the publishers wanted, they knew my final work would be more detailed – and I stepped out of the studio, into my garden.

A casual observer might have thought it a mess, but it was all planned and cultivated carefully. I liked it to look wild. There was buddleia for the butterflies and for the delicate lilac bursts, as well as a patch of red valerian, thriving in the chalky soil. Lavender in the border brought the bees. I love the smell – it reminds me of my grandmother, who made sachets of it for her wardrobes and always smelt faintly purple. I was contemplating a nap of my own in the hammock but I decided to go indoors and shower instead; the evening was so hot that I felt like sweat and dirt had created a film of filth on my skin.

I was also still feeling hungover after the wine the previous night, so I set the shower to cold, stepped under the needling water and took a sharp breath, my skin pulling and goosebumps prickling before taking pity on myself and running it back to warm.

It wasn't until I stepped out that I realised that Vivian had nicked all the bloody towels. I tried wringing my hair out and hopped a little to scatter some of the water, but I knew I'd have to run downstairs to get a fresh one.

I was halfway down the stairs when there was a knocking at the door. I swore under my breath. I scurried down the rest of the way and along the corridor and grabbed the biggest towel I had from the airing cupboard, wrapping it around myself. I put the chain on the door before I opened it.

'Hello?' I said, blinking as the low sun shone brightly into my face through the gap, blinding me briefly. There was no answer but, as my vision cleared, I saw someone standing there silently. Alex. He was dressed for the weather in cut-off blue jeans and a fitted vest top. I noticed how his muscles moved under the skin of his tanned shoulders and across his chest as he fidgeted on the doorstep, moving a heavy art folio from under one arm to the other and sweeping his dark fringe away from his forehead.

'I'm sorry,' he said in a jarringly smooth and modulated voice – I realised I had been expecting the pitched and jerking voice of a teenage boy, and his was not that. He had a man's voice, rich as cream. 'I've caught you at a bad time.'

'How do you know where I live?' I accused him, querulously, like an old woman, full of headache and annoyed that this strange person had accosted me at home when I was practically naked. I took the chain off the door and opened it further, feeling a bit foolish at peering out through the gap.

'I asked in the pub,' he replied. 'It's not a big place, everyone seems to know everyone. We've just moved here...'

'Yes,' I said, still feeling cross and discomfited, wondering if Steve had told him, angry that he would tell a stranger where I lived. 'What do you want – need, I mean? I'm sorry, I'm not at my best at the moment. Can I help you with something?'

His eyes flashed up at me from the ground, where they had previously been fixed, and I got the uncanny sensation of fingers tracing themselves the full length of my spine, a curling feeling that increased my unease further. I couldn't tell what exact colour they were.

'I can see,' he said, with a wolf grin. 'Do you want to go and put some clothes on? I don't mind waiting.' I wasn't sure what to say to that so I obliged instead, letting him in despite the shivers running up my back as I felt him watch me dash up the stairs to dress. I turned the old lock in my bedroom door as I did.

I rifled through my wardrobe and pulled out a new cotton jumpsuit that I'd bought on a whim last time I'd taken Vivian shopping. She'd been complaining that my 'look' was embarrassing. It was a bit tight for my liking, but she had approved, so I kept it on and attempted to run a comb through my mad hair.

'I was hoping you would give me art lessons,' he said, as I returned to the hallway where he was waiting for me. 'I've looked up your work online, and I really like it. I want to learn more about illustration.' I noticed his eyes look me up and down as he spoke and I felt a bit embarrassed about the jumpsuit – maybe it was too young for me.

'Oh, right. Well, I'm not sure there's a lot I could teach you, really,' I replied. 'I'm not a proper teacher. I got strong-armed into running the life classes at the hall; I've never actually had real pupils or any sort of training.'

'It can't be hard, can it?' he replied, with a smirk. 'I don't think any of my art teachers have had more than three brain cells.'

Did I like this arrogant boy? I decided to humour him.

'And how much would you pay for these lessons?'

'Ten pounds an hour,' he offered. 'For two lessons a week, and I'll keep coming to the life classes, too.'

'Aren't there other things you would rather spend your money on?'

'No. I don't care about anything else.'

This stumped me slightly. I didn't really need the money: the sale of our house in Walthamstow six years before had left us financially secure, and I really only worked to keep my mind busy and away from other things. It wasn't only that bothering me, though; there was still something unnerving me about Alex that I couldn't put my finger on. But what could I do? It felt cruel to refuse him while he was standing in front of me looking hopeful.

'Look, Alex, I'm not sure about this, but maybe we can give it a go for a couple of weeks and see if it works. For both of us. Okay?'

He smiled suddenly, properly smiled, and I was dazzled. It transformed his face, utterly, and I decided his eyes were sea coloured, changing by mood, because I had just pinned them as green but then I saw blue too, and gold. They were fathomless. It gave me a pang deep in my chest, because I didn't think he smiled much; at least, not this smile. I wanted badly to draw it.

'I've brought some of my work,' he said, hefting his folio under his arm again. 'Can I show you?' His enthusiasm infected me.

'Sure – come through.' I gestured to the sitting room and he walked in.

As I followed him in I saw he was looking at my bookshelf. I was mildly embarrassed about the eclectic nature of my collection, and for some reason hoped he had only noticed my high-brow classics, which I'd not actually had the chance to read yet, as opposed to some of my holiday trash romances, which were well-thumbed.

He put his folio down on the sofa and reached out and picked one up. He smoothed his hand along its cover and touched the edges before sliding it back into its place, then sitting down on the sofa. He liked books. I liked book people. I thought maybe he wasn't so bad, and I was determined not to let my past tar every man with the same brush.

'Let's have a look at your stuff, then,' I said, in a falsely cheery voice. 'I don't have long, though – I'm meeting friends at the pub in a bit.' This was a lie, but I didn't want him hanging around all night.

'Okay.' He looked at me with a knowing glint in his eye; I wasn't fooling him for a second with my escape plan. 'Here.'

He passed across his folio as I sat down beside him. I pulled off the elastic and opened it up. I leafed through each piece slowly, drinking in his talent. Nearly everything was in black ink or pencil, there was no colour anywhere. They were mostly observational sketches and I wondered if he took pictures of people and worked on the drawings later, because some of the detail was incredible.

'Alex, I'm really not sure what you think I can teach you,' I told him as I flicked through some simple drawings he'd done of foxes crouching in long grass. I could almost see their whiskers twitching, the movement in the page was incredible. I touched the lines of the fox's spine, almost expecting to feel silky fur under my finger. The last page in the folio was a front-on self-portrait. He'd caught the planes and angles of his beautiful face impeccably, but the almond shapes of his eyes had been shaded in an entirely pitiless black, and the effect made the skin on the back of my neck crawl.

'I'm hoping you can teach me about colour,' he said, shifting too close to me and looking down at the picture. I felt his breath drift warmly on my shoulder, smelt spearmint.

'Okay, then,' I found myself saying, swallowing my doubts. The lure of watching him draw was just too much, I was greedy for it. 'When would you like these lessons?'

'Can I just come when I'm free?' he asked me, putting his pictures back into their folder carefully. I noticed they had been ordered by size. 'I work shifts and they aren't always on the same days.'

'And you have school? College?' I asked him, but he just shrugged. Maybe he was older than I'd thought or had dropped out early. I'd never had much time for anything but art myself at his age.

'Well, I am at home most of the day; I work in my studio in the garden. But I need you to let me know at least the day before if you want a lesson, and I don't want you messing me around and going weeks without and then wanting me every day, okay?'

He smiled a sharp smile and I realised what I had said, and stammered, 'J-just take my number.'

'I've already got it, Rachel,' he said, rolling my name around his mouth. 'It was on the sign-up sheet for the life drawing.'

'Well, then, you could have just texted me in the first place, Alex, instead of turning up at my house unannounced!' I was still cross at the intrusion.

'Where's the fun in that?' he replied, the sharp smile back on his face.

With that he turned and walked away, opening the door and leaving me with another burst of hot air from outside.

Feeling a bit jittery, I returned to the kitchen and impulsively grabbed my handbag before heading out myself, locking the door behind me.

The day was still very warm and by the time I reached the pub I was thirsty. I looked around inside for Steve but didn't see him, and I supposed he might be sitting outside in the garden. I walked to the bar and got myself a lemonade. I couldn't face hair of the dog.

I carried my drink outside and, sure enough, Steve was there, laughing, in the corner with one of the regulars. I watched them for a moment, their easy camaraderie. I let myself enjoy the small happiness that having friends who can't judge you because they don't know your secrets gave me.

'Hello, trouble!' Steve shouted, looking up and spotting me lurking. 'Not brought your new boy toy, then? We just met him!' His wicked brown eyes shone with humour and he patted the seat that his friend vacated as I approached, dropping me a wink as he went. The jumpsuit was definitely too young for me, and I felt myself blushing.

I sat down and gave him a push. 'Steve! Shut up, you idiot. Did you tell him where I lived? He just wants some art lessons.'

'Yeah, with Mrs Robinson!'

I picked an ice cube out of my drink and shoved it down the back of his T-shirt, causing him to scream loudly.

'Stop it, Rach!' he said, pulling at the bottom of his top until the ice cube fell out. 'Sorry, I did tell him where you lived – he came in and asked. I didn't think it would be a problem, as he said he was going to ask you for private lessons.'

I could see him trying to keep a straight face but it bothered me that he hadn't considered my safety, or privacy. 'He just gives me the creeps a bit.'

'Maybe you need to get laid,' said Steve, stretching his arms above his head, oblivious to the damp patches beneath them.

'That's your answer to everything.'

'I know, darling, any excuse for a good shag. I'd do you but I don't like lady bits. I could give your boobs a quick squeeze if you like, though?' He made a honking motion at my chest and I slapped his hands away.

'You are a prize idiot.'

'Prize everything, my dear. When *did* you last have a good seeing to, anyway? I haven't heard any gossip about you getting rodgered, and I get all the rodgering gossip. It's the only reason I work in the bar.'

'Steve! It's not any of your business, thank you very much. I don't want you gossiping about my love life in the bar to all the smelly old farmers.'

'It's obviously all the teenage testosterone he's emitting,' he said, elbowing me in the ribs and snorting into his wine glass. 'You're not used to it. It's got you going.' More laughing.

'Steve! You emit plenty of testosterone!' I protested. 'That's really not the issue.'

'That's true, darling, but my testosterone isn't wafting your way.' He sketched a square in the air in front of him. 'I provide a safe space for ageing-spinster-born-again-virgins.'

I punched him in the arm, protesting that nearly thirty-seven did not make me ageing, and we laughed and I realised I was being stupid about the art lessons. Why wouldn't I do them? Any income is useful when you're a freelancer, Steve was always telling me sternly, thinking I was some sort of pauper. He didn't know how much I'd made on my house sale, and I let him think I was just a poor, single mum who'd wanted a fresh start out of the expensive capital. Why correct him? I didn't want anyone to know the real reasons we had left London.

'Where's the lovely Vivian tonight, anyway?' asked Steve, topping up his glass, the scent of the wine slipping through the air making me shudder.

'She's gone to Molly's,' I said, taking a swig of my own drink, lemon tingling refreshingly sour in my mouth. 'Abi and Gavin are off reviewing a hotel or spa or something and the girls are making the most of their garden, but they'll be back at ours later.'

'Do you think they'll have a wild party?' he said, the look on his face telling me he was remembering some of his own.

'No, I don't think so. I'm not sure there are even enough kids at school to have a really wild party!'

'Talking about parties,' said Steve, draining his glass, 'shall we go on a holiday? I can book something last minute, something cheap and cheerful? We could take Vivian?'

'I'm not sure I can afford it this year,' I told him, feeling guilty for lying again about my finances. I could afford it; I just wasn't sure Vivian would behave. 'And I've already booked our Dorset holiday at the end of term. Definitely soon, though – maybe a weekend somewhere? Abi and Gavin owe me some sleepovers!'

I felt guilty brushing him off, but I knew there was no way I would ever leave Vivian by herself. I didn't trust anyone else with her enough to actually go away. I briefly wondered what she was up to at Molly's, but then Steve started telling me about his latest Bristol beefcake and I was too busy laughing at his stories to think about anything else.

# Vivian

I get to Molly's at exactly six and there are already people in the garden drinking and having a laugh. Molly is in the kitchen filling a tall glass with ice and cider. She's wearing tiny shorts and a cropped T-shirt and I feel overdressed and a bit hot and cross.

'Bitch!' she says, passing me the cider. 'Did you hear me open the bottle?' She grabs me in a sloppy, damp hug and I almost spill it. She pushes me away, holding on to my shoulders, and I realise from the way she's swaying that she must have already had a few, even though it's still early.

'Are Serena and Sasha here?' I ask her, taking a gulp and trying not to hiccough or burp or be angry at her for already being so drunk.

'Yep,' says Molly, in a sing-song voice. 'Sash brought a couple o' crates and a couple o' mates. Let's go kiss some boys.'

I have no intention of kissing anyone but I follow her out anyway, lifting my hair away from my neck where I've already started to sweat.

Serena is in the garden on the swing chair staring longingly at Matthew Grey, who is here with his brother, Ben, who is one of Sasha's friends. I don't mind living here after everything went wrong in London, but everyone knows everyone and sometimes a girl just wants a secret or two or seven. Molly walks up to Serena and dumps a cold bottle on her lap, making her shriek as it hits her bare legs. Matthew and Ben both look over briefly with matching Grey grins but I notice that it's not Serena that Matt's eyes linger on, but Molly. I also notice that she's fully aware of this and she looks straight back at him with her own smile, and I'm worried. Serena has been 'in love' with Matt for years and years and she is convinced something is going to happen between them soon. Her constant wittering about how great he is makes me feel sick. They've been sitting next to each other in English this year and passing stupid notes, and while I think he probably does like her, there's no way he would go there if Molly shows any interest, and I don't like the way she's looking at him. This is trouble, and I don't like trouble.

Serena puts her drink down and tells us she's going to the loo. I think she's probably going to go and put more make-up on now that Matt is here within her reach. Her lip gloss is already an inch thick. As she leaves, Molly begins to twist up her hair, tilting one hip.

'It's too hot,' she pouts at me, her top riding up to show even more of her smooth brown belly as she pulls her hair into a messy bun on top of her head. She's still looking at Matt over my shoulder, and I don't have to turn around to know that his eyes are fixed on her slim body as she does her little performance.

'What are you doing?' I hiss at her.

'What?' she says, looking at me now, 'What's that supposed to mean, what am I doing?' Her eyes aren't properly focusing on my face: they drift from one side to the other. This is very strange behaviour – Molly doesn't do things like this. She is supposed to be a nice person. I am not impressed, and I think she has had way too much to drink.

'You're flirting with Matt, and you know Serena likes him! I thought you liked Newboy?'

The look she gives me makes me twist inside.

'Ha,' she says. 'Well, I don't see Serena's name written on him anywhere, and it's every girl for themselves, isn't it? You should know, Vivian.' She sneers my name at me and then pushes past me to go and seat herself between Matt and his brother.

I wonder what she means but then I see Serena come bounding out of the house with a smile, only to stop dead as she sees Molly sitting next to Matthew, one achingly long leg now slung over his. Serena would never have the balls to do that so I run over and hustle her back into the house before she freaks out and embarrasses everyone.

'I don't know what she's up to. You know it doesn't mean anything, Serena. She's just mucking about,' I gabble, but it's no use because Serena's amber eyes are filling with tears. This is why I'm not interested in boys. Fancying people makes you too vulnerable to being an idiot about it and humiliating yourself. I would never give anyone control over me like that, unlike my foolish mother. Love makes you weak.

'She could have anyone! Why is she making Matt fall in love with her? Everyone knows how much I like him!' Serena is staring out of the window at them and, despite my irritation, I'm finding it really hard not to laugh at the tragic look on her face.

Everyone knows her feelings except Matt, it would appear. He looks shell-shocked by the sudden attention he's getting from Molly, who is now casually trailing her fingers through the curly brown hair at the nape of his neck. As we watch he slides a tentative hand on to Molly's knee and edges it up her thigh, thumb caressing. She leans in to him, laughing at something Ben is saying, and lays her head on his shoulder. Matt casually puts his arm around her back, his other hand now on her shoulder, that thumb rubbing up and down. He almost visibly puffs up, his face lit with an incredulous grin.

Serena actually wails at this sight and covers her face.

'I can't believe this. She's such a cunt!'

She almost shouts the last word, which I have never heard her use before, and I look out into the garden in alarm, but no one has heard her.

'She's just mucking around.' I try to reassure her again, but Serena's face has gone cold and pale. Her lips are a funny colour, white under the make-up. She looks like a corpse.

'No, she isn't, Viv. I know you're her number one fan and all, but this is what she's always been like. You're blind. She can't bear for anyone else to get any attention, or have anything that she doesn't. She wants everything for herself. She was just waiting for him to start liking me back so it hurts more,' she spits out, spitefully. 'Just wait until you have something she doesn't. I'm going home.'

'That's not true,' I try and tell her. 'Molly is always nice to everyone.'

Serena just looks at me like I am stupid, which I don't appreciate. I don't try to stop her as she wipes tears away and then storms out of the house. She closes the door quietly and that surprises me; I thought she would have slammed it.

The early evening wanes into the evening proper, and the sky is starting to turn pink and purple, luminous at the edges. I'm just sitting by myself on the swing chair, watching Molly get steadily even more drunk, and more all over Matt. I can't understand it because she's never shown any interest in him before, cute as he is, I suppose, with his stonewashed denim-blue eyes and dark curls. She's pulling on one of them now and laughing as it springs back, a glossy coil. They haven't kissed yet but I can see that it's going to happen. I want to go home myself, but obviously I can't without Molly, and she's not going anywhere. Sasha and her friends left ten minutes ago, giving Molly filthy looks after Serena flounced off, and Ben has wandered off to talk to his other friends about where they are going next.

I'm thinking about going inside and watching Netflix or something when a shadow falls over me and I look up.

'Alex,' I say, without thinking. 'You got Molly's invitation, then?'

Alex smiles, and I shock myself by imagining his mouth on mine, those white teeth on my lip. Where did that come from?

'This seat taken?' He gestures to the swing seat with his bottle of beer. I shift up, willing myself not to blush. I can feel nervous sweat stinging under my arms. I glance over to Molly but she doesn't seem to have noticed anything except how funny it is to spring Matt's hair.

Alex doesn't say anything. He sits down right next to me and surveys the scene and takes a long swig of his drink. I watch the movement of his throat, the ripples of the pulling muscles under his smooth skin.

'Did you need that?' I say, the gap in conversation making me antsy.

He looks at me with cool eyes. He pushes with his feet and the seat starts to rock back and forth. 'It's hot,' he eventually replies. 'The beer's cold.'

I sit there, tense, not sure what to do or say. Alex puts his arm along the back of the chair and I'm painfully aware that if I sit back a bit the bare skin of my shoulders will touch the bare skin of his arm. There's a lump in my throat and I can feel my heart beating. It feels like it's being squeezed, folded in half, gulping for blood. I don't sit back.

'Tell me about Vivian,' he says suddenly, turning to me and startling me again. 'What do you think about living in a pokey little village, miles from anywhere with nothing to do except get pissed?'

I think I like the way my name sounds when he says it.

'Well...' I trail off, unsure of why he's interested in talking to me. 'I like it, I guess.'

'You like everyone knowing your business? What about your secrets?' He leans in slightly as he whispers the last word, and I shift away a bit.

'I haven't got any secrets,' I lie, looking away. 'It's not like that. It's more I suppose people like to feel safe, you know? We all know each other, we look out for each other.'

Alex just looks at me and takes another swig of beer.

'Where's your friend gone, then?' he says, nodding to where Molly isn't sitting any more, just as I feel my phone going off.

'Sorry. Serena had a bit of a meltdown earlier. I need to check if this is her.'

It isn't, it's Tilly. Serena went to the chippy and is apparently crying all over the chips about how Molly is behaving. They want to know what she's doing now. Molly isn't here, and nor is Matt. I don't know where they are, but I'm not telling them that. I lie instead, quickly tapping out that they are here and that nothing is happening and that they should come back. They don't want to, though. Serena is hammered and upset, so Tilly is going to take her back to her house behind the shop.

I notice that Alex is watching what I'm texting.

'Trouble in paradise?' he asks, quirking an eyebrow, and I frown, cross with him for the second time in one day.

'For someone I've just met and who just moved here, you seem to think you know a lot and you're also really annoying.'

'I like to watch people,' he says, 'it's the only thing to do here. Lots of secrets to uncover.'

'Ha! Like what?'

'Like, did you know your friend is fucking her way through the whole school?' The comment blindsides me, it's difficult not to rock back.

'What? No, she isn't, what friend? Who?' I ask, but I'm worried I know exactly who he is talking about. He just smirks a bit.

'You're a liar,' I tell him as I stand up, denying what he's saying even after what Serena said and what I've seen tonight. 'And an arsehole. You should leave.'

Alex stands up. He's so much taller than me. I can smell something earthy and almost smoky about him, which makes my mouth dry. One of my straps has fallen off my shoulder and he raises a hand and uses one long finger to gently slide it back up and I think my heart almost stops as he then uses it to trace a line along my collarbone before resting it on my throat, just for a second. I can't breathe and I think for a frozen moment that he is going to kiss me, but he just smiles his shark smile and turns and leaves.

Heart hammering, I go into the house to look for Molly. It's getting late, the light is fading and everyone else must have left when I was talking to Alex, because the garden is deserted except for beer cans and empty bottles.

There's no one downstairs so I go into the understairs loo and look in the mirror, wondering if Alex's finger has burnt me. But I look the same as always, just paler – if that's even possible. I can see a pulse throbbing in my neck and I wonder if that's where his finger stopped when he touched me.

Wandering through the empty house feels strange. Usually I like it here; it's minimalist and cool and calm, but tonight it feels charged up. No Molly. I'm going to be so cross if she's run off somewhere without me. Slowly, I gravitate toward the stairs to see if she is in her bedroom, moving as quietly as I can manage, which is very quiet indeed when I want to be. Her door is ajar and as I walk towards it I hear something, a weird slapping noise, so I creep up to look through the gap into the dim room beyond. Molly is naked from the waist down and sitting astride Matt on her bed. He's thrusting himself into her violently, his hands gripping her hips, her hair everywhere, her own hands under her top on her breasts. I can hear them both now moaning, groaning, and I should leave but I can't stop looking. Molly told us she was still a virgin like us, but this doesn't look like the first time she's done this, and Alex's words are resounding in my head. She's grinding herself onto him and her hand goes between her legs rubbing and I can hear him swearing and I have to leave, now, before I throw up every drop I've drunk tonight along with my rage that she could do this, that she's been having this secret life, risking ruining our group for no reason I can understand – she would do that, for *this*? When anyone is here to see it! Did she *want* me to see her?

I run down the stairs and out of the door. I'm supposed to be waiting for her to come home with me, but she can go fuck herself. Once she's finished with Matthew, anyway.

I stomp around the village for a while trying to calm down. I'm walking past the pub when someone grabs my arm. I spin around thinking it might be Molly, but it isn't, it's Tristan, Tilly's horrible brother, and he stinks of beer.

'Vivvy, Vivvy!' he slurs. 'Where you going, baby?' He starts to paw at my body, trying to pull me towards him, to rub himself against me. His dirty brown hair, which is usually tied back in a scratty ponytail, is loose around his face, and I have a horror of it touching me.

'Get off me!' I tell him, pushing at his chest. 'Get off!' but he's all over me. He pulls me, and I can't stop him, until we are in the alley next to the pub, where he pins me hard against the wall and starts tugging up my top, trying to get his hand in the waistband of my jeans, his fingers worming down.

'C'mon, Vivvy, give me a kiss.'

'No!' I'm shouting now, craning away from him as he leans towards me, the wet hole of his mouth rank, and I manage to kick him hard as I can in the leg and he springs back, letting me go. I can see white spots behind my eyes; I'm about to completely lose control of my temper.

'Ow, you stupid little bitch! I was just messing around, you frigid cow.'

Suddenly Molly is there too, shoving her way in between us.

'Get off her, you scumbag!' she shouts, slapping at him and barging against him with her shoulder. 'You're disgusting! Fuck off!'

He does, giving her a long look before spitting at our feet and then staggering off toward the chip shop and the house behind where he lives with Tilly and their parents.

Molly grabs me, and she's really drunk, her eyes blank and staring.

'Why did you leave, Viv? I'm staying at yours, remember? I was looking for you in the garden then I heard you shouting.' Her top is on backwards.

'You disappeared,' I tell her. 'Did you go off with Matt?'

'No, of course not,' she says, proving that even when she's wasted she can to lie to my face without even a flicker. 'He went home, and I just zonked out upstairs. D'you think your mum is in the pub? Shall we go and see? Are you okay?'

'No! Let's just go back to mine. You need to sober up.'

She shrugs her shoulders and huffs off towards my house. She falls over the stile getting into the field and I have to try and pull her up off the ground where she's rolling around, laughing like an idiot. I'm getting really cross. I'm thinking about how I could accidentally kick her in the face, but I eventually get her up and get her to my house, make her drink a pint of water and then put her into a sleeping bag on the floor of my room where she immediately falls asleep.

I think about staying up but then Mum will get home and she'll know something is wrong if I'm not with Molly and just go on and on and on, so I get changed and lie down on my bed instead. I run through some breathing exercises to try and get rid of how furious I am about this whole horrible evening, until finally I fall asleep.

I don't know how long I've been dreaming for but I wake up with a jerk. Molly is kneeling up beside me, staring at me. The edges of her face in the dim light make it look like one of those ancient Greek statues, all smooth curves and blind eyes.

'What the hell are you doing?' I whisper.

'Did he kiss you?' she says, her breath hot and sour-sweet.

'Who? Tristan? No, I pushed him off before he could.'

'No, I meant Newboy. I saw you with him in the garden, I saw you talking. Did he kiss you? Did you have your first kiss?'

'No, it wasn't like that,' I say, but I remember the way he touched me and uneasiness runs right through me, making me shiver.

'Are you scared?'

'Of what? Being kissed?'

'Yeah.'

'I don't know.'

'Well,' she says, 'I can fix that,' and before I know what's happening she brushes my hair away from my face, fingers slipping through, and kisses me hard on my mouth. For a second I think I feel her tongue against my lip, a dart of warm satin, but then she sits back before I can push her away.

'Now you've had your first kiss,' she says, giggling, and then she lies back down, falls asleep again.

I don't understand what is wrong with her. What the hell was that about? The firm belief I had in Molly, who I thought she was, is starting to erode and break away into sharp pieces in my mind. I feel unsure, like I'm losing control. I don't like to lose control. It brings back bad memories. I can't let what happened before in London with *her* happen again here with Molly. I won't. I've worked too hard.

I run my hand over my stomach and I can feel rough, sore grazes on it from where Tristan must have scratched me trying to grab me. I hate him, I absolutely hate him.

How dare he do that to me? It's bad enough when he tries to hang around with us, spotty, always foul-mouthed. He makes me sick. I end up lying awake for a long time, watching the pale light shine through the window silver onto Molly's hair.

It looks like she's burning.

# London

'Is she asleep?' Rachel had crept into a quiet house to find her mother in the kitchen, washing up.

'Yes, she went up at seven, love. School is tiring her out.'

'I'm sorry I missed bedtime again, this campaign is insane.'

'Aren't they all?'

Rachel decided not to answer the rhetorical question, which had been accompanied by a stern look. She knew her mother was unhappy with the hours she had been putting in since her promotion, but she loved her new job, and she had to prove she had been the right choice.

'How did she get on? Was she okay today?'

'Seemed to be. She's a quiet little thing at the best of times, she didn't say much.'

'I'll pop up and tuck her in and get changed.'

'Okay, love. Dinner's nearly done. I got some of those nice sausages from the butchers.'

'Thanks, Mum.'

Rachel hung her handbag on the end of the banister as she went up the stairs, pulling her hair out of its tight clip as she did. It felt dry and frizzy from the irons she tortured it with every morning, but it looked much smarter straight. She hadn't been that wild-curled art student for a long time. Pushing into her small bedroom, she cast a reproachful eye at the single bed she'd had growing up and was inhabiting again. Her little nest egg could not turn into a deposit for their own place soon enough, useful and comforting as it had been to live with her mum after everything.

She quickly took off her suit and hung it up, smoothing the sleeves and picking lint off the pencil skirt. Stripping her restrictive shirt and tights off with a sigh of relief, she swapped them for loose-fitting tracksuit bottoms and an old T-shirt. She left the confines of her room and quietly popped her head around the door to the even smaller box room, where Vivian lay sleeping.

The little girl was curled up like a bean in the middle of the bed, the covers puddled beneath her feet. Rachel padded into the room and slid her hands beneath her daughter, gently pulling her up to the pillow, tugging the covers up to cover her. She smiled, and kissed her gently on her silky head, stroked her cheek. Such a good girl. As she left she smiled again at the sight of Vivian's little uniform neatly folded on the tiny dresser ready for the morning. It didn't seem possible that five years had passed since she had come back, since Vivian had been born.

At the doorway she looked back again, feeling the tug of guilt that she was missing so much time with her, that she only ever seemed to see her asleep or to wake her up with a brief hug as she left the house. She told herself she was setting her a good example, showing her a strong and independent woman who provided for her family. It wasn't like Vivian's father ever would. Even the thought of him in their lives made her feel dizzy with burgeoning panic. They were better off like this, they were safe.

Back in the kitchen Carol was dishing out steaming mash and topping it with sausages and gravy. It really was a time warp. She felt sixteen again, caught out misbehaving as she sat down and began to eat, her mum not looking at her as she did the same; wondering if they would ever move past the parent–child dynamic. She wasn't a little girl any more.

The prickly atmosphere continued past dinner and the washing up, but was alleviated somewhat by the appearance of a large bar of Galaxy chocolate from Rachel's handbag, presented along with a gin and tonic.

'I am sorry, Mum,' she ventured. 'I know I've been taking the piss recently, but I have to be there, or it looks bad. I can't just leg it at five.'

Her mum sniffed and took the chocolate, taking the paper off and peeling back the foil. 'I'm not the one you need to apologise to. I get to see you now, but Vivian hasn't seen you since breakfast yesterday.' Carol swept the piece of fine auburn hair that always fell into her face back past her ear, and tried to straighten the frown off her face, the deep lines that appeared between her eyebrows above her glasses.

'I know, I know. I changed my meetings around tomorrow so I can take her to breakfast club. And it's Friday, so I'll have the weekend with her. I'll take her to the Leisure Lagoon, and ice cream after.'

'She'll like that,' said Carol, snapping off a line of chocolate and passing it to Rachel, who was settling in with her own drink and unsuccessfully trying to smother a yawn. 'I know it's important to you, after everything with that man, but you won't get these years with her back. She'll be grown up before you know it.'

'Mum, I know. It'll be fine, I promise.'

As Rachel let the gin and sugar do their work, the stresses of the day slipped away. They tuned into a reality

TV show and as Rachel's mind drifted to the next day's work, she gave no further thought to Carol's warning. After all, Vivian was just a little girl. School was far more exciting than spending time with her mum. Weren't friends everything at that age?

# *Rachel*

I left Steve with another one of his friends who had turned up, setting the world to rights and slurring every third word at about ten o'clock so I could get home while there was still some light. I was too lazy to go round the long, lit-street way and would always rather cut across the field, which I did, inhaling with pleasure the grassy scents of summer evenings.

I hadn't had anything to drink, so I managed to navigate keys in door with ease. I wasn't expecting the girls to be back but there were two pairs of shoes at the bottom of the stairs and all the lights were on, so I thought they must have come back early. I wondered if I would be dealing with the midnight puking club if they'd had a bit too much – it wouldn't have been the first time one of her friends had been ill. I sometimes thought I should be more firm with the drinking, but I was doing exactly the same at her age and would have felt like such a hypocrite. And after all the trouble we had to get away from in London, the awful time she had at primary school, I was just glad she had some lovely friends and I didn't want to rock the boat. And to be fair, Vivian never seemed to be drunk; she always wanted to be in control. If anyone in our house was drinking too much, it was me, as a salve to my self-enforced penance here in the middle of nowhere and the guilt I felt over letting her down so badly when she was young.

I decided to have a midnight feast of cheese and pickle on the last of the bread, and a pint of squash, and mock myself for the rebel life I was living. I couldn't help but think about Steve teasing me earlier about my sex life. I pretended I was just being coy, when in fact I was just too embarrassed to confess that the last time I had had sex was around the time Viv was conceived.

It's not a period of my life I like to think about, but sometimes I can't help but poke at it, like it's a badly healing scab that pulls and itches. Bleeds.

I met Vi's father at art college in Manchester and fell in love – or lust, probably – at first sight. He was perfect: acid green eyes against dark hair and creamy skin, my absolute favourite colour combination. He seemed to feel the same way about me and we fell into an intense relationship that revolved around skipping lectures in favour of long mornings in bed followed by long afternoons in the scuzziest dives we could find in Moss Side. Ciaran was an observational artist – he could catch someone in just a few quick strokes of a pencil, and favoured people who had been ground down by their lives. Drunks in bars and the women who paraded for their attention.

I didn't like his fixation with people who he looked down on; I didn't like that he thought he was so much better than them, when we weren't – who is? But Ciaran thought he was the next great social commentator, Lowry for the twenty-first century, dredging through life for specimens to make people 'think'. Part of me hated him for dehumanising people, but that was smothered by the part of me that wanted him, wanted him in me, all the time. I was addicted to his attention and the way he fucked me, worshipped my body like I was the most amazing woman in existence. I'd never felt before that I was the centre of someone's world and it was intoxicating and I was lost in it, in him.

He attacked me after I got my first commission. We were in our second year and I'd done a line of sketches inspired by the Cottingley Fairies hoax for a class, which my tutor had shown to a friend who was a buyer for department stores. He wanted to commission them for a wallpaper print for little girls' nurseries. It was a small fortune to me, and I had thought Ciaran would be thrilled, but I was to find out later that it didn't suit his struggling artist trope – to make money, from art? We went out to celebrate with the cheapest fizzy wine we could find, a lot of it, and when we got home, he broke a glass pane in our flat door using my head.

I wanted to leave him, of course I did – I hadn't been raised to stay with a man who hurt me, but I also hadn't been raised to understand how you can fall under someone's spell so entirely. I let him take me to A&E for butterfly stitches and then I let him take me home to bed where he made me come again and again while he whispered how much he adored me, how I was the rock he wanted to build his life on, he was sorry, so sorry, it would never happen again.

It did happen again. It always does. He smashed my hand in the same door because I had embarrassed him by talking to his friend about football. He hated the game, never watched it, though I did because I had always watched it with my father, before, and it reminded me of him. But only men should talk about football, apparently. I had shown him up. I've never watched it since, and the fingers on my left hand never did heal straight. I was just grateful it wasn't my right.

I can pinpoint the night I got pregnant with Vivian. I had offered to lend him some money, fed up of his whines of being skint. He hadn't replied, but I could feel his anger simmering and growing and I tried to distract him the only way I knew how, with my body. And I thought it had worked, until he began to be rough, using hard thrusts that hurt me and made me gasp with pain, rigid hands that left bruises. I turned my face away and he lunged, biting me where my shoulder met my neck, so hard I thought he had taken a piece of me. He finished with a bloody-mouthed shout, slapped me and then left me there, in our bed, bleeding.

I didn't even leave him to protect her initially, I was that worn out and weak, still in love with him despite his fists and his teeth and the words that hurt worse than either. I thought we could have a family, that the baby would fix everything, fix him, but when I told him I was pregnant he was beyond furious. He didn't want a milky sow hanging around his neck, a baby to throttle him with inanity and despair like he'd done to his own father, a talented musician who never made it after being 'trapped' by his mother and himself. That beating was the worst, including several kicks to the stomach that I thought had ended everything. I should have gone to the police but instead I ran home with nothing except bruises and scars, and shame, to London to live with my mother again in her little house in Walthamstow, praying that he wouldn't follow me.

By some miracle, despite weeks of bleeding, I didn't lose Vivian. My fairy commission was enough to get by on while I slowly built us a life, painted a fantasy. Vivian never once asked me about her dad, although I was expecting it, planning for it, and she looked nothing like him at all, which was the purest sort of relief. I didn't want to see his acid eyes ever again.

I had thought I would never want to be in love again, or even have sex with anyone ever again but, as always, thinking of Ciaran, of his hands on my body, stirred something dark inside me, and I went to bed and masturbated until I fell asleep, dreaming of dark wings and sharp teeth, of wicked hot breath on my neck and of cold, clever fingers between my legs.

–

When I woke up I felt overheated and sweaty and guilty about going out yet again the night before, and an echo of the strange dreams followed me around until I dispelled them with a cold shower. There were no movements from Vivian's room so I peeped my head round the door ever so quietly. They were both in her bed, cuddled up together, which I couldn't imagine was making them hot at all and I smiled before retreating downstairs for tea and toast, which I took outside into the garden to have while I listened to the birds waking up.

–

I was working on the final draft for the book when I heard someone pad into the studio behind me. It was Molly, looking pale, her eyes black and smudged with make-up, her long hair straggling down her back.

'Are you okay, sweetheart?' I asked her, putting down my pen and turning to her. She looked at me, her throat moved but she didn't say anything. I put my hand on her shoulder, and she stepped into me, putting her head down next to mine, her arms round me. I could feel her shaking. I put both my arms around her and hugged her. 'Darling, tell me, what's wrong?'

'Nothing, I'm sorry,' she said, pulling away and scrubbing her eyes with the heels of her hands. 'I'm just a bit hungover. I think I need to go home and sleep it off.' She looked so sad, I had to try and not laugh at her woebegone expression.

'I'm not very sympathetic if it's self-inflicted, Molly' I told her, and she managed a small, tight smile. 'Are you sure you don't want to stay for breakfast? I can make pancakes?'

'I'm sure.' She sniffed. 'Can I have another hug?' I obliged, happily. I never got any affection from Vivian, and often worried that Molly didn't get enough from her mother. She spent so much time at our house I did wonder if she saw me as a substitute in some way. As she left I glanced up at Vivian's window and saw a flash of her pale face looking out at us, and my stomach dropped. I knew she would be jealous, and I didn't want that.

Molly left using the back gate and I went back to the house. I put more bread in to toast and flicked the kettle back on, calling to Vivian as I did. She eventually slouched down the stairs, but didn't come into the kitchen. I took her breakfast into the front room instead, where she scowled at me.

'I'm not hungry.'

'Fine, I'll eat it,' I replied, sitting down on the armchair and tucking a leg up. 'What's up with you this morning? Are you feeling hungover, too?'

'No.'

I ate the toast as slowly and loudly as I could manage, watching Vivian. She was deliberately staring out of the window but I could see a small muscle twitching in the soft skin under her jaw.

'Do you have to make so much noise? You're a grown woman.'

'I can do what I like in my own house, Vivian. Are you going to tell me what was wrong with Molly this morning? Have you had a row? You know you're supposed to tell me if you're feeling out of sorts about anything.' I watched her breathing steadily, exactingly. Controlled and even, in and out.

'No, we didn't have a row. She just got really drunk yesterday. It was gross.'

'Was she ill?'

'No.'

'So, what happened? What was gross?'

'Nothing, Mum! For god's sake not everything is a massive issue. Just leave me alone for once.'

It was like getting blood from a stone. Feeling my own frustration bubbling up, I left her to it, resolving to keep a close eye on her in the coming days, monitor her moods.

I spent the rest of the weekend pottering around in the garden being ignored by my daughter, as usual, trying to rescue my poor plants from the heat. There was a hosepipe ban, so I put a bucket in the shower and collected what I could from there and other waste water, and I was fairly pleased with my efforts – everything seemed to be alive and still thriving despite the drought. I knew I'd need to keep on top of it, though; last summer, the heat was a killer.

# Vivian

As soon as I wake up a black mood envelops me. I don't want to go to school today. I don't know what to do about Molly. I saw her, out in the garden with my mother on Saturday. She thinks she can have her, too. Does she want everything that doesn't belong to her? Maybe Serena was right about her. Maybe I have been blind.

Our phone chat was completely dead the whole weekend and that's never happened before. It always annoyed me, pinging all the time, never leaving me alone, demanding my time, but now it's silent I miss it: absence leaves a hole.

I get ready for school slowly; I've been awake for hours already. Mum is already pottering about – she gets up stupidly early, too – I can hear her making tea, the roil of the kettle. Why is she drinking tea when it's already boiling outside? I feel like we've been transported to some Louisiana swamp. There's probably an alligator at the bottom of the garden. With any luck it will eat me on the way to school. I imagine it slithering out of the undergrowth to snap me in its mouth, crunch my bones, make me bleed red rivers into dying grass.

'Viv, do you want a cup of tea, babe?' her voice echoes up the stairs as she hears me come out of my room.

'No.'

'Have you got time for breakfast? I've made some porridge if you want some?'

Porridge? Is she mental? It's about eighty degrees already; I don't want bloody tea and porridge. I walk into the kitchen and grab cereal instead, to have with icy cold milk like any normal person. I can feel my mother's eyes on me, tracking my movements. I sit opposite her at the table, our actions in tandem, spoon to mouth to bowl to mouth. Her brain is ticking over, I can see it. I've been too moody this weekend, she's going all suspicious.

'You feeling a bit better today?'

'I was fine yesterday.'

'It's hard to tell when you ignore me so thoroughly.'

'Whatever.' I know I shouldn't wind her up because she could really make things difficult for me if she wanted to, like she used to; demanding all my passwords, searching my room, just watching me all the time, but I can't help it when she's just so bloody annoying. I'll be nice to her later and she'll forget about it with any luck. I never understand why the girls always row with their parents – all you need to do is pretend you like them and you'll get away with everything. It's not hard. Well, usually it's not hard, but I am in a bad mood today. Just want to have finished school already so I can go to university and leave her here and never come back. She picks up the breakfast things and plonks them noisily in the sink. I leave without saying goodbye.

Molly is usually waiting for me by the back gate in our garden, but I sent her a message this morning telling her I was going in early so I didn't have to see her straight away. I'm not particularly early but I'd rather walk on my own today. The air is buzzing with bugs and light is streaming through the trees, striping the air and making my eyes water. It feels damp already, like the inside of a lung or something, spongy. Humid. Horrid.

As I make my way through the trees I catch sight of a couple ahead of me through the leaves so I slow down enough to not catch up with them. I don't want to speak to anyone, and I think it might be Molly, but I can't see who she is with so I move off the path and behind the big bramble bushes that line the way so I can eavesdrop on her from the side. It's fun creeping through the forest to spy, though I'm worried about getting snagged up in all the thorns.

I see a shaft of sunlight beam off a golden head. That is Molly, but I can't make out who she's with yet – is it Matthew? He's on the other side of her but there are too many leaves here. Is she talking about Serena? Maybe she's trying to fix things. Then I see him through a gap, his clear profile. It's not Matthew. It's Alex.

I hear her laugh, loudly, an incredulous laugh. I know all of Molly's laughs and that one means that someone is telling her lies. I'm so caught up in trying to listen without being heard myself that I get caught on a bramble branch, and it whips around onto my face as I try and pull it off, leaving a scratch. I can feel spots of blood raising themselves along it like fire beacons. Fuck! It really stings. I'm lucky it didn't go in my eye. That would have been karma, wouldn't it? By the time I have extracted myself from the stupid blackberry bush I've lost them.

After a quick trip to the bathroom to wash the painful scratch on my cheek, I go and find the girls. I don't want to act like there is anything wrong, but it's difficult for me not to be stiff and uptight at the best of times, let alone when everything might be blowing up. This is all salvageable as long as Molly doesn't keep being a freak. They are standing in a huddle in the hall, our usual spot. Serena looks angry, hissing at Molly, who is doing a remarkable job of looking bewildered. She's trying to brazen it out, the liar.

Then everything goes into a painful slow motion as Matthew walks past me, towards them. I've never noticed before but he walks with a funny kind of bounce on his heels. With his springy hair, it makes him seem like a puppy. Serena spots him coming and goes rigid like a mannequin, Tilly's knuckles turn white on the strap of her bag and she turns her face to let her hair fall between her and the scene that's about to happen. She hates confrontation. Molly hasn't seen him yet, and his hand reaches for her shoulder, to tap, stroke almost.

'Hey, Molly!' He sounds so happy. Idiot.

Molly just turns around to face him, raising an immaculately arched eyebrow, with what looks like a practised sneer on her perfectly made-up mouth. A pale pink dagger. I've never seen her look at someone like that before. I resolve to practise it in the mirror, because if a look could kill, it would be that one. I can almost see Matthew withering on the spot with embarrassment.

'Can I help you with something?' She tilts her head slightly, points her sharp chin.

Matt just stands there. I can't see his face, but I see his hands: his fingers twitch and then compress and clamp together, make fists. A hot red flush creeps up the back of his neck above the white collar of his shirt. Molly is still looking at him like she's just found him on the bottom of her shoe. Serena and Tilly don't say anything; their eyes flick between the two of them like they are playing tennis and they are the spectators watching the ball ping back and forth.

Matthew doesn't say anything else; he turns sharply on his heel and walks back toward me. His face is pale but there are high spots of colour on his cheeks and he looks like he's going to be sick. His eyes meet mine for a moment but then slide away, ashamed. Did he see me on Saturday, watching them through the door? Watching him? He steps around me, leaving me with a citrusy scent to follow back to Molly, who has turned back to the girls with a flick of her hair.

'See? I told you nothing happened. He was just trying it on with me, grabbing me and stuff. You didn't see it right, Serena – if you hadn't run off like a kid you would have seen it, too. Wouldn't she, Viv?'

She looks at me now, blue eyes telling me to toe the line. I could break her right here, if I wanted to. For a second I taste domination, bittersweet, addictive, but then I spit it away. Not yet.

'Yep. Nothing happened, Ser. He's a dick.'

Serena looks at me for a long moment, like she's making her mind up about something, then plasters on a thin smile, glossy but false, teeth behind it.

'Yeah. He's a dick. Come on, Tills, we're going to be late.' She grabs Tilly and drags her away to registration without waiting for us to follow. Molly is still looking at me with a small, pleased smile on her face. She doesn't thank me for saving her slutty arse and I realise with a sinking feeling that I'm stuck. I can't now tell anyone what really happened without looking bad myself for lying in the first place; I'm caught in the spiderweb of her untruth. Hopefully it will all just blow over. I don't like change. I want things the way they are.

'What on earth have you done to your face, Viv? It looks like a cat has scratched you.' She raises a hand and gently touches my cheek. I manage to not lean away.

'I caught it on a bramble in the garden. Mum has been letting the blackberries run wild. Can I borrow some concealer for it at break?'

She drops her hand and frowns, briefly, then changes the subject.

'Sorry I had to go early on Saturday, I didn't want to wake you up. You were snoring like a hippo.'

'I do not snore!'

We laugh and I feel a bubbly relief that maybe it's going to be okay and that nothing is going to change. I decide not to ask her what she was talking about with Alex; I try to tell myself it probably wasn't anything interesting and I don't want her to think I was sneaking around following her and I don't care what he says, anyway. It doesn't stop suspicion from joining those jagged thoughts in my brain, though, the new niggling lack of trust I have in who she is, and what she might do. Were they talking about me?

'I'll put some make-up on it later for you; let it dry a bit first. Let's go.'

The rest of the day seems pretty normal. We all sit together on our table at lunch – it's the best table, where you can see everything that's going on, no one else would dare sit here – and we all laugh and chat like usual. The girls are concerned about my 'poor face' but Molly has done a pretty good job of covering it up.

'OMG, guys, I've got the best gossip,' says Tilly, in between shovelling bites of limp orange pasta into her big mouth.

'What?'

She just chews, trying her best to look mysterious.

'Tilly! Spill!'

She looks around quickly and then leans in, as do we, three blonde heads and my mousey one.

'I heard Chloe crying in the bathroom to Becky that her period was late.'

There's a collective intake of breath, with a delighted undertone.

'No! I thought condoms were vegan-friendly?' I say, and to my great satisfaction the other three start honking with laughter. I don't always get it right humour-wise, but that was a good one.

'She's a fucking idiot if she is pregnant,' says Molly, picking the salad out of her sandwich. 'We all had to do that horror show of a sex-ed lesson trying to put those rank minty condoms on bananas. My hands stank for ages. So, it's not like she doesn't know.'

Tilly and Serena look at each other, just for a second, but it's a loaded look. Molly obviously knows what to do, doesn't she?

'Didn't Daniel break his?' I try and distract them. 'I remember one of the boys definitely broke theirs being stupid.'

'Yeah, it was him,' said Tilly, turning her attention back to us. 'I bet it was him – I bet he broke one putting it on and just didn't tell her and now she's going to have his vegan baby.'

'But babies drink milk, so how can a baby be vegan?' says Serena, looking a bit confused, which isn't unusual.

'I think you can drink human milk okay, just not milk from other animals,' I tell her.

'Urgh!'

We all look a bit revolted at the idea. I don't like the thought of pendulous breasts full of milk, leaking everywhere. Imagine the mess and the nasty sour smell. Disgusting. I can't imagine anything worse than having a screaming baby stuck on you all the time, sucking the life out of you.

'Well, who cares if she is or she isn't. Chloe is a stuck-up cow who doesn't even live in the village,' finishes Serena, which is a bit rich as she's only just counted as village as her house is way out, but none of us mention that. She's right about Chloe, though, she is stuck up.

We have PE at the end of the day – as if Mondays couldn't suck any harder – and have to play rounders. Serena is pitching the ball and it's my turn to bat. Instead of throwing the ball underarm like she's supposed to, she looks at me for a second and then lunges, lobbing it hard, straight at me. I try and jump out of the way, but I jump into it instead, and it cracks right on the bony part of my hip, and I scream.

'Sorry, Viv!' she shouts, with a laugh in her voice. 'Was that a bit hard?'

I have tears in my eyes, because it really bloody hurt. I look around to Molly, who is watching from the side lines. She isn't doing PE because her mum always writes her a note to get her out of it because she hates getting all sweaty. All sweaty doing PE, anyway – she didn't seem to mind the sweaty exercise she was doing with Matt the other night. She doesn't say anything, but her mouth is a thin line. The ball gets thrown back to Serena, who throws it properly underarm this time, so that I can hit the ball and run.

Maybe everything isn't going to go back to normal after all. Maybe I'll need to fix it.

# London

Was there anything more boring than watching your kid play on the park? Rachel was itching to get out her Black-Berry and check her emails, but it wasn't in her bag. She'd left it on charge in the kitchen and forgotten to bring it. She looked around instead at the other families in the park, faces in the crowd. Sometimes, even now, she'd see one like his, and feel her stomach drop, or imagine eyes on her back, like the unwelcome weight of a palm between the shoulder blades.

'Mummy!' commanded an imperious little voice from the top of the slide. 'Mummy, watch me!' To Rachel's horror, Vivian twisted at the top and threw herself down it backward, ending up sprawled on the tarmac.

'Vivian!' she shouted, running over to scoop her off the ground. 'You aren't supposed to go down the slide like that!'

'Why not?' asked her daughter, seeming unperturbed by the nasty graze on her shoulder, which Rachel was inspecting as she pulled her away. 'It doesn't hurt. It's boring doing it the normal way.'

'Well, we'll have to go home now so I can clean this. You're bleeding.'

'No! I don't want to go home yet!' Vivian began to tug at Rachel's hand, leaning away and letting her legs go limp so all her weight was on her arm. She screamed, 'You're hurting me!' Several faces turned their way and Rachel could feel heat creeping up the back of her neck and into her cheeks.

'You're hurting yourself!' she hissed, mortified by her suddenly kicking and screaming child. 'Stand up properly!' As suddenly as the tantrum had started, it stopped. Vivian stood up and pulled her hand away with a sharp jerk, her features stony, her mouth in a distinct pout. Rachel picked up her hand again. 'We can come back later, or Nana will bring you, okay? I might need to do a bit of work this afternoon.'

Vivian didn't say anything; she was silent the short walk home, not even asking for a Mr Whippy as they passed the ice-cream van that had pulled up by the gates to the park and was already surrounded by a gaggle of excited children and harassed parents digging into their pockets and bags. *Suit yourself*, thought Rachel. *Always cutting your nose off to spite your face.*

Back at home, and as soon as Rachel had finished cleaning the nasty scuff on her shoulder with an antiseptic wipe, which she accepted without even a murmur though it must have been sore, Vivian jumped down from the kitchen counter she'd been lifted onto and ran out and up the stairs to her room, shutting the door just too loudly behind her.

'What's all that about?' asked Carol, coming out of the front room where she'd been watching her soaps. 'Is she okay? I wasn't expecting you back yet.'

'She scraped her shoulder and didn't want to come home to clean it,' said Rachel. 'She had a right shit fit in the park. Have you seen my phone? I need to check something.'

'What happened to your free weekends?' asked Carol, turning away with a sniff. 'I'll go and check on her. And no, I haven't seen your phone.'

'It was on charge,' Rachel said to her retreating back, looking at the wire which was still plugged in, but was devoid of her phone on the end. She looked around the kitchen, lifting and moving various magazines and other detritus. It wasn't there, and flipping all the cushions in the front room didn't reveal it either. She'd put it on charge last night, she knew she had. It had been almost dead. She tried calling it from the landline, listening for vibrations, but there was no sign of it and it went straight to voicemail, her own voice asking her to leave a message.

Running up the stairs herself she went into Vivian's room, where her mother and daughter were sitting on the bed. Vivian was still in her silent sulk, sitting stiffly on Carol's lap as she fussed over her shoulder and stroked her hair.

'Vivian, have you seen Mummy's work phone?'

Pale grey eyes just looked at her coldly, her face unmoving.

'No? Not been playing with it? You know you aren't supposed to touch my work phone.'

Vivian just turned her face into Carol's chest, refusing to look at her mother any more.

Stamping back down the stairs into the kitchen, Rachel looked around again, rooting through drawers and opening child-height cupboards. No sign of the phone. As she stood, a thought occurred to her, and she moved to the back door and tried the handle. It was open.

'Mum!' she shouted, 'did you leave the back door open again?'

Carol came down, Vivian trailing silently behind her.

'Did you open it this morning or has it been open all night again?'

Carol had the decency to look guilty rather than deny it outright. 'Rachel, I'm sure—'

'Sure what? That some crackhead has run in and nicked my phone? Like last time, when my bag went? And your sunglasses? It's probably the same person! They probably think this house is a guaranteed mark! *Mum*, for god's sake, anyone could have come in.'

'I thought I locked it… I was sure I did… I had to open it when I was cooking dinner, but I thought I locked it…' Carol trailed off, put her hand to her mouth.

'Silly Nana,' said Vivian, smiling.

# Rachel

'Vivian! Are you awake yet, darling?'

I heard movement from her bedroom, so despite the lack of a reply I decided she must be awake. I set some breakfast stuff out for her, cereal and the juice she liked, and then went upstairs to get my bag together for London. I really didn't want to go, but the author of *Prince of Dark Wings* was really keen to meet with me in person and talk through the draft sketches I was doing. The publisher had paid for my train tickets, and I could be there and back by tonight.

I hadn't been back to London in almost six years. I could almost taste it in my mouth, that dirty, grey city-slick over everything, cigarettes and traffic. I'd found it so enticing once, the city pulse. Not any more.

Vivian mooched into the kitchen and winced as she sat down.

'Are you okay, Viv?'

'Yeah. I just banged my hip at school yesterday.'

'Ouch. Let's have a look?'

She unwillingly slid down the side of her skirt and untucked her school shirt to show me a nasty green and purple bruise. There was so little to her that she often bruised badly, from even small knocks. When she was little her shins had always been so mottled with bruises of varying ages that they looked like storm clouds.

'That looks really sore, darling – there's some arnica cream in the bathroom cabinet you can put on it—?'

'I'm sure I'll live, Mum.' She rolled her eyes. I gritted my teeth and took a breath to smooth away the irritation. Why did Vivian always have to make her disdain so clear? I'd literally given up everything I'd ever worked for to keep her safe, and she treated me like I was just some nuisance. The lack of respect – gratitude, even – was beginning to grate more each day.

'I need to go to London today, babe, so make sure you take your keys to school. I probably won't be back 'til late so you'll have to fend for yourself. Maybe have Molly over or something, keep you company? She can stay over if you like, I don't mind. There's stuff in the fridge.'

'I'm sure I'll cope. Why do you have to go to London?' She looked uncomfortable at the thought, and I understood how she felt. Bad memories. Police. Hospital smells.

'I have to meet with the author of *Wings*.'

'Sounds boring.'

'Probably. We can do something this weekend, if you want? Maybe we could go to the cinema or something, go for dinner in the city?' I felt bad that I had been seeing so little of her; I could feel her slipping away from me and it frightened me. She just shrugged.

We finished breakfast and I dropped her off at school on my way to the station. As she went in I noticed Serena and Tilly by the door. They looked at her walking up and turned away. I couldn't see if Vivian had noticed or not but I felt another small pang of concern, and really hoped that everything was okay in her group. Vivian didn't cope well with changing friendship dynamics. I worried at the thought like a bone all the way to the station, and through to London. I was already suspicious about her behaviour over the weekend, how she had holed herself away brooding over something. I remembered how badly she had been bullied before, how eventually even her best friend had deserted her. Not that I had known what was happening until it was too late to do anything about it. The ever-present guilt – how badly I'd let her down – it stung.

–

The sights and smells of my abandoned home town pummelled me as soon as I got off the train at Paddington. The heat amplifies London. Emotions run higher, happy laughter outside pubs can turn to violence in a flash, temper running just beneath the surface, an undercurrent of disquiet. The stink of bins catches at you just as you breathe in, turning your stomach. How had I ever loved this place? Already I was longing for the clean scent of the fields and woods, of new-home. A rash of sweat broke out under my arms and on my back. I was going to be a complete mess by the time I turned up at the publishers.

The meeting was near Euston, a stone's throw away from where I had worked as a campaign manager before we left London. I'd been so happy in the huge ad agency. Every day was different, fast, clever. I'd felt important, an important cog in a top-class engine. I had worked so hard, given up so much to get to where I did. No one had even called me after I left. No one had cared. I wasn't important at all. I spent every second on the way to the meeting praying that I wouldn't bump into anyone I knew. Not that they would likely remember or even recognise me, after six years in the wilderness.

Walking into the offices of the publishers I felt light-headed, almost out of my body. I was worried about the meeting, about conversing with people. I had cloistered us away from situations where new people might be. I wasn't anxious that my work wasn't good enough, more that I wasn't. I didn't feel like a fully formed human being any more, there were so many parts of me missing, gouged out of me. I could barely breathe; all the fear we'd run away from rushed back. I knew the danger was no longer here, but my body thought otherwise. I managed to present myself at the desk in reception and the trendy, bespectacled man behind the desk, whip thin, offered me a cold drink of water. It felt amazing, that first cool sip. That, and the blissful air conditioning helped me pull the fractures back together.

I made it through the meeting, long and boring as it turned out to be, without collapse; I left the building to start my journey home on a high. I had done it. I'd come back to London and survived the experience. I almost enjoyed the walk back, weaving through the crowds, slipping through easily like the native I had been, descending into the underground. It wasn't until I'd been on the tube for twenty minutes that I realised, pulling my head out of my book, that I'd gone the wrong way. In unthinking relief, my feet had taken an old, well-trodden path from Euston. I had got on the Victoria Line; I was heading back to Walthamstow.

I couldn't stop myself in the end. I got off the tube at Walthamstow Central, stepped out onto the road opposite the bus station, my heart fluttering. I wanted to see. I wanted to see again where I had lived, all those years of my life after my father died and my mother was broken, and after Vivian was born. I wanted to see my old house. I slowly walked up St Mary Road, cutting through on East Avenue to Orford Road. So slowly.

Would anyone recognise me now, out of my sharp suits, my straightened hair and those pretentious horn-rimmed glasses that I hadn't even needed? I was such a fool. Pretending everything was perfect.

There was the old deli on the corner. The Queen's Arms had been renovated, gastro-pubbed. People were seated outside the tapas restaurant enjoying the evening sun with large glasses of wine and bottles of beer. I watched a couple sitting together: she was tracing pictures on the condensation that misted her glass, and he was looking at her with a vague expression of amazement that someone as pretty as her was sitting there, with him. They both looked so happy. I wondered how their story would play out, where they were in it: the beginning? The middle? I didn't know where I was in my story; if it was even my own any more, or if I was just a bit part in my daughter's. I wanted a drink, badly, but I was too afraid to stop anywhere. I couldn't risk being recognised. I couldn't bear the looks I might get. I put on a pair of oversized sunglasses that I had bought for Vivian and then adopted because she refused to wear them. They suited me well enough. The glasses and wild curls, I hoped they would make an adequate disguise.

I made my way down Beulah Road looking at all the little cottages as I always had, so cosy and safe looking; imagining the happy, normal families inside the old brick and whitewash walls. Most of the houses on Maynard Road were bigger, except the one we had lived in, squeezed in like an afterthought between two existing ones. I stopped outside, on the opposite side of the road. I didn't want to get any closer. The roses in the front garden were blooming as well as they had ever done, the lavender spraying out through the fence. My mum had loved those flowers and I was glad they were still being cared for. My heart ached for her, as always. You don't realise the enormity of someone's presence in your life until they are gone, and all you are left with is a hole. And my mother's death had been such a shock – she'd been young, really, still fit and healthy. I miss her every day. I miss her love, the scent of her embrace.

A tatty red car had pulled up a few spaces away from me. I was vaguely aware of a dark-haired man in the driver seat, but it was the slim blonde woman whose appearance punched me, stole the air out of my lungs. It was Lucy. Her face had aged, it was hollow and worn. She looked awful – why did she still look so awful, after all this time? Surely things would be better by now? What had happened?

I didn't stay. I turned and I ran. I always run.

## Vivian

'Why has your mum gone to London?'

Molly is lying on my bed, kicking her legs off the side, making a mess. She makes a mess everywhere she goes. They follow her around, messes.

'She's got a meeting with an author. She's doing the pictures for their book.'

'A kid's book?'

'No, it's for our age.'

'Oh. Aren't we a bit old for pictures in books? I thought she just did the covers?'

'That's what I said. I think they are trying to make it a thing again for older books, too. I wish I could draw like she does.'

Molly looks at me, pinning me with her eyes. I don't like it when she looks at me like that. I can never figure out what she is thinking.

'You've got other talents, though.'

I think this is where you are supposed to be self-deprecating. I know I have talents.

'Hardly.'

Molly spins on the bed and hangs her head over the side, looking up at me upside down. Her hair spools onto the floor and I can't help thinking it will get everywhere. I'm always finding long, golden hairs all over me, like she's marking me with them. Little golden chains.

'You have plenty of talents. You're an amazing actress, aren't you, Vivvy?'

'You're the one doing drama, Molly. I hate drama.'

'No, you hate dramas, not drama. But you're acting every day, aren't you? Pretending you're like us.'

'What?'

'Pretending. You pretend to like the boys we like, the clothes, the shows, and try and fit in, but you're not like us at all, are you?'

'I am like you! I'm completely normal, stop being a dick, Molly!' Worry is bubbling inside me, where has this come from?

'Don't worry, I still like you, Vivian. I don't think you're dangerous. You make me laugh. And you'd never hurt me, would you?'

'Dangerous? What? What the fuck are you on about today? You're being really weird. Why would I hurt you?' Panic beats its drum in my throat. What does she know? Has she been speaking to my mother about me? I remember how cosy they had looked out there in the studio, together, without me. But she wouldn't say anything, I'm sure of it.

Molly just hangs upside down like a bat, looking at me. Why would she think I was dangerous? Deep down I can feel a secret part of myself coming apart, trying to escape, and I have to breathe in very slowly to keep it together. I pretend to write something in my book. We were just reading passages from *Macbeth* to each other before she started on this. I stare at the page, watch the words swim.

*Fill me from the crown to the toe top-full*
*Of direst cruelty.*

I'm gripping my pen so tightly it's hurting my fingers. It would be so easy. It would be *so* easy. But then I would be right back where I started, before we left London. I don't ever want to go back there.

'Do you like Alex? He's up to something, you know. He was talking to me about you.'

Mercurial as always, Molly switches topics as quickly as changing a TV channel. She always does this to me, tries to shake me up. I'm much too clever for that trick. This is what she really wants to talk about. I can ignore the rest – it was the wind-up, she was just making it up to try and catch me out, no one knows anything. *Breathe. Relax.* Alex is the trigger here, and that I can deal with. Relief makes me light-headed and colourful spots dance behind my eyelids like sprites.

'I'm not interested in him, so he can be up to whatever he wants.' *Breathe out, feign boredom.*

'Why not? It's not like you don't get asked. Tommy asked you out last year, and he's quite fit.'

'I just don't want to do any of that stuff.'

'What stuff?'

'You know!'

'No, what?'

'Molly!'

'Vivian!'

I swear to god, one of these days…

'Haven't you even thought about it, though? You must think about what it's like. Everyone does. It's perfectly normal, you know.'

Maybe I *should* think about it. It all looks so disgusting and dirty, though. I just can't see how it would be nice in any way. I haven't figured out yet what I'd get out of it; it always looks like the men are doing all the enjoying. I'm not doing it unless I get something out of it, too.

'And if you went out with Alex everyone would die of jealousy.'

'I suppose.' I change the subject. 'Do you think Serena threw that ball at me on purpose in PE? I've got a massive bruise.' I slip down the side of my shorts for her to see, and she purses her lips and frowns.

'Ouchie. That looks sore. No, I don't think she wanted it to hit you. She was just being a dick, trying to make you jump out the way. I don't know. Don't worry about her, she'll get over herself.'

'I hope so. I don't like it when things are all messed up.' I look down at her. 'Your head is going to pop if you hang there for much longer, Molly.'

'Blood flow is good for the complexion, Viv! You should try it.' She laughs.

Molly finally hauls her now very pink face up from where it was hanging and flops back down on the bed. I can see a sheen of sweat on her skin and it's getting on my sheets. I'm going to have to change them now; I won't be able to sleep in them, otherwise. I feel itchy already. If it's not her revolting hairs, it's her sticky skin.

We both get back to our books, but something she said is distracting me. Would people look at me differently if I was with Alex? Would I be the most popular one? We scribble for a while longer before Molly starts to get antsy again.

'Let's have a drink.'

'What? A drink drink? It's Wednesday, Molly, we've got school tomorrow.'

'So? A couple won't hurt. I'm bored. Go on, Viv, you're no fun any more. I only brought a couple, and I'm staying over, and your mum's out...'

I am not boring! I don't really want to but I guess a few won't hurt.

'Okay, but I don't want to stay up late!'

'Yeah, yeah,' says Molly, as she runs out of the room and down to the kitchen, taking her bag – which I now realise is clinking – with her. She comes back with pint glasses full of bright pink fizzy cider and ice. Passing one to me, she holds the other out, too.

'Cheers!' she demands, pushing her glass against mine. We drink. It tastes a bit funny; I tell her I don't like it and she rolls her eyes, so I just drink it, and I drink the other two she makes as well.

After the third one, I try and stand up to go to the bathroom and I stumble against the doorframe on the way out, feeling dizzy suddenly. I don't like it. I feel a bit sick.

'Are you all right, Viv?' asks Molly, when I come back. I can feel a slick of sweat on my top lip gathering in the dip beneath my nose, matching ones at my ears, on my neck. Everything is a bit fuzzy. Am I drunk? How can I be drunk? I don't usually feel like this after three – I never have more than three for precisely that reason.

'Vivian,' says Molly, her voice sounding a bit like it's in a bubble, 'why did you and your mum move here? Why did you leave London?'

'She didn't like her job,' I lie, not liking the conversations tonight. I hate talking about London. She knows this. Why is she being so weird and nosy all of a sudden?

'Alex was asking me why you'd come here. I don't think I like Alex,' she says. Back to this again. The constant change of subjects is making me nauseous.

'What? Why not? I thought you thought he was sex on legs.'

'No, he's fit but I don't like him. I don't trust him, I don't think you should trust him, either. He's shady.' Her voice trails off as she shifts closer to me on the bed. I hope she's not going to get all touchy-feely with me. 'Do you like him?'

'I... I don't know, I haven't really thought about it...'

'What?' Molly sways towards me, crawling up the bed to where I've had to sit down, my head nodding, flopping. I jerk it back up. 'He's interested in you, in some weird way, how can you not be interested, too? Vivian, do you think you might be gay? I don't mind, you know I love you, right?' I can feel her breath on my cheek, and I lean away, almost falling off the edge of the mattress.

'I'm not. I don't fancy anyone. I just don't think about it.' My head is pounding now, and I can feel my eyeballs, the pressure of them, the size of them pulsing like rotten grapes in my skull. 'Moll, I think that cider is off, I feel really weird.'

'You should think about it,' she says, reaching out a hand. I jump up, and stumble.

'Get away from me,' I say, just before I have to run to the bathroom to be sick. 'Get away.'

# London

The hot steam from the oven fogged Carol's glasses as she pulled out the tray with the fishfingers on. 'Argh!' she said, as she turned to the table. 'I'm blind!' As the lenses cleared she saw Vivian's friend Lexie was giggling, and, watching her, Vivian began giggling, too.

'Are you both really hungry?' she asked.

'Starving!' said Lexie.

'Yes, starving!' said Vivian.

'Can you eat *three* fishfingers each? Three whole fishfingers, and chippies, and peas?'

'Yes!'

'Yes!' came the little voices.

Lexie was in Vivian's class, and she'd surprised Carol a few days earlier by asking if the smiley blonde girl could come for tea one day. 'She's my best friend,' Vivian had claimed.

'Is she? How lovely!' Carol hadn't said as such but she was very relieved to know Vivian had a friend. She'd been more worried than she'd admitted to herself or Rachel, who didn't seem to be worried at all, about Vivian starting school. Nursery hadn't been the greatest hit, and she'd wondered if school would be any better.

Now, Carol enjoyed the fact Vivian was chattier than usual because of her guest. She slid the crumbed fishfingers off the tray and onto the plates and cut them into mouthfuls, adding the chips and peas. 'Make sure you blow on it,' she warned. 'Who wants ketchup?'

'Me, please!' said Lexie. 'Thank you.'

'I want ketchup too, Nana,' said Vivian.

'Really?' asked Carol, looking at her as she pulled the bottle from the cupboard. 'You don't like ketchup.'

'Yes, I do!' she insisted.

'It's my favourite,' said Lexie. 'I love ketchup. Mummy says I would put ketchup in my cereal if she let me.'

'It's my favourite, too,' said Vivian, though Carol noticed later that she hadn't actually eaten any of the sauce she'd insisted on squeezing onto her plate.

The girls were playing in Vivian's room when the doorbell rang.

'Hello! How have they been?' Lexie's mum was standing on the doorstep.

'Good as gold. Come in. Have you got time for a drink? Tea? Coffee? Wine?'

'Ooh, go on, then. I'll have some wine, if you are. Liam is with his dad this weekend, and he's taking him to Silverstone tomorrow. Lexie's a bit little to be interested, so we're having a girly weekend. He'll have her next weekend instead.'

Carol smiled faintly at the ins and outs of split parenting. Not a choice she'd had after Rachel's dad had died; there had only been her, having to hide her grief to support her little girl. Even now, it was her whole focus. Two years to herself while Rachel was at university and then she'd come home beaten up and pregnant, expecting Carol to pick up the pieces. 'Well, you'll definitely want a wine, then. They're playing upstairs. Come through.'

Lucy sat down at the table and looked around. 'I always love walking down this road. We're only around the corner, on Eden. I wondered what this one would be like inside – it's bigger than it looks from the outside, isn't it? Ours is like that, bit of a Tardis. Have you lived here long?'

'Thirty years now, and Blackhorse Road before that.'

'Wow, a long time! You're a proper East Ender. So, did Rachel grow up here?'

'She did, before a bit of art uni in Manchester. She went to Henry Maynard School, too.'

'How lovely! Is Vivian enjoying it? I can't believe reception is going by so quickly.'

'I think she is now she's made a friend. Lexie is a credit to you, by the way – she's a sweetheart.'

Carol took a bottle of wine from the fridge and poured it into waiting glasses.

'Thank you. She is a love. She was still a baby when her dad left, it didn't seem to affect her too much. Liam's a different story unfortunately – he can remember us together and it's difficult for him. Is Vivian's dad still in the picture? She told Lexie she didn't see him.'

'No, thankfully,' said Carol with a frown, as she sat down and passed a glass to Lucy. 'Rachel is well out of that.'

'Sorry, I shouldn't have asked. I talk too much, and don't think; that was rude of me. What is it she does? Rachel?'

'Don't apologise, it's fine, honestly. She's in advertising,' said Carol, making air quotes with her fingers. 'Something artistic. She got a promotion, recently, and it's taken up a lot of her time.'

'I don't see her a lot at school. But she seems lovely, and it must be exciting, advertising. I'm an accountant, can't really get much duller. But at least I can work around the kids.' Lucy smiled and lifted her glass to drink.

'Speaking of kids...' said Carol, as feet thundered down the stairs.

'Mummy!' shouted Lexie, as she bounded into the room, throwing herself onto Lucy's lap. 'I missed you!'

'Hello, darling, have you had a nice play?'

'Yes. We had fishfingers and we played with Vivian's phone.'

'Vivian's phone?' said Carol. 'Vivian, what phone were you playing with?'

'It was just pretend, Nana,' said Vivian, who was giving Lexie a look.

'No, it wasn't,' said Lexie, oblivious. 'Vivian's got a phone. A black one, with lots of buttons.'

# Vivian

'Oh god, my head really hurts.' I open my eyes and then shut them straight away. 'I think my teeth have melted.'

'Yeah, I don't think you brushed them last night, you were so wasted!' Molly has the temerity to laugh at me, when she was behind this.

'Did you spike those drinks, Molly? Why?' I put my hands over my face, fan my fingers so it's covered and press down so it doesn't slide off when I sit up. I'm going to assume this is my first and last hangover. I'm never letting that sneaky bitch make me a drink ever again. Snatches of last night seep into my brain: what Molly was saying about me, asking me if I was a lesbian. What is wrong with her? All any of that stuff does is cause trouble. Look at how much she's fucked everything up.

'Can I have a shower first?' Molly asks, ignoring my question and stripping off her night clothes. She has no modesty whatsoever, and I have to avert my eyes from the expanse of skin while she grabs the towel I put out for her. 'Do you think your mum will make pancakes?'

'I don't think she's up. I didn't hear her come home, did you?'

'Yeah, I heard her come in. It was late though.'

'Well, maybe, I don't know...'

Molly sings in the shower, badly. She might be good at a lot of things but her singing could strip wallpaper. It wakes my mother up, which I suspect was her intention, and I hear her moving around in the kitchen in between verses.

By the time I am finished in the cold shower, which fails to cool me down but at least makes me feel cleaner, and slightly more alive, Molly has already disappeared. I get ready and slink down the stairs, soft feet, so I can snoop. They are laughing together, not talking, so I go in. Neither of them takes any notice of me standing in the doorway: I am invisible.

'Wait, wait!' says Molly, who has hold of the frying pan and is trying to flip the pancake. 'Yay!' It flips in the air, she catches it perfectly, and she puts the pan back down and catches my mother in a hug, which she reciprocates. This scene of domestic bliss makes me feel sick, so I cough, and they see me and step apart. I hate pancakes.

–

The school day drags as the remains of my Molly's-fault headache rolls around in my skull, squashing and squeezing my brain. She is as perky as ever, laughing and joking, while I feel vile and moody. It's harder to behave when I am not feeling straight. All of them tease me at lunch for being hungover.

'You look as rough as a badger's arse,' giggles Tilly, covering her mouth like she always does when she laughs, ashamed of her teeth.

'At least I don't smell like one, like your disgusting brother!' I snap, and enjoy the offended look on her face. I cannot stop myself. 'Are you rancid on the inside, like he is?'

'What's that supposed to mean?' she asks me, eyebrows gathering above her watery eyes in a frown. 'He's not that bad! That's out of order, Vivian – I was only teasing you because you're hungover for once, instead of us.'

'Truth hurts, huh?'

'Fuck off!'

'Molly knows all about how rancid he is, don't you, Molly?' Her face is a picture, but I don't really understand why: she knows what he did to me the other night, she was there! I open my mouth to say I don't know what when she stands up and grabs me by the arm, pulling me out of my chair and hurting me. I swing my other arm and slap her, hard, on her bare bicep. The noise of it rings around the room. Serena and Tilly are aghast, stupid eyes wide.

'Vivian Sanders! Molly Barnes!' The strident voice of Mrs Barker shouts out across the canteen, making us cringe. 'Come with me, right now!'

The walk is sullen. I didn't mean to hit her, she was hurting me first. They always hurt me first – it's not my fault if I lash out after, is it? I can feel imprints of hard fingers circling the thin muscle of my arm: little burning spots. My jaw hurts where I have been gritting my teeth. Molly hurt me. She is trying to steal my mother: every time she sees her I catch her all over her, in the studio, in the kitchen, and now she hurt me. I don't like this Molly.

Mrs Barker takes us into Mrs Brondsbury's little office next to reception. I don't know where she is, but her stink lingers. Coffee and stale cigarette smoke. I can feel a slick of sweat start up on the back of my neck, and I have to tense to not heave up my lunch on the carpet.

'It was my fault, miss,' says Molly, stepping forward in front of me. 'I was pulling her, it was my fault.' I can see the welts my fingers have left on the silky skin of her upper arm, white blending to pink, strangely beautiful.

'I saw her hit you, Molly. And not gently.'

'It didn't hurt, miss, it was my fault.'

Mrs Barker looks unconvinced. I just look at the floor, though I can feel her eyes on me, suspicious. She's never liked me, not since Mum came in and had a meeting with her because she was worried about bullying, like at my old school. God knows what she blabbed on about. I am so cross at myself for not keeping it together. At least Molly is admitting that it's all her fault, which makes me inclined to forgive her for yesterday's transgressions. Maybe.

'Both in detention tonight, please. I won't have fighting on school grounds. I'm frankly disappointed in you, Molly.'

Why isn't she disappointed in me? I've never had a detention in my life!

# Rachel

I always enjoyed it when Molly stayed over, but it made me feel guilty too, because I would always catch a secret part of myself wishing Vivian could be more like her. I loved my daughter madly, but I longed for an easier, more tactile relationship. I missed human touch. Vivian hated it when I tried to hug her, or kiss her – anything at all really. She'd always been like that, even as a small child, pushing me away. She allowed it as she got older, sometimes reciprocated and did *try* to be affectionate – her friends were good for her like that – but I could always sense the tension it sparked in her. I didn't know if it was just me, or if she was like that with everyone. The psychiatrists at the hospital told me that she had delayed empathy. One suggested that she had an attachment disorder, that I was not loving or caring enough, that perhaps bringing her up without any contact with her father and then working too much had scarred her. I was never sure, and I didn't believe their suggestion that she might be autistic, either – she was who she was, and I had to love her in spite of what she had done, because I had brought her into the world. Nothing seemed to be holding her back from life now anyway, and I had given up everything to devote myself to her full time, like a proper mother. And I was always watching.

I didn't see Alex that week at the Thursday life class, where Geoff was magnificent as always, and I assumed he had changed his mind about coming along, or having lessons, and I was surprised at the pang of disappointment I felt. I found myself thinking about him and wondering what he might be working on as I was in my studio.

After school on Friday Vivian rolled in and was about to run up the stairs when I caught her. She'd been avoiding me all week, hiding in her room like a little mouse.

'Darling, come and have a drink before you disappear into your pit.' Her face creased with annoyance as I deliberately offended her – she was obsessively neat.

'Ugh, Mum, I've got loads of revision to do. We've got exams next week.'

'Yes, but it can wait ten minutes while we have a chat, can't it? You've been holed up in your room all week. It's not like you – you're all usually out and about.'

'Yeah, I just said, I've got revision?' She looked at me again like I was an insufferable moron then sloped into the kitchen, begrudgingly plonking herself at the table. I moved in behind her and made us both a squash with ice from the freezer, enjoying the crackling noise the ice made in the tall glasses.

'So,' I began, 'how is everything at school? Are you worried about the GCSE mocks?'

'Not really.' She lifted a slim shoulder in a shrug, tucked her hair behind her ear.

'Why were you back from school so late yesterday? You didn't really answer me when I asked you at dinner. What's going on?'

'Nothing. I was just hanging out at Molly's, we were revising. Sorry, I meant to text you.'

'Are you out with the girls tonight?'

'No. But I'll probably go out for a walk or something. I need to do some sketching for our art coursework.'

'Is everything okay with you guys? I haven't seen much of anyone this week.'

'You saw Molly, didn't you? You two were having a lovely time flipping pancakes yesterday,' she said, looking into her drink, a small frown on her face. 'Everything is fine.'

'Are you sure, Vi? You know you can always talk to me about anything at all, anything you want to?'

She looked up at me with her funny half-smile. 'Yes, Mum,' she said, with a fake-weary sigh. 'I know you are the super-cool young mother that I can talk to about sex, drugs and rock 'n' roll. But I'm not having any sex or drugs, and rock 'n' roll is shit, so I'm fine, okay? Are you going out tonight? I wouldn't mind the TV to myself.'

'Is that a hint? I could pop out to the pub, I suppose. I didn't go yesterday after class. Steve probably missed me.'

'I'm sure he did. You should go out, I'll be fine.' She picked up her squash and gave me a rare kiss on the cheek before going upstairs. Everything seemed fine, but something she said had left me with the unsettling image of her watching me cooking with Molly from the kitchen doorway, silent and jealous, on the outside. I needed to be more careful of her feelings.

# Vivian

Mum taps on the door and tells me ten minutes until dinner, so I shut dull *Jane Eyre* which I'm revising from and pick up my phone instead. There aren't any messages. Everything has been really weird since last weekend, and the fight yesterday made it even worse. We've all been kind of acting like nothing happened, and that everything is normal, but it's like we're all dancing on ice without knowing the steps. It could break at any second and then we'd all drown, freezing in dark waters. I still have a bruise on my hip from where Serena threw the ball at me – I know she did it on purpose, but what did I do? I wasn't the one who went after the boy she liked; I just lied for Molly.

I haven't seen Alex all week. I haven't stopped thinking about what Molly said about him fancying me, and about what being with him might mean. I wonder where he might be, and if he's with someone already. I decide I don't like the imaginary girlfriend I've concocted, unless it turns out to be me, of course.

'Viv!' shouts Mum from downstairs. 'Tea's ready!'

I leave my phone on my desk and go downstairs to eat. I decide I can't be arsed to do any more revision tonight. Mum – who is looking a bit glammed up for once, which is weird – leaves to go and see Steve and tells me she'll be back before ten, so I can take over the front room and binge-watch my shows. I'm feeling pretty smug about getting rid of her for the evening so easily, without getting an inquisition.

I make myself some popcorn and a drink and I've literally just sat down when the doorbell goes. I really hope it's not for me, as I've had enough of this week and for a second I think about just sitting here quietly, but no doubt Door Knocker's next step will be to peep in the window right at where I am, so I get up and answer the door.

It's Alex.

'What are you doing here?' I ask him. I realise I'm still angry about what he said about Molly last weekend, even though it might have been true. 'Here to tell more lies about my friends? And how did you know where I lived?'

He shrugs, looking irritatingly cool and collected in a white T-shirt and cut-off grey jeans. I'm a sweaty mess and I wish I'd had another shower and not eaten so much of Mum's lasagne. He's caught me off-guard, which is rude.

'I know where everyone lives. It's not a big place, is it? Can I come in?'

I begrudgingly agree with this statement, and I step aside to let him come in. I catch that earthy, smoky scent again as he walks past, and the clean smell of his skin, and I feel my heart beat faster. His dark hair curls at the back of his neck onto his collar and I have to stop myself reaching up and threading my fingers through it. What is wrong with me?

He walks straight into the front room like he owns the place, flops on the sofa and starts eating my popcorn.

'You didn't answer my question,' I accuse him.

'Which one?' he replies, throwing a piece of popcorn in the air and catching it in his mouth, like a dog. 'Okay, I was bored, I wasn't lying about your friend, and I already

96

told you I know where everyone lives. What are we watching?'

I'm mildly embarrassed by the 'recently watched' list that pops up as I turn the TV on, so I quickly flick to movies.

'I don't really want to watch a film,' Alex says suddenly, turning to look at me. He takes the remote from me, fingers brushing mine, and switches off the TV. 'Has your mum got anything to drink?'

Feeling a bit like I've fallen asleep without realising and gone into a lucid dream, I go into the kitchen and open the fridge. There are a couple of bottles of white wine in there and I know there's a box in the cupboard too, because Mum gets a wine club thing, so I think I could pinch some and she wouldn't notice, even though I haven't really drunk it before as we usually get cider. I grab a bottle and two glasses and go back in to the front room, trying not to shake with nerves. I don't like not knowing what to expect.

Alex is looking at our books.

'I like that one,' he says, pointing at one of Mum's. I don't see which and I don't really care, because books are boring. I sit down and he takes the bottle from me so I can put down the glasses. He pours us both a glass then goes and puts the bottle back in the fridge.

'Warm wine is the worst,' he says, coming back in and sitting next to me, closer than he was before. 'So, pretty little Vivian, tell me everything about you.'

'I don't think there's much to tell.'

'You don't sound like you're from here. You haven't got a farmer twang.' He's leaning back on the sofa, scuffing lines in the suedey material, then rubbing them out again with his long fingers.

'No, we moved here from London. We've been here since I was nine.' I find myself leaning back too, mirroring his position. I read somewhere that it's what people do, to make other people feel comfortable. I don't, but I don't want him to know that.

'Why did you leave?' He looks so directly at me, and I try to do it back.

'Why do you care?'

'Just trying to make conversation.'

'I saw you trying to make conversation with Molly the other morning.' As usual my mouth snipes quicker than my brain can think. He laughs.

'Ah, Molly. She's really pretty, isn't she? I bumped into her on the way to school.' I don't like him saying Molly is pretty. Is he here with me because he wants to get in with her? Jealousy pricks me. It's always Molly.

'I've not seen you walking that way before,' I tell him.

He just smirks, and changes the subject back to London, again. 'I'm from London, too. Why did your mum want to leave? I don't know why anyone would choose to come here if they didn't have to.'

Despite the repetitive questions, which annoy me, he's surprisingly easy to talk to. He asks me loads more. People usually just want to talk about themselves, integrate themselves by comparing their experiences to yours, take over. We talk and talk for ages. I do eventually tell him about where we used to live in London and I even talk a little bit about how awful it was there, about the bullying and how the other kids were so horrid to me. I'm telling him about Tristan trying to touch me last weekend after the party when I notice that his eyes have gone all flinty; he looks angry.

I swallow more of the suddenly sour-tasting liquid in my glass – the last of the bottle I see now, empty on the table next to us – a bit disconcerted by the look on his face. We both put our glasses down at the same time, and then he reaches out, pulls me towards him and kisses me, hard. He drags me up onto his lap and I go with it willingly, feeling a rush that surprises me, straddling his legs like Molly did to Matthew, wrapping mine behind him. When he crushes me against him, pulling my hips down, it almost steals my breath. He slips his hands under my top, smoothing them up and down, and it feels like they are big enough to circle my waist entirely. His thumbs rub the skin at edge of my bra, back and forth, bumping along my ribs.

His tongue is in my mouth properly now, and I always thought this would feel completely disgusting and cold like a fish, but it isn't. It's hot and fierce, and I want it all. I drag my fingers through his hair, pulling on it, and he tips us over on the sofa, and he starts to rub himself against me through our clothes, and I realise that he's got an erection and it's the best feeling ever, that I'm doing this to him, that he wants me – me! Not Molly, *me*.

His hands are in my hair now, twisting fingers, tugging, pulling. I wrap my arms around him and pull him down against me, like he could melt into me, like every inch of our bodies could touch all at once.

The friction he's creating between us as he rocks his hips between my legs is building up into something that I've never felt before. I can feel a flush rising up my chest, and I'm making stupid noises in my throat because my mouth is still full of his and I can feel that something, something is about to happen inside me when he suddenly stops and pulls away. The disappointment is crushing. I can't speak, I can't breathe, I could scream.

He looks at me and his eyes are darker than ever and his hair is sticking up where I've ruffled it.

'I'd better go,' he says, dipping his head and kissing my collarbone and nipping at my shoulder. I want him so badly to keep touching me it is literally hurting; I want to pull his head and his mouth back to me, but he sits and then stands up, arranging himself in his jeans, running his hands through his hair.

'See you later, Vivian.'

And then he's gone, leaving me feeling frustrated and more than a bit drunk. Did any of that even happen? Are we together now? I don't even have his phone number!

I'm furious he's just come over and done that to me – who does he think he is? – and I need some air, so I decide to go to the Lav and see Mum and Steve. They will probably be pissed by now and won't notice if I'm being weird. My legs are shaking as I get ready to go.

The field is getting really dusty now, the path is almost bare apart from some raggedy, yellow stalks of grass. The air is humming with heat, it matches my insides. I never thought that anything people did together looked enjoy-able, but maybe I was wrong. Maybe I would like to do those things. With Alex, if it feels like that. I can't believe I *liked* it.

I'm almost at the pub when I bump into bloody Tristan again, sitting on the bench by the duck pond, and he's just as drunk as he was last week, but not so amorous this time, thank god. He looks up at me as I walk towards him, briefly confused, but then he focuses.

'Where's your little blonde friend today, Vivvy?'

'Shut up, Tris. I don't want to talk to you.'

'You're as stuck up as she is. Happy to fuck me when she wants it though, isn't she? Likes a bit of my cock when it fucking suits her.'

'What are you talking about? Shut up, Tristan, you pervert!' I shout at him now, head hurting and feeling sick from the wine, remembering now the look he gave Molly last week. Surely she wouldn't go there – not with Tris, of all people? He's Tilly's brother! Even if he was attractive, and he is not, that's so gross. Something clicks in my head. This explains our fight in the canteen. Molly thought I knew about her and Tris, the dirty bitch! I'm utterly revolted at the thought of Molly, beautiful Molly, polluting herself with this horrible, grabby-fingered goblin.

'Ask her,' he says. 'Ask her, and when she lies, ask her how many moles she's got on the inside of her leg. I know how many, because, because I saw them when she was sitting on my fucking face!' He stands up and staggers off, almost falling. 'And tell her I'm going to tell everyone what a slut she is! You can't just go around fucking with people's heads, using people. See how fucking popular she is then!'

He's almost in tears as he stumbles off, his shoulder bouncing off the wall of the pub. I forget about going in to see Mum; I should go and find Molly and tell her what he's saying about her.

It's not far to her house and when I get there I go straight around the back because I know that if she is home, then she'll be sunning herself like a cat in the garden, as always, and I'm right. She's lying on a sun lounger on her front in shorts and nothing else, reading *Jane Eyre* in the last of the evening light.

'Put some clothes on, Molly!' I yell at her, covering my eyes. Now that I'm here it suddenly occurs to me that I have no idea how to speak to her about this. Do I just say, *Hey Moll, how is it having sex with every boy that moves? Is there anyone left you haven't felt up? By the way, our best friend's brother — you know, the really manky one with the horrid, greasy hair who spends his days getting intimate with dead chickens — is about to out you as a big slag to the whole village.*

'What's wrong with you?' she asks, pulling on a vest top. 'You look all hot and bothered, what have you been up to?'

'Nothing,' I say, immediately defensive, putting my fingers to my hair to make sure it's straight.

'Liar,' she says, seeing straight through me in a second. 'Tell me.'

'I haven't been doing anything! I was at home revising, then I was going to go and see my mum in the Lav and I bumped into Tris again, and he was drunk again and...' I trail off.

Molly's eyes suddenly go very cold, blue chips of ice gleaming. 'And what, Viv?' She leans towards me and tilts her head to one side. 'And. What? Did he touch you again? Because I will fucking kill him if he did.'

'No,' I blurt out, 'he says it's you who's been doing the touching.' I look at the ground because I don't want to watch her lie to my face again, it makes me so mad.

'Ugh,' she says, leaning back on her sun lounger and stretching her arms above her head. 'Please. We hooked up once when my parents were out and I was bored. It didn't mean anything, and I'm sure he's exaggerating what even happened and there's no way anyone would believe I'd touch him with a barge pole, even if he did say anything.'

This I can agree with.

'Why did you touch him with a barge pole?'

'Like I said, I was bored.'

'So much for your virgin status, you liar! I think Tilly would be upset if she found out. And I think Serena is still upset about last week, you and Matt.'

'What with me and Matt?' she says, and I look up. She's got a coy look on her face and it doesn't suit her.

'You know what,' I say, looking away again. 'I heard you in your bedroom with him, that's why I left.' I don't confess that I watched, and that I think about what I watched. 'This is why you hurt me yesterday, isn't it? You thought I was going to tell Tilly about you and Tristan. You thought I knew about him, as well as you and Matt.'

'You do have a nasty habit of finding things out.'

This is true, but I've clearly taken my eye off the ball recently if she's been managing all this extracurricular activity without me knowing. 'Who else have you been doing this with? Why?'

She jumps off the lounger, putting her hands on my shoulders and looking down at me. I can see her nipples through the thin white material of her vest top and I think she knows it.

'Vivvy, Vivvy, it doesn't mean anything. Serena doesn't know for sure anything happened, I'm not going to tell her and neither are you. That goes for that piglet Tristan, too.' She pokes me hard in the chest. 'And at least they know where to put it now!' She laughs and I feel angry, again. I think she is being blasé about what Tristan might say, and I worry about what might happen, that this might be the final straw for our group, even as she wraps her arms around me, presses herself to me, and tells me everything is fine.

I don't believe her. Something needs to be done.

# London

Rachel had needed to run to make the meeting, and when she arrived she already felt wrong-footed, and on edge. She didn't like Vivian's new year three teacher; in fact, she thought she was a bitch, and probably in the wrong profession. Why teach little kids when you clearly didn't have the right temperament for it? She shifted uncomfortably on the tiny wooden chair outside the classroom where she was being kept waiting – deliberately, no doubt.

'Mrs Sanders, would you like to come through?'

'It's Miss, actually.'

'My apologies, Miss Sanders, come through.'

Rachel looked around the room. It hadn't changed in the twenty-odd years since she had last seen it herself: words stuck on the walls, splashes of colour in paintings, messy handprints with names beneath. Nothing seemed different at all, except the size of her arse on the ridiculously small chairs.

'Thank you for seeing me, Mrs Sanders,' said the teacher.

Rachel felt the beginnings of a headache bloom above the clench of her jaw. 'No worries,' she lied. 'You said there'd been an incident you wanted to talk to me about—?'

'Yes, well. More of a series of incidents, really.'

'Go on.'

'We lost one of Vivian's classmates for an hour today.'

'I beg your pardon? You lost a child?'

'Not quite. Vivian had locked him in the PE cupboard. She didn't tell anyone this, despite us clearly looking, and asking the class where he was. We were very worried.'

'It took you an hour to find him? Was he not shouting?'

'The sports hall is kept locked outside PE lessons. Vivian stole my keys from my handbag and lured him inside on the pretext of pulling a prank. She locked him inside the cupboard, locked the hall again, and put my keys back in my handbag. He was extremely upset by the time we found him. He was on the verge of wetting himself.'

Rachel pressed her lips together to stop herself laughing with shock. The little madam!

'We'd called his parents – can you imagine how worried they were? I have given Vivian lunchtime detention all this week, as we do not suspend year three children. But this isn't the first issue we've had. We had the biting incident last year – which we chose to move past – and it's not the first time Vivian has taken things that don't belong to her.'

Rachel felt aggrieved on behalf of her girl. 'Look. She's only seven, and she's highly intelligent – you've said so yourself. Do you think maybe she's bored? Obviously I will be speaking to her about this, and we'll come up with a suitable punishment at home, but I do think there's something you need to work on here. The biting clearly has nothing to do with this, I don't see a connection.'

'Mrs Sanders, I really do think you should consider taking Vivian to a child psychologist – I—'

'It's Miss! And you're joking! A psychologist, for pulling a prank? That the boy was in on, from what you've just told me.'

'The boy wasn't aware that he would be the "prank", Miss Sanders. It concerned me that Vivian thought it was funny to leave him for so long. She is still denying having anything to do with it, though obviously the victim has identified her.'

'Victim! They're children, not murderers! Look, this was clearly unpleasant for the little boy who got locked in, but it was obviously a joke gone wrong. My daughter does not need to see anyone. Is this *victim* one of the children who has been bullying her, per chance?'

'We haven't seen any evidence of bullying. I have been watching. I wonder if Vivian's idea of bullying and actual bullying are the same thing. We'll be keeping an eye on her.'

'How do you even know for certain it was her?'

'Well, like I said, the victim—'

'So, it's just his word against hers? It could be him lying and saying it was her because he doesn't want to get a friend in trouble?'

'Well, I doubt it, what with the past history...'

'So, a half-hearted nip on the arm of a kid who was bullying her and now she's prime suspect for everything? That doesn't seem fair. Look, I'll talk to her and try and get to the bottom of it, but I think you need to think about how you're treating her. She isn't a bad kid.'

Miss Avon looked like she wanted to say more, but instead she stood up and gestured to the door. Rachel left.

–

Carol was in the kitchen when she got back, dropping a teabag into a mug. She looked at Rachel expectantly, an eyebrow quirked in a question.

'Don't ask!' said Rachel, as she sat down and put her face into her hands. 'Where is she?'

'She's upstairs playing. Should we talk about it?'

'Talk about what? It wasn't really anything, just a silly prank she took too far, if it even was her. According to Miss Dipshit, she locked some boy in a cupboard, probably one of the ones who've been teasing her, not that they ever fucking do anything about *that*. It's ridiculous – how were they allowed to sneak off together anyway? It's their fault.'

'Locking someone in a cupboard doesn't seem that extreme—?'

'Well, he was in there for quite a while from the sounds of it. They thought he'd run off, called his parents and everything.'

'God, that's awful! Why would she let it go that far?'

'I don't know!' Rachel threaded her fingers into her hair and pulled at it, groaning.

'Don't do that. It's not the first time you've been up there, is it?'

'That wasn't her fault, either! That horrible boy she bit had been teasing her for weeks – she'd already told you about it, though you neglected to tell me, didn't you? I'm always the last to hear anything about my own child!'

'Well, you're never here, are you? It's probably a cry for attention!' The accusing tone stung, and Rachel flinched, hot tears starting as her temper flared.

'I need to make money, Mum! I have to feed and clothe us! I'm not neglecting her, I spend every spare second I have with her – I don't have a life of my own outside work, or being here. What else am I supposed to do? I suppose you still think I should have just got rid of her, don't you?'

'Rachel, keep your voice down! She'll hear you!' Carol hissed, her face a picture of hurt. 'How dare you throw that in my face, after everything I've done for you? How dare you.' She slammed her hand on the work surface, the noise making Rachel jump.

'Mum, I—'

'Don't. I'm going out. You can feed *your child* and put her to bed. I've had enough of you not listening to anyone but yourself.'

'Mum, please – I didn't mean it…' But Carol pushed past her, picked up her bag from the hallway floor where she always left it, and walked out of the door.

Rachel took a steadying breath before steeling herself and heading upstairs to speak to Vivian – what choice did she have?

# *Rachel*

I was up first thing that Monday. It was unusual from the very beginning because Vivian had beaten me to it; she was already in the shower, even though it wasn't yet six. I hoped she hadn't been stressing about her exams or whatever it was going on with the girls. She buzzed around looking for things after breakfast, and then she was out the door with barely a bye.

I was in the studio later, finishing the fourth version of my third plate for *Prince of Dark Wings*, when my phone pinged with a message. I didn't recognise the number but I assumed it was mystery boy Alex, because it apologised for the last-minute request and asked if he could come over now. I agreed, as I needed a break from drawing wings. The detailing on the feathers was imprinted on my eyeballs. I texted him back offering to make him a cup of tea.

I went into the house and put the kettle on, setting out two mugs with teabags and sniffing the milk as I always do, even though I'd only bought it the day before. It's something my mother always used to do, but I don't think I ever did it myself until after she passed away. It's funny how we remember people.

There was a knock at the door and sure enough it was Alex, dressed for the ridiculously still-bloody-boiling weather in shorts and a vest top. He looked tanned and had that glow of vitality about him that somehow disappears over the years. I wonder when I lost mine.

I asked him how he took his tea — typical teenager: milky, two sugars — and then I took him out to my studio. To my gratification, he made a low whistle.

'This is awesome,' he told me, immediately nosing into everything like a magpie, picking things up and inspecting them from end to end before getting into something else. 'The light is amazing.'

'That was the plan.' I was pleased that he immediately grasped how I had put it together. 'I can't draw unless I have natural light. I'm a snob.'

'Who can?' he asked me. 'It's hard to catch shadows without the light.' He'd brought his portfolio again and I hoped there might be new sketches in there to look at.

'I thought maybe you might like to start with one of your sketches and pull a little bit of colour in from there?'

'It always looks like a cartoon if I try and add colour,' he griped good-naturedly. 'It just doesn't look natural.' He put the folio on the workbench and opened it, fanning out the work inside it.

'Start with muted colours and build up,' I suggested, picking out one of his beautiful fox sketches. It looked like a work in progress and he hadn't done much shading, just careful quick lines that captured the crouching intensity of an animal poised to run. 'Do you want to try the paints? This would look lovely with a wash of colour.'

I got out some old watercolours and palettes and told him to go and get himself some water from the kitchen. He came out of the house carefully carrying two jam jars of water — he'd spotted the stack obviously, and was clever enough to bring two at once. The look of concentration on his face reminded me of Vi when she was little, trying to tie her shoelaces. I felt myself warming towards him, and I wondered why it was he had disconcerted me so much before. I still couldn't remember who he reminded me of, and so decided it wasn't anyone, that I was imagining it. I put it out of my mind.

We settled easily into our work, engrossed in what we were doing. I had opened the doors of the studio wide in an attempt to let the air in, but there was no breeze to be found and I felt more than one slip of sweat trailing down my neck. Alex looked as cool as he always seemed to, but he must have been feeling it because in one quick motion he pulled at the material of his top and lifted it off his torso, screwing it up and using it to rub at his face and neck. I couldn't help but look at him with an appraising, artist's eye. He was superbly formed, with a perfect dip of muscle above his hips which edged above the denim of his shorts. He wasn't overly muscled, I doubted he was a gym bunny, but I could see a natural definition on his flat stomach and his arms were not thin. I imagined he had a wiry strength. He could probably lift me easily.

That errant thought made me jump, and I realised that there was an eye peering at me past the white of his top, and half a crooked smile, too.

'Checking me out, Rachel?' he teased, and before I could answer he absolved me and my blushes. 'Don't worry, I do that all the time. Stare at people. It's a sketcher's habit, isn't it? There's a bloke at work, he has the most amazing curly hair. I'm always looking at it, it makes my fingers itch wanting to try and draw it. He probably thinks I fancy him.'

'I know what you mean. I always want to draw my daughter. I'm always staring at her, too. She hates it.'

'You don't look old enough to have a daughter. You barely look older than me.'

'Oh, flatterer. I'm old enough to be your mother.'

'You'd be a young one – I'll be twenty next year.'

We settled into another comfortable silence – I was glad he wasn't a chatterbox – and worked side by side for a while. I don't think he really needed my expertise so much as my encouragement: he had an incredible natural talent. Colours are always tricky, though. We were talking about blending techniques when my phone buzzed again and I picked it up. It was a message from Steve. Just one line. *Call me.*

Warning pheromones started bursting in my body. Something was wrong, I could feel it. I don't know how, but I knew. Swallowing against a suddenly dry throat I took my phone outside and called him.

'Steve? What's happened?'

'Oh, sweetheart. Are you at home? I've got some bad news.' I felt tears prickling at the back of my eyes and my throat felt tight as he continued. 'I've just heard – you know Tilly Beaumont's brother, Tristan?'

'Yes, of course I do. He takes Vi to school sometimes with Tilly.'

'He's been in an accident in his car. He didn't make it, Rach. He lost control of his car and crashed. His brakes must have gone or something, I don't know, it was such a shit heap!' He said the last bit angrily, and I felt the same way. He was only seventeen! How could he have been gone, just like that? I'd seen him on Friday sitting by the green. I was hollowed out by shock, eviscerated.

'Oh god, poor Tilly and her mum and dad, they must be devastated. How did you find out?'

'Geoff came in. He saw the police leaving the Beaumonts' house, and he knows one of the detectives, who told him. Bob's just gone past. He must be on his way to get Tilly from school to tell her.'

I felt a bit sick that I must have known about her brother before she did, and I immediately started to worry about Vivian. Would the school tell them straightaway – should I go and get her? Would they come home? I said goodbye to Steve and I walked back into the studio, where Alex was still painting. He looked up and I knew he must have been able to see on my face that something was wrong and it occurred to me that maybe he knew Tristan – they would be about the same age. I felt a pain in my chest that they might be friends and now I would have to tell him that Tristan was dead.

'What's wrong, Rachel?' he asked, putting down his brush and walking over, wiping his hands on a cloth. 'What's happened?'

'I've heard some bad news, Alex. Do you know Tristan Beaumont?'

'No. I don't think I've met him yet. The name is familiar, though—?'

That small pang of relief was the thread of feeling that caused a cascade of sudden grief for Tristan, who I'd known since he was a gangly, cheeky eleven-year-old; for Tilly, who had lost her brother; for his lovely, lovely parents, and I couldn't stop it rushing out.

'He's dead. He's been killed in a car accident.' I choked the bitter words out and then the tears followed them.

Alex went distinctly pale, then stepped toward me and wrapped his arms around me. He was so tall that my head fit into the dip beneath his collarbone and he held me silently as I wept, one hand tentatively stroking my hair.

I let him do it for a minute, breathed in his scent, before I gently pulled away; it felt inappropriate, I barely knew him.

'I'm sorry. I think I'm going to have to go and get my daughter from school or something, I'm not sure; I need to call them. Can we pick up the lesson another time, I don't know – I'm so sorry.' I repeated myself and wiped my cheeks and he looked at me with his sea-storm eyes, his face taut with concern, with shock, something.

'It's fine,' he said quietly, reaching out to cup my shoulder and squeeze it gently. 'I'm so sorry, too. I know what it's like to lose someone too soon. I feel awful for his family. I hope your daughter is okay.' He turned away and gathered up the things he was using and took them back into the house. I stood there, useless for a long while, still unable to take in what I'd just heard, before I walked into the house too. Alex had gone already, but I noticed that he had washed up the mugs and the palettes from the painting, and his small kindness touched me.

I picked up the phone and dialled the school number. Mrs Brondsbury the school receptionist picked up after several rings, and I could hear from her voice that she'd been crying. Not wanting to upset her further – it was such a small school, she must have got to know them all so well, watched them grow – I quickly explained that I'd heard the bad news and I wanted to know what they were planning to do, if they were going to tell the kids or send them home.

'We're going to pull them into an assembly in an hour,' she replied, tears in her words. 'We'll have to tell them, and we'll offer to get them in with the school counsellor if they need it. This is so awful, I've known that boy since he was a naughty wee scrap. We'll let them go home early if they want to, afterwards. Was Vivian close to him?'

'I don't think so, not recently,' I replied, 'but she's very close to Tilly, and he would give them lifts to school and whatnot. It's going to hurt, I'm sure. So I should just wait here?'

'Yes. Just wait there, she'll be home.'

# Vivian

Tilly's dad came in to school and took her out of our classroom.

'What's going on?' Molly whispers to me, as the teacher closes the door behind them.

'I don't know. I'm sure we'll find out soon enough, though.' This is all very exciting.

'I hope she's all right. Bob looked awful.' Her pretty face creases with concern.

As I thought, we all get hustled into an assembly after lunch. Mrs Barker is standing on the stage in the hall. All the college kids are here too, which is unusual. It's stuffy and tight in here, with dust motes dancing in the sunlight that streams through the windows. I watch her as she clears her throat and takes a deep breath, clasps her hands in front of her.

'I'm sorry to have to tell you all that I have some very sad news.'

There's this weird collective intake of breath, and I can almost feel everyone's pulse pick up, smell the sweat that's springing up on their bodies. It's completely silent and still in the room, but swollen to bursting at the same time.

'We have learnt this morning that Matilda Beaumont's older brother, Tristan, was killed in a car accident on his way to work today. We realise that many of you knew Tristan, and because this is a tight community, we are all going to be greatly affected by this tragic loss. Please, please know that any of you can come and speak to a member of staff if you are struggling. We will be arranging for counsellors to be available for you, but for now we feel that as long as there is someone there and if any of you want to, that you can go home to be with your families.'

Shock blows around the room, people reel back in their seats. Lots of the girls start to cry – Chloe is being ridiculously dramatic, sobbing and wailing, even though she didn't even like Tristan as far as I'm aware – and the boys are all pale. They are all frightened. Death can come for anyone, it doesn't care how old you are. I can feel myself trembling.

Serena has gone an awful green-grey colour, and Molly is silent, her eyes fixed on the floor.

'Come on,' I tell them, 'let's go.' I have to get out of this room.

We're walking out of the hall when I spot Alex. I realise I didn't see him in the assembly, he must have slipped into the back, and I'm going to ignore him but as I walk past he grabs my arm.

'I'll come and see you later,' he murmurs, and then he's gone.

Molly watches this exchange with a black look on her face, tight-lipped. He's intruded on our private moment.

We make our way out of the school, out of the claustrophobia of everyone else's emotions spilling everywhere. It's hot and sunny, and the sky is blue. It's weird that Tristan is cold and dead when everything else is so alive and bright. You'd think the birds would stop singing or the breeze would stop blowing, but nothing's changed out here.

Serena is crying now, without sound. Tears are running down her face and dripping on to her shirt. We all say we are all best friends, but I know she likes Tilly the best, and I think that she must be feeling her reflected grief as well as her own pain. I wouldn't know, personally. Molly stops and grabs her in a hard hug. I put my arms around both of them. This is going to bring us all back together after the mess Molly made of everything, I know it. And I'm certainly not going to miss Tristan or his disgusting, grabbing hands.

'I can't believe it,' whimpers Serena, her voice thick with snot and tears. 'Tilly could have been in that car, too, if she hadn't come to mine to revise yesterday. We're not usually allowed sleepovers on Sunday, but we begged. I can't believe it.' Her voice trails off as the significance of this sinks in. I hadn't even thought about Tilly possibly being in the car. She must have had a fairy godmother looking out for her today.

There's a heavy quiet over us as we walk slowly away from school, towards my house. I think about asking them to come in but I can't bring myself to do it. I can't cope with all the brewing emotion, the tears, the wailing, the mucus. I don't like it when people aren't in control of themselves, it stresses me out. Mum is always too emotional. She's going to be awful when she finds out about Tristan. I decide just to get that over with and, after another uncomfortably long hug with Molly and Serena, I go in to the house.

Mum is sitting on the sofa, staring at nothing, hands in her lap. She must know already. This bloody village!

'Vivian, darling, oh god, are you okay?' She jumps up out of her seat, and starts to hug me and pat and clutch at me, like she's checking me for holes. I let her do it even though she knows perfectly well that I don't like it.

'I'm okay, Mum, I wasn't close to Tristan. I'm more upset for Tilly, and Serena is taking it really hard, too. We don't know what to do for Tilly.' I manage to gently remove her hands and get her to sit back down on the sofa.

'You can't do anything, darling. Nothing is ever going to make this better for her. You just need to be there for her.'

'Okay, Mum.' I think to ask, 'Are you okay?'

'Yes, darling, I will be, of course. I just feel so awful for Tilly and Bob and Maureen. And you were in that car last week! I can't bear it.' She catches her breath, her hands at her face.

'Mum, please, don't get yourself upset – I can't cope with it when you're upset.'

'I know, I know – I'm sorry. I'll be fine, I promise. I'll go and put the kettle on and make us some tea.'

I can hear her crying in the kitchen, but I don't go in. I don't know what to say to her when she gets like this, without getting angry at the pointlessness of it all, and I can't let her see me angry.

She's on at me again when she comes back in, sitting down too close to me: 'Vivian, are you sure you're okay?'

I shuffle up the sofa away from her. 'I'm fine, Mum, I told you. I didn't even like Tristan.'

'What?' The look on her face makes me realise that wasn't the right thing to say, even though it's the truth.

'I didn't like him.' I say it again anyway, mutinous.

'That, that isn't really the point, Vivian.'

'I already told you, it's horrible for Tilly, but I don't really care that much because he wasn't very nice to me.'

'So he deserves to be dead? Because you didn't like him?'

I just roll my eyes. She's such a drama llama, it drives me insane. He practically raped me, I'm not sorry he's dead and I won't say otherwise, not to her anyway.

'He was seventeen, Vi, he had his whole life ahead of him!' Tears are running freely down her face now, her stupid nose is pink and I can't bear it, can't bite quick enough to keep the words in.

'Why do you make everything about you? He was my friend's brother – this isn't about you! Just shut up!'

She reels like I've slapped her, but she does shut up at least, and we sit in silence. I put the television on and pretend to watch it.

The afternoon and evening drag. It's so uncomfortable. I can see the words that Mum is desperate to say to me itching under her skin, but she bites her lip. I'm older now, I know how to look after myself. I can handle this, obviously. But I don't think she can. It's always about her. Blaming herself for everything – she loves it. She thought everything that happened in London was her fault, how bad it got without her even noticing because she was so wrapped up in her crappy career. If she knew the whole story her fucking head would explode. It's not long before a glass of wine appears, the bottle tucked down the side of the chair for easy access. She didn't used to drink so much: that's a hangover from back then, too.

Eventually, I tell her I'm tired and want to go to bed. She asks me if I want to sleep in with her, but I can't imagine anything worse than her tossing and turning and kicking and breathing on me all night under the pretence that it's comforting for either of us. I want my own bed, my own room, my clean space.

I'm finally in there, tucked away safely from her histrionics and thinking about everything that has happened and what might happen next when something flies in through my open bedroom window and lands right on me. I jump up, terrified it might be a moth – I hate moths, nasty dusty dirty fluttering things – but when I turn the light on I see a pebble on the bed.

Alex is outside my window. He waves and I put my finger to my lips – Mum is still awake. I want to sneak out but he'll have to wait. She's had most of two bottles of wine tonight, bloody alchy, so I can't imagine she'll be awake for much longer. He points to the back of the garden, then goes and climbs into the hammock. He's a lot better at it than Mum is – she always falls out the other side at least twice. I watch it swinging gently for a minute, nursing the small excitement inside, before switching off the light and climbing into bed. I hear Mum coming up the stairs and the door of my room swings open quietly – I oil it so it doesn't creak – and she shuffles in. I force myself to relax and breathe deeply and not react when she reaches out and smoothes my hair, her hitching wine breath swarming all over me. Eventually she shuffles back out and stumbles around the bathroom and into her own bedroom.

When she finally goes to sleep – goes quiet, at least – I creep out of the house. I skip the second-to-bottom step that creaks and walk the edge of the hallway for the same reason. It's exhilarating after the depression of the day, sneaking out. He must like me. He wouldn't be here if he didn't really like me. He'd avoid me, people always avoid grieving people. Misery is catching, it seeps everywhere, sticks to everything, makes it dull.

The hammock is swinging slightly and the ropes are rasping on the branches. I can make it out because the moon is so bright tonight, it catches the shapes of the garden, plays tricks with them. I run to the hammock before I freak out completely, even though I know perfectly well there isn't anything there except us, shadows and heat.

Alex smiles up at me as I reach him, his face silver.

'I think there's room for a little one.' He reaches up and steadies me as I clamber in next to him. There's not a lot of room but I'm not going to complain about being pressed up against him, half on top of him. My body fits perfectly along his, my shoulder under his, my head nestled into his neck. I've never felt comfortable being near anyone, but this is different, somehow, I can cope with this. Maybe because I want to do this. After the endlessly horrible, miserable day, to finish it here, with Alex, looking at the stars, it's perfect. He takes my hand in his, threads our fingers together. They look like pearls in the moonlight.

# Rachel

Vivian decided to go into school the day after Tristan's accident, though I wanted to keep her at home. I think she'd had enough of my concern. The shock of the accident seeped into me, it froze my bones. I couldn't stop thinking about how Maureen must be feeling. What if it had been Vivian, in that car? I saw her, over and over, crushed, bleeding. I couldn't stop. I kept picking at those images, deliberately hurting myself with them.

I knew from sorry experience that Tristan's family had suffered a horrible trauma losing someone so close to them, and that it was going to change everything for them for ever. I've always known that life is cruel, and fragile. I was seven years old when my dad went out to meet friends one night and never came back. I was cross, sulking he was going out without me and leaving me and Mum by ourselves, and I refused to say goodbye or give him a kiss, and then he never came back. I remember the policemen on the doorstep, deep voices. Mum slowly crumpling to the floor as they asked her if they could come in. I was sitting on the stairs, looking out through the door at the lashing rain, neon light on puddles hurting my eyes. He'd been hit by a speeding car on a crossing in town. I had delayed him. I had kicked off, made him late, sulked, cried. If I had just let him go, he wouldn't have been there, at that moment, on that road. I had killed him as surely as the car had.

It's taken me most of my life to try and forgive myself for ruining those last moments I had with him, to try and stop blaming myself for the horrific accident. I know my mum never blamed me, but it's always there, that lumpen guilt, that pain. Sometimes I think that's why I stayed with Ciaran for so long, that I thought I deserved everything I was getting, that I was being justly punished. I still don't think I'm capable of having normal relationships with people. Our therapist in London, the one who recommended a fresh start, I knew she thought it was all my fault, what happened with Vivian. That I had neglected her somehow. I just didn't want to smother her like I had been smothered, in a cage made of my mother's fear of losing me like she had lost my father. My disinterest in the minutiae of my daughter's life had allowed what happened to happen – I always thought it was more my fault than hers.

I was quite literally saved from that spiral of dark thoughts by the bell. Well, the tone on my phone, which trilled and told me that someone was thinking about me. Alex, as it turned out, wanting another lesson, that day if I could manage it. If I was okay. I wasn't in a good place, but I knew company would force me back to a safer one. It always did. I wondered if he knew that, sensed that I was vulnerable. Maybe. It was enough to get me up, washed, dressed, anyway.

–

'Rachel?' He stood in the doorway of my studio, taller again than I remembered every time I saw him. His hair was still damp from his shower and it curled slightly, flopping into his eyes. I had to resist walking up to him and brushing it away. He was puppy-like in his enthusiasm to get started again on his foxes; he'd sketched out a new one especially. At first, he was content to stand beside me quietly and watch as I painted, keen eyes taking in ratios and blending. He was a quick study, soon using the same techniques to mix a beautifully rich russet red for his fox. He followed up with creamy paws and tipped perky ears with black, using the same for the eyes that looked up at us from the page, peeping through green stalks of long grass topped with feathery tufts. It was so joyful, alive. He was so incredibly talented.

'Are you feeling okay, Rachel?'

'Hm?'

'Are you feeling okay? After yesterday, I was worried. The accident.'

'Not really, darling.' The endearment slipped out easily, and I saw him glance at me, and felt embarrassed.

'And your daughter?'

'I'm sorry?'

'Your daughter, is she okay?'

'Well, yes, I suppose she is. I guess that's a relief.'

'Really?' His unbelieving tone caught my attention.

'I'm sorry, I don't know what you mean.'

'I was wondering why it would be a relief. I thought she would be upset – isn't she friends with Tristan's sister?'

'I, well, I guess it just hasn't really sunk in yet. She struggles with expressing her emotions sometimes.'

'You don't seem like that. Is she not like you?'

'No, we're very different in a lot of ways. I definitely wear my heart on my sleeve.' I thought again about her callous disregard of Tristan, of the tragedy of him losing his life at such a young age. It must have shown on my face, a grimace, because he turned away. Should Vivian have been more upset? Was it wrong to judge her for not being upset by Tristan's death? I couldn't actually remember how she'd reacted when Mum had died. Everyone reacted differently to grief. Vivian had always been a stoic, inward-looking child, bottling everything up until... well. She wasn't like that now.

'Maybe she takes after her dad?' He put down his paintbrush and looked right at me, tilting his head as he waited for my response. My mouth went dry, and before I could answer he said, 'My mum raised us on our own, too. I wouldn't know if I was like him, either. My dad, I mean. I don't see him any more. I haven't seen him in years.'

I felt sick at the thought of Vivian being like her father. It was a thought I had spent a lifetime trying not to have, to not let poison my mind.

'No, she's not like him. She's her own person, that's all. She's just processing it all in her own way.'

'Everyone is different I suppose,' Alex said, putting down his brush. 'Shall I make us a cup of tea?' His hand reached out, slipping across the small of my back briefly as he passed me, not waiting for me to answer, leaving me with dark thoughts.

—

'I haven't put sugar in this one,' he said, as he came back into the studio, eyes on the tea in his hands. 'I can go and put some in, though, if you want?'

'No, it's okay, I'm sweet enough.' I felt silly immediately after saying it, but it was something I always said. I couldn't remember who I had got in from. Maybe one of my parents' sayings, nestled into my memory, a small treasure. He just laughed.

'What are you working on at the moment? Are these from a fairy tale?' He started nosing through my sketches, completely at ease with his surroundings. I was impressed with his confidence, the way he moved as though he belonged exactly where he was in every moment of his life. I was always so awkward, shy at his age. Easy pickings for Ciaran. He flashed into my mind, unwelcome, and I shuddered. Ever observant, Alex was there again with his cool hand briefly on my shoulder. He didn't say anything, only smiled gently until I answered.

'Kind of. I'm doing illustrations for a book. There's an indie publisher in London trying to bring back the concept of drawings in books. Lots of old stories have them, but they cost so much extra to print it fell out of fashion.'

'I think it's great. I love those old books with illustrations. We had some at home.'

'Where did you live before?'

'Here and there.' He turned away, picking up his palette. 'I just need to go and rinse this off.'

I watched him walk back to the house, back straight, easy strides. He didn't have that bouncy teenage boy walk. I thought to ask him how he had ended up here in the village, about his mum, but by the time he got back I was entirely engrossed in drawing Arabella walking through the veil from her world to the Fae kingdom of her future, and I had forgotten.

# London

Carol was beginning to wonder if she'd offended someone. Usually, when she came to pick up Vivian, some of the mums would wander over, make the usual small talk about that week's spellings or a lost piece of kit, but for the past couple of days she had found herself standing alone.

It wasn't even that people weren't speaking to her: judging by the quick looks and nods in her direction, they were speaking about her instead. About her, or her granddaughter. The cupboard incident had obviously not gone under the radar. Carol felt the invitations for Vivian's birthday party burning a hole in her handbag. Taking a breath, she walked over to a group of the girls' mothers.

'Hi, Alicia,' she ventured. 'How are you?'

'Fine, thanks,' said the other woman, sliding her eyes to those of her companions and back again. Carol had to stop herself from frowning at the rudeness. She was far too old for schoolyard antics, and she thought the women in front of her should be, too.

'I've got some invitations for Vivian's birthday here. I've got one for Sophie – shall I just give it to you?' She started to feel in her bag for the hard edges of the little envelopes. Alicia reached out a hand, a patronising smile appearing. 'We can't make it,' she said, eyes again straying to those of her friends. 'Sorry.'

'I haven't even told you what day it is,' said Carol, feeling an embarrassing flush running up her chest, anger heating her.

'Sorry,' said Alicia, who looked anything but. 'We're busy. Actually, I think we all are, aren't we, ladies?' The others at least had the grace not to say anything; they just looked away, leaving Carol rooted to the spot with shame.

'Have you got Lexie's there?' came a voice from behind her.

Carol turned, feeling shaky and sick, to see Lucy, who was smiling in the manner of someone who was gritting their teeth. She stepped in, put her arm around Carol's shoulders and walked her away across the playground.

'Ignore those nasty bitches,' she whispered. 'They think their shit doesn't stink.'

Carol found herself laughing because mild-mannered Lucy was not usually a swearer. 'Thank you,' she said. 'Do you think things are that bad with Vivian? She hasn't said.'

'Lexie said none of the other children are speaking to her after she locked Jaxon in the cupboard. She said she doesn't seem that bothered, though, and that boy is a complete toerag.'

'She never said. I asked her if everything was okay and she said it was fine.'

'Maybe she thinks it is fine. Does she know she's having a party?'

'Not really – I was thinking we could just do something at our house, cake and games... I can understand the kids being a bit mean, but why is Alicia being such a hard case?'

'Jaxon's mum is her bestie, isn't she? They went to the girls' school together. Makes them think they're Walthamstow Village royalty.'

'Village royalty!'

'I know. Pretentious cowbags. Look, why don't we do something with just the girls for Vivian's birthday? I'm sure she'd prefer that, anyway. We could do an old-school birthday, with a cinema trip and McDonald's.'

'Thank you, Lucy. That sounds perfect. I really appreciate it.' Carol could feel a lump in her throat and her eyes felt tight. Poor Vivian! No one wanting to come to your birthday party was every kid's nightmare. What was she going to tell Rachel? It might be better if she thought this was her idea, not that she had even mentioned doing anything for a party.

'Chin up, it'll blow over. It was a stupid prank that she didn't know how to stop. No one died!' laughed Lucy, shaking her thick blonde hair over her shoulder. 'Look, here're our girls.'

Carol turned to see Lexie and Vivian walking out of the class, hand in hand, and she thanked her stars that at least Vivian had this one loyal friend.

'Do you want to come back to mine for a sneaky wine?' said Lucy, nudging her. 'I can give the kids dinner.'

'Yes, please,' said Carol, thanking her stars again that maybe she had a loyal friend, too. She'd been lonely since Rachel had got her promotion, and since she had taken on so much childcare her old friends had drifted away, full of plans for cruises and jaunts that Carol couldn't go on. None of them were even grandparents yet, let alone full-time ones. It wasn't exactly what she had planned for her retirement, she thought, watching the two little girls skipping up the road.

## Vivian

I don't know why I bothered coming into school today. Hardly anyone is even here – they are all skiving because of Tristan. The people who are here are miserable and everything feels so heavy. We don't have any air conditioning so wherever you go it's like walking into an air bath, but no one is getting clean: half the boys stink, and I've already been in the bathroom twice to check that I don't, too.

We are supposed to be having our mock exams soon, so I walk around the school looking for somewhere to revise where other annoying people aren't already slobbing about. All the other years are in their lessons and the year elevens have finished their exams and don't even have to be here, so lucky. I quite like this, though, wandering around aimlessly. Without really realising what I'm doing I end up in the art block. There's no one here. I'm alone except for the lingering smell of paint and glue, sharp in my nose. Feeling my pulse pattering with the small illicit thrill of sneaking where I shouldn't, I look through all the work that's been put out for display. Everything is pretty standard clunky rubbish, apart from one drawing but I don't think it's finished, so I don't know why it's here. It's a sketch of a girl, but she doesn't have any eyes. The rest of her is perfect, but she hasn't even had eyes drawn that have been rubbed out – there's just an untouched, creamy space under each arched eyebrow and above high cheekbones. She seems familiar somehow. I can't stop myself taking it, rolling it up and hiding it in my bag. I haven't stolen anything for a long time. It's the sort of thing that gets you noticed for the wrong reasons, however much fun it might be, but I want it.

I wish Molly was here. The buzz of stealing the drawing fades quickly. I'm so bored and I'm no good at talking to people unless they talk to me first, which they don't if Molly isn't with me. If it wasn't for Molly, I don't know if anyone would ever speak to me. I wonder if they'd speak to me if Alex was my boyfriend. I bet they would. I think about going home, but if I did I'd only have to see Mum and she's probably still revelling in having something to be all sad and moody about. Why did Tristan have to go and die? What an idiot. Any *normal* person would have just broken their legs or something.

The rest of the day drags and drags and I spend most of it sitting in the library, watching people. Chloe is there for a while, counting on her fingers and chewing on her nails. Becky is scribbling away next to her, head close to the paper, leaning to one side like the scratching of the pen is a language that maybe she could understand if only she can get close enough. She's making revision flash cards. I don't need those. I can remember pretty much anything once I've read it, though eventually I'll forget it if it's something pointless. What's the point of memorising loads of dates of when boring dead people did stupid shit in real life? It's not going to help you budget your crappy wages from your dead-end job, is it? Not that I'm going to have a crappy job. Once I've figured out what will make me the most money with the least amount of effort I'll be set. Probably banking or hedge funds or something. I thought about studying law, but I don't think I'd like the hours you have to work. I'd also rather have a job where you don't have to speak to idiots, but I'd imagine being a criminal lawyer might be interesting. Or a psychologist, full to the top of everyone's darkest, slimiest secrets. Maybe that. Not that any of the ones I spoke to were particularly clever: they sucked up everything I told them and just regurgitated it in a way that made them sound clever, but certainly didn't fix me in the way they wanted, the way I made them think they had. There's nothing about me that needs fixing.

I've texted Molly again, but she still isn't answering, and I don't know what to say to Tilly so I haven't sent anything to her. I guess we'll get her some flowers or a plant or something useless that's supposed to make you feel better. I might have a picture somewhere with Tristan in it. I went through a phase of taking photos of everyone, secretly, if I could. Posed photos are the worst: you can't see people when they are posing. I'll have a look later. Maybe, if I can be bothered.

'There you are.'

After I get down off the ceiling a warm thrill runs through me. It's Alex, he must have been looking for me. He's not supposed to be in our library, he could get in trouble.

'Hey.' I brush my fringe out of my eyes and peep over to where Chloe and Becky are sitting. They've both noticed, perking up their ears. Alex slides into the seat next to me and puts his arm over the back of my chair and both their mouths drop open at the same time. This. Is. Amazing. They are looking at me! Alex doesn't notice, he just trails a finger over my shoulder, back and forth. I can feel it through the thin material of my shirt and my chest gets tight. His touch burns me. I can feel heat creeping up my neck and before it can reach my cheeks, I reach up with my hand to link it with his.

'Shall we go somewhere else?'

Picking up my bag, I smirk at Chloe and Becky and then I follow Alex out of the library and into the blinding sunlight. It makes me sneeze, like it always does, and then he sneezes, too.

'You've got it as well,' I tell him, wiping my eyes and laughing.

'Got what? Hay fever?'

'Oh, maybe, no, I thought it was the sun? The light makes me sneeze. It's a genetic thing – photic sneezing. My tear ducts are a bit wonky and when the sun makes my eyes water a bit goes the wrong way and makes me sneeze.'

'Ah, I do have that! I thought everyone did it. I thought it was your eyes protecting themselves from the light. You can't sneeze with your eyes open.'

'In case they fall out?' I laugh. 'Nope. We're special. Apparently you have a fifty per cent chance of getting it from your mother. Does your mum sneeze? Mine does.'

'I hadn't noticed.'

I notice his mouth press when I mention his mother, so I make a note not to ask him about family any more. What do I talk to him about, though? It's not going to be easy, even following up on the world's most boring sneezing conversation.

'How has your day been?'

'Fine. Great. Everything going to plan.'

'What plan?'

'Ah, wouldn't you like to know!' He slings his arm around my shoulders again, pulling me to him before dropping his hand to mine and gathering it up.

I don't like it when people have secrets. I want to know about everything. I don't mind if people still think they have secrets after I have found out about them, though. That's just useful. I'm still not sure what else to do about Molly's secrets. At least Tristan's can't hurt me any more. Us, I mean. Tristan's name in my mind seems to have transferred itself to Alex's mouth, and he asks me about him.

'How are you feeling? About the accident?'

'Awful, it's so sad. He was only seventeen.' I find my mother's words coming out of my mouth: something tells me they are more palatable than my own thoughts, which are basically I wish everyone would stop fucking asking me. I don't see the point of grief: everyone dies eventually.

'It's all right if you don't care, you know.'

'What? Of course I care. That's a weird thing to say.' It is weird, but it also makes me feel good, because of course I don't actually care that much and am just waiting for everything to go back to normal. It intrigues me to think he might go against the grain as much as I want to.

'Well, you told me, didn't you, what he did to you the other week. That was well out of order. Maybe bad things sometimes happen to bad people, too.' He's looking at me as he says this, and he looks... I don't know. I find it hard to tell how other people are feeling sometimes. I'm not sure what he wants me to do so I don't reply.

We walk out of school as the bell rings for the end of the day, and gravitate to the tree where we first spoke. The trunk is broad enough for us both to sit back against the rough bark. We are holding hands and mine is starting to feel sweaty and I don't want to feel gross so I take it back under the pretence that I need to tie back my hair using the bobble that's currently digging into my wrist.

Alex leans over and kisses the patch of skin behind my ear I've just exposed, then the inside of my wrist where there's a red line, and a live wire shoots right through me. I want to feel his hands on me, which is troubling because I don't like being touched. I can only think that my attraction to him, his mystery, is overcoming my natural inclinations about germs and romance and things. Even I am not immune from biological urges it would seem.

I don't know if he's pretending not to notice the effect he's having on me, but I'm exasperated when he turns away, leaning back and closing his eyes. I take the opportunity to study his face. Nothing is out of place. Usually when you look at someone for long enough, you start to spot flaws or anomalies – something. Molly has a freckle on her lip line that fractures their shape. Serena has a cowlick that means her hair never falls straight, however much she attacks it with products. Tilly's nose has a scarred bump in the middle from when she went over her handlebars after her bike chain fell off when we were kids. She'd been mean to me all that day, I remember. There was blood everywhere.

I'm looking and looking. I have an eye for detail, I notice things, but his face is just perfect. He's got thick – but not too thick – eyebrows that don't have any nasty stray hairs in the middle, or on his brow bone. They are lighter than his hair, more brown than black. He's got eyelashes that would put mascara out of business if girls had them. I trace the lines of his face with my eyes, follow creamy smooth skin over his cheekbones. No nibbled dry patches on his lips. Even though his hair is dark, his skin isn't. He's got the same sort of tone as Molly: lightly tanned, but in a blond person kind of way. I could look at his face all day, but the best part of it is currently hidden under shut eyelids, delicate and pale with a fine tracing of blue: ink dropped into milk.

'Vivian, are you staring at me?' He speaks in an amused, low rumble and one green-gold eye pops open looking right at me, caught in the act. I open my mouth, but my words aren't working, and then he puts his hand behind my neck and pulls my lips to his and it doesn't matter any more.

—

I walk in through the back gate of the garden thinking of nothing but a cold shower. The short walk through the woods back from school has left me with a tickle of sweat on my lower back and more gathered at the place where my hair meets my neck. I feel dirty, and sticky. Alex didn't seem to mind the heat, he never looks anything but chilled. He didn't walk me to the gate because he had to go back and get something he forgot from college, but that was fine because I don't want Mum to know about him. I know she'll think he's a complication that I might not be able to handle, but I'm practically a grown-up now. I'm nearly the oldest in the year: I'll be sixteen in a couple of months. He kissed me again before he went, and it made me want more of him.

I see Mum in the studio and before I can sneak past she spots me too and waves me in. Ugh, I just need a shower! She catches me in a sweaty hug, and I can't help but shudder with disgust. She notices, and lets me go with a pathetically forlorn look on her face.

'Hello, darling. How was it? Were the girls there?'

'No. Hardly anyone was. It was fine, though, I just revised. I think they are just going to drop some of our exams, or push some back. It doesn't matter to me, anyway.'

'Not everyone is like you, Vivian.'

I look at her as she says this, surprised by the snap in her tone, but her eyes have drifted back to her painting. She's used my face again for the girl in the book. She always does. Her paintings sell really well because people want the illustrations or the cover art as prints, and I hate it. I don't want my face on the walls of strangers' houses. What might my painted eyes be seeing? At least she's changed my hair, though I expect that's because of a description in the book rather than any effort on her part. I look ridiculous with that massive, braided mess. Are those bells? Imagine having bells in your hair – everyone would be able to hear you coming.

'Mum! It looks like me again! I asked you not to!' I hate the whine in my voice, but this is a conversation we have had several times and she *still* does it.

'Sorry, darling. I can't help it – you're always the first face in my mind.'

'Well, can you paint me out of it, please? Gross. I need a shower.' I notice a different painting set up on an easel. 'I like that fox, is he going in the book?'

'Ah, no, that's a different project.'

'It's really good. He looks like he's going to jump off the paper.'

I manage to make my escape and run for the bathroom. I wonder if Alex will come back tonight? At least I finally have his number. I'll have to think of something clever to text him. Something to make him want me.

# Rachel

I don't know why I didn't tell Vivian about Alex coming over. I wasn't sure if he went to the school or not – he changed the subject when I asked him – and frankly I thought she might be embarrassed if she knew a boy from school was coming for lessons. I imagined they would bump into each other soon enough anyway, in such a small place. Alex was handsome enough to be noticed wherever he went.

I suppose a small part of me just wanted something new for myself. Everything I did was centred around Vivian, her and her feelings. I had given everything up to look after her properly, but maybe it was time I had something too. It was nice to have a new friend, unconventional as it may have been, considering the age gap. There weren't any other creatives in the village either, so to have someone to really talk to about something I loved without having them look bored enough to cry was a real treat. I was thinking of all the different artists I wanted to talk to him about, the books I could lend him. I had flights of fancy about going to his first exhibition, wandering around with a glass of champagne and telling people that I had helped him when he was a young man. He was capable of a career as a painter, I could see it in him already. It distracted me momentarily from thinking about Tristan, but unfortunately that didn't last.

I had meant to go to the supermarket before Vivian had got home, but Alex hadn't left until two and it had slipped my mind, the distinct lack of any sustenance in the house. I called up to Vivian that I was heading out and asked her if she needed anything and got the usual noncommittal grunt in return. She would probably text me something when I was in the car on the way home and then be furious when I turned up without it. Well, she had legs, so she could get herself to the bloody shops on the bus if she needed something. I was getting more annoyed with her by the day.

I'd managed to choose the wonky trolley as always at the shop, and was trying to unfold my shopping list one handed when I banged into someone by accident.

'Oh, I'm so sorry...' Then my words dried up. It was Maureen, Tristan and Tilly's mum. I felt sorrow like a stone plunge into my stomach, closing up my throat. I didn't know what to say to her, though I desperately wished I did. I could barely cope with the burden of my own issues and always went to pieces when confronted with the raw and bleeding aspect of someone else's emotions.

'Maureen, I...'

'Don't, Rachel, please. It's fine. I wouldn't know what to say to me, either. I don't even know what I'm doing here!' She gave a short, almost hysterical bark that was nearly a laugh, nearly a scream. 'I forgot my list. I forgot my bags. I can't remember where I've parked.'

'Oh, god, Maureen, can I help? Can I give you a lift home? Maybe Bob could come and get your car later, I could bring you some shopping...'

'He's a mess, Rachel. He's completely destroyed. He's lost his boy, our boy!' Pain ravaged her voice, ripped at it with cruel fingers. Tears spooled in her eyes, spilling at the first blink down her plump red cheeks. 'Oh, I'm sorry! I'm so sorry!'

'Please don't say that, Maureen, please, let me help, let's find your car, I can drive you home and I'll come back for mine. Come on, darling.'

I abandoned my trolley and she let me lead her out of the aisle and through the gust of air conditioning by the door, into the still baking, glaring sunshine. I had to hold her elbow and gently guide her steps; she was blind with tears. I gave her a tissue from my bag but she just clenched it in a white-fingered fist and let them run down her face, quiet but wrenching sobs shaking her shoulders. I couldn't speak past the lump in my throat. There weren't many cars in the car park, but I knew their car and it was easy to spot: a huge, bashed-up, ancient Land Rover. I had no idea how the hell I was going to drive it but Maureen wasn't in any fit state to and I couldn't speak to call Bob.

I had to take her handbag and get the keys out, help her climb into the cab. I don't think she knew where or even who she was by that point; she wrapped her arms around her waist and bent herself double, making small noises full of hurt. I felt every one. I managed to get her seatbelt on her and I started the car, the clutch stiff beneath my foot. A small, irreverent thought wormed its way into my brain, that Maureen must have a left thigh of steel, and for one horrifying second I thought I would laugh, but it whipped itself away as quickly as it arrived. I stalled at the lights on the way into the village but eventually made it to the turning off the high road where the chippy was, the forlorn 'Closed' sign hanging askew in the door. I don't know how I got her out of the car, or to the door. It burst open as we arrived and Bob stumbled out, whey-faced and wild.

'Mau, Mau! Where did you go, where were you?' Behind him was Tilly, ashen. She looked up at me and attempted to smile but failed utterly, merely twisting her face. Maureen just staggered past them and up the stairs, followed by her husband. I had to pass the car keys and Maureen's handbag to Tilly who took them silently from me and went slowly up after them, leaving me to shut the door as quietly as I could manage.

After I left them I had no idea what to do with myself, so I walked over to the pub in the hope that Steve would be in the bar. Thankfully he was. He took one look at my face and jumped up from behind his laptop and pulled me into a hug.

'Darling, what's happened? You look awful.'

'I saw Maureen at the supermarket. She just fell apart in front of me. I had to bring her home in her Rover – I don't even know if that was legal! I was probably driving it illegally, the police will have to arrest me!' I tried to laugh, but it burnt on the way out into a sorry squeak.

'I'm assuming you've left your car at the supermarket, then?' he asked, voice muffled by my hair as he gently rocked us from side to side. I nodded onto his warm shoulder, which was more than a little dampened by my onslaught.

'Come on then, trouble, let's go and get you your car back.'

'And some food?'

'Don't push it, darling, you know I get all mine delivered. I can't stand the supermarket, everyone shoving around like sheep, desperate for the last packet of Hobnobs. It's like the apocalypse in there. Deranged.'

Steve always made me feel better and he did lift my spirits temporarily as he drove me back to the shop and, despite his protestations, came in with me while I bought some bits, talking to nearly everyone who walked past us. Steve was a village 'lifer' as he put it, and as the owner of the only pub, he probably knew every single person who lived in a ten-mile radius. As well as my own shopping I bought some extra milk, tea and bread – basics I thought the Beaumonts might have run out of, plus some things they could cobble an easy meal out of.

Steve noticed, sharp-eyed as ever. 'You're a sweetheart, you really are,' he said, arm around my shoulders. 'How is Vivian getting on? Is she coping? I hope this all isn't going to set you back.'

'What do you mean, set me back? Set me back where?' I had never told Steve about what had happened in London.

'Sorry, love, I don't mean anything by it. But you were always so wound up over Viv before. You wouldn't let her out of your sight.' He looked embarrassed, but I knew perfectly well what he was getting at, and he had a point.

He thought I was paranoid about her safety, I was worried about mine too: I had felt a threat hanging over us for days now, but I didn't know what it was, only that I was out of sorts and nervous.

'I think she's going to be okay,' I offered, wondering again if that was actually a good thing. 'I'm worried for Tilly, though. I can hardly bear to think about what she must be feeling.'

Steve just gave me a wan smile, and we went to the tills.

After Steve left me in the shop car park with another one of his firm hugs, I put the shopping in my boot and

I drove back to the chippy. I rang the doorbell. Tilly answered, her eyes raw and red, and I silently gave her the shopping bags. She took them with another small twist of her mouth and shut the door. By the time I got home I was crying again myself. I knew what that pain felt like. I knew it would never leave them, only hide itself in small spaces of their hearts like a cancer.

I didn't sleep that night.

When Vivian was in the hospital I had asked my doctor to prescribe me sleeping tablets because I hadn't been able to close my eyes without seeing horrific images. I'd wandered around my empty house, devoid of my mother and Vivian, alone with my thoughts and ever increasing paranoia and fear. The pills had given me a temporary respite from it, wiping out the day and smothering me with a chemical blanket. They didn't stop the exhaustion, but at least the intrusive, dark, night-time thoughts, the guilt and the fear, had been banished.

I hadn't needed them for years. I'd thrown away the last few I'd had in a fit of optimism the year before. I wished now that I'd kept them. I lay in my safe bed, in my safe room, my safe home, but I wasn't safe from myself. I wasn't safe from the scratching, hissing torments that crawled through the gaps in my subconscious, twisting every positive thought I'd ever had. I had let Vivian get in that car. I had known that car was dangerous. Why had I never said anything about it? What if she had been in the accident? I had failed, again, as a mother. I couldn't protect her. I knew I was feeling sorry for myself, hijacking another family's sorrow, making it all about me. I was one of those awful, weak people who can only cope with grief by causing themselves more pain.

I drifted off as light began to creep into my room, and what little sleep I had was full of screaming brakes, wet roads, neon lights and the sound of a child, crying on a staircase.

# London

The house was silent.

'Hello?' called Rachel, as she pushed open the door, tugging her key out of the lock and putting it back in her bag. 'Mum?' Everything was still, she could feel that the house was empty. She pulled out her phone, but there was no message. Not that her mum was particularly good at texting; the mobile Rachel had bought her was probably switched off and abandoned somewhere in the house like it usually was. No note in the kitchen.

The skin on the back of her neck prickled as she moved through the downstairs. No sign of Vivian's school bag. They must have gone somewhere after pick up. But it was late, nearly bedtime. *Past bedtime*, said the snide voice in her head. *You timed it on purpose so you didn't have to do it.* She picked up the landline to call Carol, but then spotted her mum's mobile sitting right next to it, and swore under her breath. For want of anything else to do she went to the kitchen and looked in the fridge, pulling out a bottle of wine and pouring herself a large glass, which she carried through the front room and drank standing up, watching out of the window. The nights were drawing in.

As the minutes ticked by Rachel felt her nerves getting tighter. Where were they? What was her mother thinking, keeping Vivian out like this? She had a swimming lesson in the morning, she needed to be at home in bed. Then the voice again, not so snide this time: *What if she can't come home? What if he's come? Taken them?* Her stomach clenched around the wine she had drunk, and she sat down, put her glass down. She was being ridiculous. *Breathe*, she told herself. There was an explanation, they were together somewhere. Carol had probably taken her out for some tea, a Friday night treat. She stood back up, forced herself to go upstairs and get changed. They'd be back any minute.

Wrapped up in her dressing gown, in her most cosy pyjamas, soft fabric comforting against her skin, she had just flicked off the light to her bedroom when she heard the front door go. She ran to the top of the stairs, and to her horror felt her slipper catch against the carpet runner and felt entirely weightless for a second, falling, before managing to grab the banister with a lurch, her heart hammering. How many times would she have to tell her mum it needed re-pinning? She could have broken her neck. The door rattled as she found her feet and her mother came in, shutting it behind her.

'Mum! Where have you been? Where's Vivian?'

Carol looked up and smiled beatifically. 'Hello, my lovely!' she said, before walking suspiciously steadily down the hall. Legs still shaking from the near-miss on the staircase, Rachel followed. *'Mum!* Where's Vivian?'

'Oh,' said Carol. 'She's at Lexie's. She's having an over sleep. Sleep in over. Sleepover.' She laughed.

'Mum! Are you pissed?' said Rachel, worry swiftly being replaced with acute crossness. 'Where have you been? Where's all her school stuff?'

'At Lexie's. We went after school, for a quick cup of wine. Tea. And wine.'

'It's nearly nine o'clock! I was getting frantic!'

'Didn't think you'd be home yet, love, have you been here long?' Carol had found the wine that Rachel had left on the side and poured the rest into a glass, before pulling open a drawer and tugging out a sheaf of takeaway leaflets. 'D'you fancy a pizza? Starving.'

'No, I don't! Mum, you have to take your mobile, you could have sent me a message to let me know – I was so worried! I thought something had happened to you. I thought...' She trailed off: Carol was paying her no attention at all, her narrow focus now on choices of toppings on the leaflet which she was holding almost to her nose. Rachel put her hands to her face and sighed heavily through her fingers, letting the fear ebb away with her breath. She couldn't let it take control of her again, everything was fine. 'Actually, Mum, I could murder a pepperoni passion. You have to phone them, though.'

Later on, in front of the TV and full of pizza and garlic bread, she thought to ask her mum how Vivian had been at school, but Carol had fallen asleep on the other chair, her glasses slipping down her nose, and she was starting to snore. Laughing softly, Rachel covered her up with the throw, gently took off her glasses and put them on the coffee table, and went to bed.

# *Vivian*

'I can't stop thinking about him,' says Molly, who has managed to drag herself to school today looking suitably miserable.

'Yes, it's very sad,' I tell her, trying not to sound bored. She's sitting next to me at our lunch table, moving food around on her plate with the tip of her fork. I have already eaten all mine. 'Try and eat something, Molls.'

'I haven't been able to eat anything since Monday. I'm just not hungry.'

'Well, you'll have to force yourself, then. You're as bad as my mother.'

'What's that supposed to mean?' She looks up at me, a line between her eyebrows.

'My mum. She's been a complete nightmare this week. She didn't even know Tristan that well. He was my friend's brother. I don't know why she has to be all fucked up about it.'

'It's called empathy, Vivian. Do you know how bad you sound right now? It's probably making her think about her dad's accident. You know, your granddad, who never got to see her grow up, or meet you? Your nan was only in her fifties, too, wasn't she, when she died? That was another accident, wasn't it? It's bringing it all back for her. You're such a bitch sometimes, I don't know how you came out of her.' Molly's face has gone white; it makes her eyes really stand out. She's beautiful even when she's furious. 'You must know how scarred she is by her past – you went mad at me for asking her about it that time.'

Well, it's private. It's none of Molly's business, our past. I wonder if she's ever noticed my mother's literal scars, nosy cow that she is. I'm picturing the thin white line that runs along the edge of my mother's scalp (*'Oh, I don't remember, darling, I think I did it when I was little'*) and about the crooked fingers on her left hand (*'I shut them in the car door and I didn't get them fixed because I was pregnant with you, and then I just never did. They don't bother me.'*) There's a crescent moon where her neck meets her shoulder too, but you can only see it when she's tanned. I wonder what it feels like to bite someone that hard, feel their flesh split between your teeth. What it tastes like, that much hate.

Molly is still wanging on when I refocus on her. I lose track sometimes.

'You're so lucky to have a mum like her, and you just treat her like shit. It's not fair!' Oh, great, here we go with the Molly sob story. *My mummy doesn't love me, boo hoo hoo.*

'I don't treat her like shit, Molly. Where's Serena, anyway? I thought I saw her this morning.' I can tell that Molly doesn't really want to change the subject, but I'm bored of it.

'No, I haven't seen her at all, she must be hiding somewhere.' She starts poking at her lunch again.

This is just another symptom of how messed up everything is. This is Molly's fault. If she'd kept her legs shut none of this would have happened.

'It's our anniversary soon,' mumbles Molly through a mouthful of food that she's finally put in her face.

'What?' I hate it when she talks while she's eating.

'Our anniversary. Six years since you moved here.'

'Oh, right. I didn't know you kept count.'

'It's not hard to remember, really. We should do something, with Tilly and Serena too. I think we should all do something soon anyway – we need to do something for Tilly.'

'Yeah, definitely.' I can't imagine anything worse. 'Have you got your history mock now?'

'Yeah. I'll see you later.'

I watch her as she stands up with her tray and walks away from me, slim and light-footed. People move out of the way to let her past without even realising it. I can see that her whole life will be like that, people stepping aside while she gets everything she wants. I wish she hadn't mentioned the anniversary. It means that this time six years ago, I was in the hospital.

That's not something I want to remember.

—

I'm walking past the college's common room after my exam when I see Alex bound out, turning away up the corridor. He doesn't see me, and I'm about to call out to him when I see Molly come out too. Her shirt is half-undone, and she goes after him.

If she thinks she's going to do to me what she did to Serena then she's got another think coming, and it won't be a good one. Rage bubbles up and heats every part of me as I follow them.

# Rachel

I woke up with a start, and a headache. It was later than usual, and the sun shining on the side of the house had turned my room into a sauna. I had to get up and change the bed clothes, they were grimy with the sweat of a restless night of fretting and nightmares.

I managed to shower and choke down some breakfast, clearing away the remains of Vivian's morning meal. I didn't understand why she was so anal about tidiness everywhere else but refused to do the bloody washing up. My conversation with Steve was playing on my mind and once more I started to dwell on my relationship with my daughter. Was I too controlling of her? Did I trust her? It was all so hard. I've always felt that there's this monumental lie that people tell you about motherhood. They tell you that you will love your child beyond anything in existence, that the moment you set eyes on them, you will be swept away on this sea of everlasting joy and adoration. The agonies of birth brushed under the carpet, forgotten in an instant. Rubbish.

My whole pregnancy had been difficult. Recovery from the beating Ciaran had given me was stifled by crippling morning sickness. My mother, horrified by the state I had shown up in, wanted me to get an abortion. ('*He did this to you? Ciaran? Rachel, there are options these days, love, you don't need this reminder of him your whole life. Nothing* comes of a bad seed except poisoned fruit – you are still young, there will be time.') I ignored her of course, revelling in the suffering I so deserved.

And if I'd thought the pregnancy was rough, it was nothing compared to the birth.

Two days and nights of contractions, painful enough to keep me awake, but not to bring her. Six hours of fruitless pushing, I could feel her moving down, and then up, down and then up. Like the world didn't want her. The midwife had no choice really, but to cut me. I can still hear the snap my skin made. The low cry from Mum as the blood came. That agonising rush, pushing involuntarily when I wasn't supposed to, the great splitting pain of it and then she was there, on my chest. This skinny, slimy, purple creature with staring, filmy eyes, rolling wildly. Gasping. We both gasped for air, fought for it, looking at each other.

I felt nothing.

There is a photo somewhere, that the midwife took for me. I am on my back, naked, with Vivian on my chest, slick against me, no space between us. I am staring lifelessly at the ceiling, limp, exhausted beyond all feeling. I looked decayed. Where was that joy I had been prom-ised? That light in my face? It wasn't there. When you are broken, utterly, there are no spaces for love to crawl in, just a vacuum where nothing can live.

I had to have surgery to mend the damage the birth had caused me; had to have, in the end, the epidural that I'd refused out of fear during the labour itself. By the time I was wheeled out of the operating theatre and back up to the ward, Mum had bathed and dressed Vivian. She looked like an actual baby, tiny pink and perfect. I still didn't love her, but I marvelled at that perfection, had some weird pride in her creation, that small miracle women perform every day. I searched her face for Ciaran's, but I never saw him. Not on her face.

It did get easier, I suppose. She was difficult those first few months, screaming for hours on end while I rocked her and shushed her, fed her biting mouth, frantic that she might be ill, that I was failing again. It took Mum storming in one night, knackered from the screeching echoing around the house ('*For goodness' sake, give her here*') and taking her away from me, just plonking her in her crib, holding me back while she screamed in a back-arching, kicking temper until finally she just settled, fist in her mouth, gumming it angrily, panting. Then she slept.

('*Some babies just don't want to be held.*')

After that, she was an easy baby and toddler. Self-contained, content to play by herself for hours. I was so happy and proud to have such a perfect little girl, it was such a relief after the traumatic years of my relationship with Ciaran, the pregnancy, birth. She healed me. I finally fell in love with her, felt the tendrils of that all-encompassing adoration I'd been told was mine by right.

It wasn't until she went to nursery that the problems started to occur.

There was an incident with a little boy. They'd had a childish falling out over a toy and both been ticked off. Later on, Vivian had gone over to him while they were all supposed to be having a nap, taken off her pants and deliberately urinated on him. A nursery worker had seen her do it, and she'd laughed it off, so I told myself it was meaningless. I carried that conviction for years. *It doesn't mean anything. She's her own person. There's not a problem.*

All the niggling issues at school that I was called in for, I dismissed as nothing. I ignored it all. And I knew that if I ever told anyone about how I had felt about her those first years, they would think I was a terrible mother, an awful person. Who doesn't love their baby? They would blame me. And at least I loved her now, I told myself again. I was fixing things, making them right.

I rubbed my face, trying to dispel the crowding thoughts as I went out into the garden, and then almost screamed as someone came at me from my studio – Alex, again. Cross at him for frightening me, full of painful recollections, I was harsh.

'Alex! Do you not remember me specifically asking you to text me if you wanted a lesson? I don't want you creeping around in my garden when I'm not here!'

'I'm sorry, I didn't want a lesson, I just wanted to pick up my picture. I was going to work on it at home, I just thought maybe you were out here.'

'Well, I wasn't!'

'I can see that. I'm really sorry,' and he turned sharply and left, leaving me feeling even worse than before for shouting at him when he hadn't actually done anything wrong, except look for me where I'd told him I could usually be found.

I spent the rest of the afternoon indoors, watching rubbish on TV and playing stupid games on my phone. I didn't have the energy for anything else.

–

'Prosecco's on me tonight, my darling. I fancied a change,' said Steve, popping the cork with an efficiency born of many years' practice. I watched the liquid bubble and froth in the tall glasses. We raised them silently, clinking them together, our thoughts a few houses away, where the oppressive sadness of the shut and silent chip shop pervaded the little high road like the weather, heavy, smothering. Even sitting as motionless as possible I could feel sweat tickling my hairline and pooling beneath my breasts.

'Do you know it's cooler in Barcelona than it is here?' said Steve, taking a long sip of his drink. He paused, waiting for the inevitable burp from the fizz. 'It looks like this weather is in for the long haul. The green will be a brown by the time I get back. Everything is baking to death.'

'What do you mean, "get back"? Where are you going?'

'I got a last-minute deal on a trip to Gran Can, darling. I'm going with Bill.'

'Bill? Bill "onions" Bill, who is about seventy, Bill?'

'Yes, what of it? I'd rather be going with you, boring only-going-to-Dorset-this-year girl.' He picked up his drink and stared into it. 'To be honest, we were chatting in the bar about everything, and both of us wanted to get away for a while.'

'Oh god, Steve! You'll give him a heart attack!'

'Rubbish! We'll have an amazing time. We're only going for a week, anyway. I'm assuming you can keep yourself alive for that long without me?'

'I guess I'll have to! I can't believe you're deserting me though…'

Steve gave me a sly look. 'Well, I'm sure your boy-toy will keep you occupied!'

I didn't even grace that with an answer. He just laughed.

'When are you going?'

'First thing tomorrow. Can't wait. You'll have to come next time – you can ditch Vivian with Abi and Gavin for a change. It's about time you gave the poor girl some space.'

'Yeah, yeah, I know. Over-protective mother, can't help it.' That again. I forced a smile and sipped my drink, trying not to wince at the taste, acid on my tongue.

We spent the rest of the evening like we usually did, chatting about anything and everything, the easy and comforting company I'd come to take for granted.

If I'd known it would be the last time I would ever see him, I would never have let him go.

# *Vivian*

When I get home from school I go straight to my room and I lie on the bed. The window is open, but it just lets in more heat. It presses down on me, as heavy as sand, burying me alive. I let my mother bury me on the beach once; it was supposed to be fun but I have never felt so terrified. I don't feel frightened now. I am trying to sort through many different emotions, but fear is not one of them. How I feel about Alex. How I feel about Molly. Alex and Molly. Molly and Alex. What they were doing, together, in that room. I let different images, scenarios, run through my head, to try and detach myself from them. I don't want to think what I am thinking – I don't want to think about a room with no windows. My phone buzzes insistently with messages from Molly but I ignore it. She has betrayed me, she has hurt me like Lexie hurt me. She wants what is mine.

Nothing else happened when I followed them. Alex disappeared, so I just ended up behind Molly as she was looking for him, trying to sniff him out like the bitch that she is. I tailed her back round to the school entrance, where she stood, waiting for me. I watched for a while, saw her texting me, saw her get cross that I wasn't there for her at the exact moment she decided to remember me. She's a hypocrite. Tells me he likes me, that I should like him, then goes after him. I am starting to think that I hate her.

When Mum leaves to go to the pub yet a-bloody-gain I quickly get changed, because I have a feeling that Alex isn't going to be far away. Since the first night he came over – the day Tristan died, I suppose – we've been meeting up every day after school, or at night when Mum has gone to sleep. We haven't really done anything except talk a lot and kiss, but I have decided that I want to do more. I don't know for sure what he was doing with Molly in that room earlier, if he was reciprocating (because I have no doubt about what she was trying to do), but I want to put my mark on him before I deal with *her*. He's mine.

I'm debating over lip gloss when there's a knock at the door – I knew it – and I run down and open it to see Alex standing on the step, leaning casually against the frame, his dark hair falling into his eyes. He reaches up and sweeps it back, his eyes flicking over me as he steps into the room, gathering me up and kissing me hard. In between the fluttering in my stomach and the usual sudden smoothing out of anything I had in my brain, a niggling thought manages to remain and wonders why he always turns up after my mother has already left. Obviously I don't want her to know about him, because she will make a fuss, but does he sit somewhere and watch the house? I feel excited that I'm worth stalking, and that surely he doesn't want Molly instead of me, and my mood picks up even more when he lifts me easily and carries me into the front room, collapsing us both onto the sofa, laughing in a breathless way that doesn't leave much room for anything else. I wrap my legs around him and pull him towards me as hard as I can manage, but he wriggles away from me as usual, and sits up, pulling my legs away and tucking them over his own so I'm lying back and he's looking down at me. I'm not happy.

'Don't you want to?' I ask him, trying to pout like Molly does.

'Are you feeling all right? You look a bit weird.'

'Alex! Answer the question. Don't you want to? You know?'

'Want to what?'

Jesus, he's as bad as bloody Molly. I could strangle him!

'Stop it. Have sex with me. I want to do it with you.'

'Viv, you're only fifteen. Aren't you worried about getting in trouble?'

'No, why would I? I don't care about that stuff. I'm on the pill, if that's what you're worried about.' My mum took me to the doctor's about my horrible periods last year and they'd prescribed it. Convenient, now I thought of it. Surprising that my mother didn't think of this. Unless she didn't think of this because she thought no one would want to have sex with me, which is rude, but not beyond the realms of possibility. Always thinking I'm still the vulnerable little girl of her imagination.

'I'm not worried about that.' He leans back, eyeing me sideways. 'But I think you care about what people think about you, don't you?'

'That's a strange thing to say.' He really is a complete weirdo sometimes.

'Have you been in trouble before? Like, proper trouble?'

'With police and stuff?' I frown at the even-odder-than-usual turn of conversation.

'Yeah.'

'Why are you asking?'

'I'm just interested. I want to know everything about you.'

He follows this up with leaning over me and kissing me, nuzzling into my neck and ear. I don't like it. I want the fierce kisses, not soppy bullshit. I shrug, hunching my shoulders, forcing his face away, pushing him until he's sitting up again. Why would he think a fifteen-year-old girl would ever have been in trouble with the police? I mean, obviously I have, which makes me unusual. Maybe he knows that. Maybe he is unusual too, which is why he's asking. He knows we're the same. I decide to touch on honesty.

'When I was younger, once, but it wasn't my fault. It was this other girl. Everything that happened was her fault. She ruined my life, but I don't want to talk about it. I told you before, I was bullied.'

I don't think he was very happy with me pushing him away, because suddenly his face seems to fold in on itself, his expression. His lips almost disappear into a white, pinched line and the tendons on his neck stand out. I lie very still and listen to the small sounds he is making as he breathes in slowly. He brings up his palms and scrubs at his face and hair, making it stand up. When he moves them again the expression is gone, although his eyes are still very dark – the glints of gold and blue have disappeared into the deepest green. He's got such amazing eyes.

'I can't stay tonight,' he says, sparking a painful disappointment in me. 'I have some work I need to do, but I'm free tomorrow. We could go for a picnic or something?'

I swallow my annoyance that he's leaving and my confusion about how he reacted to me pushing him off, watching him as he stands up on his long, lean legs in one smooth movement, sweeping mine to the side as if they weigh nothing.

'I know somewhere,' I tell him, anxious suddenly that he's going so quickly. 'I used to go there all the time as a kid, to the woods. I can text you where to meet me?'

He smiles, tightly, and then he's gone, leaving me to brood.

I usually hang out with Molly on a Saturday morning, but I haven't called her today to ask what's she's doing because of my Alex plans, which have not one iota of room for her. I ended up telling her that I had to hang out with Mum last night. I hope Molly didn't see her out. I know she's getting suspicious about what's going on with me and Alex, but this is my new secret. I'm sick of all hers.

I think it will be fun to get him completely lost in the woods today so I can have my way with him. I don't understand how I've gone from being uninterested in sex to completely dying for it in less than a month, but I'm not going to complain – it's good to be normal, right? I just want him to make me feel good. I know he can. I keep remembering that feeling, the first time we kissed, him pressed against me. I want it again. It will be the longest we have spent together, I will make sure of it. He's always dropping in and out of my life, teasing me, not letting me know anything about him. He's a puzzle that I need more time to solve, to break. I will find everything out eventually, he can't get away from me now.

I'm meeting him at eleven out by the copse so I while away a bit of time replying to the girls. Our chat has been really quiet again this week, despite Molly's best efforts, but there are messages on my phone from this morning. Molly wants us all to go to her house later for movies and a sleepover, just the four of us. Tilly hasn't been at school but she is coming back on Monday. She says it's horrible at her house with her mum crying all the time and her dad drinking too much. I tell them I will come later but I'm going out first, and Molly immediately texts me privately asking what I'm doing and who am I doing it with, but I just don't reply. I decide to leave my phone on my bed while I'm out because I don't want any disruptions, or Molly tracking me down with that app that tracks your GPS location. Why I let her persuade me into that one I don't know. I wouldn't put it past her to turn up at the worst possible moment and ruin everything.

I tell Mum that I'm going to Molly's and I'll be there all night and she just nods at me without smiling. I practically sprint out of the door and away from the cottage, out the back gate past the studio. It occurs to me maybe I should have gone the other way as this is the opposite direction I should be going in but I don't think she's clever enough to notice that. She'll be painting soon and that always makes her forget everything; she goes into a weird dream state, you could say anything to her and she wouldn't even notice or remember.

Alex is waiting for me in the car park next to the woods where we'd arranged to meet. There aren't any cars here, as usual – it's not a busy spot really except the odd dog walker. We're so far away from anywhere else that no one bothers. There's nothing special here to see. It's why I like it so much, you can feel like you're the only person in the world. I can't wait to take him to the stream, it's the best spot in the whole woods, and exactly where I want to be with him.

He kisses me when I get up to him and then grabs my hand. 'Ready?' he says, tickling me with his smooth voice. 'Are you planning on getting us lost in the woods?'

'Only if you annoy me. I might leave you in there. You could be lost for days.'

'Remind me never to annoy you, Vivian.' He laughs.

The woods here aren't big enough to get lost for days unless you are a complete idiot, but there are plenty of private spots to find and I quickly take us off the path toward my favourite one, pointing out the landmarks as we go. Molly and I found it, years ago, when we were still into playing outside and walking through streams and catching bugs and things. It was our secret place, but we haven't been here together for ages now. I don't know if she comes here any more, though I do occasionally when I want to be by myself. If it all gets too loud.

We walk for about a quarter of an hour, talking easily and stopping now and again to look at things, or just to kiss each other. Alex presses me hard against a tree at one point, and I wrap my legs around him as he holds me up. I want him to have me right there, but he pulls away like he always does and laughs at me. I think he must know exactly what he's doing to me. I think he's just winding me up, like I'm a toy he's playing with. Every time he kisses me or touches me it feels like he's adding branches to a fire that's just building up inside me. I can hardly wait to get there.

'Your friend has been texting me,' he says, suddenly.

'What? Molly?' My stomach twists viciously. 'What about?'

Alex just laughs. 'You know what. She's very persistent, isn't she? I had to run away from her yesterday, in college. She tracked me down and tried to molest me.'

I was right then, about what she was doing. She's trying to steal him. The thought of Molly and Alex together hurts my head. It's a black thundercloud in my perfect day. I put it to one side but I will have to do something about it later. He's mine. She can't have him.

Finally we get to the bank, and I choose to properly forget about Molly, pushing away the simmering anger I'm feeling for later. It's an open spot, just big enough for me to put down the blanket I brought with me in the dappled sunlight. The wide stream spins and whirls by, and the small sounds of the woods stop while their inhabitants decide if we are a threat or not before starting up again. It's warm and it's calm and it's completely perfect. Alex sits down and asks me if I want a sandwich, pulling his rucksack toward him. I kick it away to the side. I sit down over his lap.

'No, I don't want a sandwich,' I tell him, taking off my top just to make things really clear. 'I want you. Here. Now.' And I push him down and I kiss him.

# Rachel

Vivian went to Molly's for a sleepover on Saturday and I had to stop myself from calling Abi to check that she was there, that she was safe, telling myself that I was being paranoid. I knew that she would go mad if she thought I was checking up on her. I also knew the chances were that Abi wouldn't even be there, anyway. I paced around the house instead. I started jobs and left them half done, taking everything out of the airing cupboard and then just leaving it all in a pile. I needed to wash it all again. Then I decided to clean the bathroom, properly clean it. I sprayed everything with bleach and I scrubbed and scrubbed, but nothing was clean, and the skin on my hands started to split and to bleed. I didn't know why they were so dry. I thought I would have a shower, and clean the inside of the glass door at the same time, but the hot steam kicked up the chemical smell and it got in my mouth and in my eyes and it hurt, and I sat down in the hot bleach and I cried and cried. The arguments with Vivian about Tristan had sent me into a tailspin. I had thought everything was fine, that she was fine, but I had seen a flash of the anger that terrified me. There was no one I could speak to about my worries – I'd pushed people away and kept them at distance. I felt abandoned somehow, dragged back into a dark place I thought I had escaped from.

After I managed to pull myself out of the hissing water, I scrabbled around for my phone and I sent a message to Alex, apologising for the day before. I told him he could come any time he wanted to, later even, if he was free.

I managed to get dressed, just pulling on some of Vivian's short-shorts and a vest. Why was it still so *fucking* hot? I was sick of it. I went out to the studio; I had no idea what time it was or what the hell I'd been doing all day but I hoped that working – I was so behind on my work, I'd been throwing away page after page all week – might calm me down. I took a glass of wine with me. I took the whole bottle.

I picked up a new sheet of paper and I decided to work on the penultimate plate, the one of the prince and the girl, Arabella – whatever her bloody name was – breaking apart after their first kiss. She's pushing him away; he's desperate to control her, to hold her to him. His hands gripped her waist, her long, loose hair whipped at their faces. Dead, grey trees tore at a sickly yellow sky. It was a dark image, desperate love in the heart of it.

I always gave my drawn girls Vivian's face. I couldn't help it, even though it drove her mad. Delicate arching eyebrows, clear cool eyes and a slightly pointed chin. Perfect cupid-bow lips. But I just couldn't get her right, and was about to scrunch and rip the paper up in a childish, screaming tantrum when I heard a cough behind me and I spun around, heart in my mouth. Alex.

'You nearly gave me a heart attack!' I screeched at him, voice rusty and breaking.

'I'm sorry,' he said, palms lifting. 'I got your text, so I came. I was worried about you yesterday. I wanted to check on you – it didn't seem like you were feeling yourself.'

'Not myself?' I swung round, glass in hand, almost spilling wine everywhere like a drunk. 'What would you know, Alex? You don't know me! You have no idea what I'm really like, do you?' I could feel my pulse pattering under my skin, everywhere; I was going to have a panic attack and, oh, I couldn't, I couldn't go through this all again... Then he took my wine away and caught my shoulders. His hands were cool, and it was enough to start to snap me out of the spiral. His thumbs gently stroked up and down on my bare skin.

'Rachel, look at me. Look at me right now. Breathe with me, Rachel, please.' I looked at him and he was pursing his lips and taking slow, deep, exaggerated breaths which I copied, just to humour him but actually I needed them, and I stopped shaking and I tried not to cry. He held my gaze with his pretty eyes.

'How did you know how to do that?'

'Family issues.' He didn't elaborate.

'Thank you. I'm so sorry. I'm fine now, honestly. I'm glad you came over,' and I realised I meant it. His collected, still presence was far more soothing than the wine or the drawing was. He smelt faintly of salt and I thought of the sea rushing over the shore. I was jittery still, but I wasn't going to break.

He used his fingers and thumbs to gently knead the muscles above my collarbones. He ran his fingers over my shoulders and back up to my neck. A thumb came to a stop over my still hammering pulse and pressed gently. His eyes darkened and his lips moved but no words came out.

Starting to feel more than slightly uncomfortable I pulled away and turned back to my picture. Alex followed my gaze. He dropped his hands.

I suddenly saw, with a dawning horror and huge embarrassment, that I had drawn the faery prince with his face: slashing eyebrows, ocean eyes, full lips, a shock of dark, silky hair. It was quite clearly him. It was only then that I realised that the reason I was so angry at my inability to draw Vivian's face on Arabella was because I hadn't drawn her face at all.

I'd drawn mine.

I turned around, and pushed past him out of the studio.

'I think you should go now, Alex. I'm completely fine and I have a lot on today,' I shouted over my shoulder as I ran into the house, away from him, away from the sudden, shocking, creeping slick of *want* that swept through my body. He was a teenage boy, what the fuck was wrong with me? I was weak with it.

I got into the house and I ran up the stairs and I stood in my room, gasping, my hands in my hair. I couldn't pull any air into my lungs. I was such an idiot! Where had this even come from? I tried to brush it off, scrape it away, but it was like drowning in oil. No desire, or desire suppressed for years, had caused a storm of need in me that was almost impossible to bear. I wanted something for me, just once, for me and not Vivian. I wanted *him*.

And then, inevitably, I turned around and I went back down the stairs, back out into the garden where he stood, waiting for me. Cool, clever hands reached out to my shoulders again, fingertips smoothing, and I reached up to him, the nerves in my fingertips rejoicing in the feel of his skin, his hair. I looked up into his perfect face, and his sea-glass eyes, and I pulled his mouth down onto mine and I was lost.

# Vivian

I get to Molly's a bit late, and I have a leaf in my hair. She plucks it out and raises one eyebrow at me; which is annoying on so many levels, not limited to the fact I can't do that.

'What have you been up to, bitchy?' she asks me, with a twisty smirk on her face. She looks pissed off, but I decide that I don't care because I am feeling completely awesome after my afternoon with Alex, although I'm starting to wish I'd just gone home so I could relive it over and over. But I guess that, in theory, I should be here – if not with her, then with my other friends who need my 'support', or whatever.

'Serena and Tilly aren't coming,' says Molly. 'Tilly didn't feel up to it, so Serena has gone there instead.'

Oh.

'I wasn't sure if you were going to come or not. I did call you.'

'I left my phone at home.' I knew I should have gone back and got it but I hadn't wanted to ruin my morning by potentially having to speak to my mother. It's bad enough I'm here with this traitor.

'All day? Have you not been back to get it? Where have you been? What have you been up to, Vivvy? Why are you being so mysterious?'

Her blue eyes are flickering all over me now, needling, and I feel like she can see right through me. She pulls me into the house. I can smell pizza cooking and my stomach gurgles loudly.

'Been working up an appetite, Viv? I think you should go have a quick shower before we eat. You stink.'

I don't stink, but I obey orders, then return to the kitchen where she grabs a tea towel and manoeuvres the pizza out the oven. She slices it with a pizza roller – I wish we had one of those – and she plonks it down on the table. She's already got out ketchup and mayo, which she proceeds to squirt all over her half.

'I have no idea how you are so skinny,' I tell her, sitting down next to her and picking up a slice. I try and eat it too quickly and the hot sauce burns the roof of my mouth, right behind my teeth. It will blister, I know, and I will have a tender raw patch for the next few days.

'Ow.'

'You should blow on it first, Vivvy,' Molly snipes at me. 'I thought you were getting good at blowing?'

I decide to ignore this, though I do blow on the pizza.

We eat the rest without talking, and then Molly gets up to get us drinks. I can hear her poking around in the utility room, then she goes into the loo. On a whim I slide her phone toward me over the counter and tap in her passcode. There are no messages from Alex, but I see lots from Serena. Molly wasn't telling me the truth about why the others aren't coming tonight. Serena's been speaking to Matt. She knows what happened and she is not happy about it. That's why her and Tilly aren't here. This is the end of everything now. She's destroyed us, ruined us. Another black mark for Molly, who has clearly been getting away with things for far too long. I hear the flush and I push the phone away, my hand shaking. She comes back with wine and I take a deep breath; I need to calm down and stay in control.

'Are we allowed to have this?' I ask her, knowing that Abi can be a bit funny about us drinking. My mum is desperate to be a relaxed, uber-cool mum, but Abi has no such qualms, despite the buggering-off-all-the-time tendencies.

'Who gives a fuck?' is her succinct reply. 'They're out 'til after midnight as they've gone off to do some restaurant in Bath for the stupid blog.' She pours us large glasses of wine, the liquid glugging out of the bottle. I look at her face, notice that she looks flushed, and a bit smudged. I think she has been crying. I don't feel sympathy. This is all her own stupid fault.

I sip the wine. It isn't the same as the one I drank with Alex our first night. I think about our kissing on the sofa and what we ended up doing this afternoon that was even better. When I look up, Molly's eyes are boring into me again.

'You're screwing him, aren't you?' she says.

'I don't know what you're talking about.'

'Liar, liar, pants on fire. You're screwing Newboy. There's something wrong with him, you know. He asked me all sorts of weird things about you.'

'Like what?'

'Like where you're from, who your dad is, if you even know who he is. Why you're so fucking weird.'

'I am not weird! And he doesn't think I'm weird, he gets me!'

'Clearly there's something wrong with him then!'

'What, there's something wrong with him because he's not interested in you? Because he wants to know about me, instead?'

She gives me a cool look.

'No, I just don't trust him. He's creepy.'

'How do you know what he is? Have you been hanging out with him?'

'No. He's probably going to get kicked out of the college because he's never there.'

'I see him there! You're just jealous!' I say, before realising that she has been manipulating me into admitting there is something going on between us.

'So, is he any good? Big dick? Did you suck him off?'

Hearing her reduce my afternoon into small, dirty phrases is making me even more cross, so I tell her if she doesn't shut the fuck up then I'm leaving, and that nothing has happened anyway. I know she doesn't believe me and instead she immediately follows it up with another sucker punch. The Molly one-two.

'You know I could have him any time I wanted, don't you?'

'What?' I have to close my eyes for a second to keep the hate in.

'Alex. He doesn't want you. We practically fucked in the common room yesterday. He was all over me.'

'Why are you saying this? You're a liar. You just said you didn't hang out with him, but now you're fucking him in the common room?'

Molly shrugs, and sways slightly. Is she drunk again? She is! I wonder how much she has been drinking recently. It's as if alcohol has taken away the old Molly and replaced her with this new one that I don't like. That I don't like *at all*.

'Not lying. I thought you would want to know. He's not trustworthy.'

'Molly, I really think you should shut up.' She won't. She has no idea how angry I am.

'What are you going to do about him? I think you should dump him. Don't make me prove he's just the same as all the others. He wants me as much as they all do. It's all they want.'

Her eyes are appraising my face as I listen to this. Is this a threat? Is she actually threatening me? Would she actually try this now she knows I am with him? Can I be sure she won't? Oh, Molly. You stupid girl. I won't be threatened.

'I don't know why you are saying all this, Molly. It's none of your business.'

'I thought you might actually be upset for once,' says Molly, sipping her drink, eyes sliding away.

I remain still but my mind is frantic. Am I supposed to cry? Thinking about what Molly said makes me feel furious so I try to push the thoughts away. I need all of this to stop. How did I end up with such a shit best friend again? I feel like I have been fooled, like she has always been this person underneath, that she's just fake niceness varnished over a hateful, green-eyed thief. She is jealous of me, of my boyfriend, of my mother. She wants what's mine. But she is not going to have it.

Molly goes and sits in the front room, flopping down onto the sofa and spilling wine on herself, but she doesn't notice. I sit and breathe for a minute, trying to calm down. I need to pretend everything is okay while I come up with a plan, so I go and sit down next to her, and I grab her hand to make her think I'm not angry with her. She doesn't say anything, but I see her relax. We finish watching a film we started weeks ago, when things were still perfect, and drink more wine before going upstairs. I ask to borrow pyjamas and she gives me a scrappy little lace nightie which I'm not sure about. She's wobbling about all over the place, she must have been drinking all day. Part of me wants to just go home, but then there will be the inevitable inquisition from my mother. And I haven't decided what I need to do about Molly yet.

'This is a bit small,' I tell her, holding up the nightie by its tiny straps.

'It gets hot in here. You know I can't sleep with the window open.'

No other bed wear seems to be appearing so I put it on in the bathroom, use her mouthwash to get rid of the taste of pizza and wine and go and climb into bed. She faffs around for a while in her ensuite (cleanse, tone, moisturise, brush, brush, braid) before coming back and pacing around her room for a bit, switching on the fan she's got on the desk to move the stuffy air in useless circles. Her plait is as thick as my wrist at the top and it tapers down to a whip of gold at the bottom which flickers side to side as she walks, a cross cat's tail. Eventually she jumps on the other side of the bed and crawls up to get under the sheet. It's hot enough to sleep without it but she can't sleep without some sort of covering, I don't know why. Maybe she doesn't feel safe in the place she's most meant to, at home, at night, in her bed.

There's enough light in the sky outside gleaming through the gaps in the curtains for me to see Molly's profile next to me. Her eyes are still open and she's staring into the dark above her. I don't want to talk about Alex again but I can feel the words bubbling up in my mouth so I press my tongue onto the smooth, sore, burnt spot behind my teeth and I taste metal instead.

I don't think I'm going to but at some point I actually fall asleep listening to Molly's breathing. Maybe it's the change in it that wakes me up, or it's the dream I'm having about Alex running his smooth hands over me, shoulder to hand, hip to knee, breast to waist. I wake up, and it's Molly who has her hand on me. It's underneath my nightie and flat on my breast bone. She knows I'm awake.

'I was wondering if you had a heart, Vivian. I was wondering if there's anything inside you at all,' she slurs, before slipping her palm sideways, cupping my breast, her thumb brushing over my nipple. I have no control over it stiffening and I'm frozen and I don't know what to do. I can feel her breath on my cheek, smell sour alcohol, and she slowly moves her hand over my ribs and down my body.

'Please, don't,' I tell her. 'Please.' But she puts her hand over the top of my underwear, her fingers resting between my legs, applying the faintest pressure.

'Did he touch you here, Viv?' she whispers, hot mouth at my ear. 'Did he kiss you here? You know I could kiss you there and it would be better than anything he could do?' Her lips brush my neck and I suddenly regain control of my body and I jump up, pushing her away so violently she knocks against the wall.

'Why are you doing this?' I shout at her now. 'Are you mental? You've fucked everything up! Everything was perfect, why have you fucked it up?' I run into the bathroom and I put my clothes on, throwing the scrap of nightie into her shower. I can't stop the rage spilling over and I lash out, sweeping everything from the windowsill to the floor; I lose it, just for a screaming second, and then perfume smashes at my feet in a cascade of bright glass and the scent stings my eyes.

I go back into Molly's room and she's just lying there, on her back, with the light from the window shining on her face. I can see the silver track of a tear slipping over her cheek but I don't care. I don't say anything.

It's in this moment, watching her cry in the gloom, that something whirrs and clicks in my brain, the way she's been acting. It is just that, isn't it – an act. It's an act for me. She's in love with *me*. She doesn't want Alex, he's not shady – she just wants me for herself! All this time, she's been playing up – why the hell did I not realise sooner? I could have used this. All that power over her, and I never realised; I let the control slip through my fingers and now we are here and Molly has thrown everything away and it's too late. Now she's nothing to anyone, and I'm afraid of what she might do next.

I won't let her ruin me like Lexie did.

# London

'What's wrong with her now?' asked Rachel, as she walked into the house past Vivian, who was running up the stairs.

'She's got a face on because I keep telling her she's too young to dye her hair,' said Carol, wryly. 'She's even younger than you were when I told you the same thing, and you pulled exactly the same face.'

'Why does she want to dye her hair? She's only eight!'

'She says she wants to have yellow hair like Lexie.'

'To go with the blue shoes and the sparkly blue ruck-sack like Lexie?'

'Mmm,' said Carol.

'Even if it was blonde it wouldn't look like Lexie's, hers is so long and thick. I wouldn't mind her hair myself! Vivian's is too fine, I'm not sure she's going to get it to grow past her chin any time soon.'

'Takes after me – Vivian? What have I told you about eavesdropping?'

'I came down to see Mum,' said Vivian, who had been listening from the foot of the stairs. 'Is that why my hair isn't long? Because it's like yours? It won't grow?'

''Fraid so, my love! It'll grow more when you're older. It's just fine,' said Carol, pulling on the tips of her own short bob ruefully.

Vivian frowned. 'What time am I going to Lexie's?'

'I'll drop you off,' said Rachel. 'I'm going out for a drink; I need to get ready first, though. And you should count yourself lucky that you got Nana's lovely shiny brown hair and not Grandad's curly hair, like mine!' She ruffled Vivian's head, grinning down at her.

Vivian just pulled a face, and leaned away. 'Get off. Hurry up, Mummy!'

'Go and get your bits together, okay? I'll jump in the shower.'

—

Rachel pulled back the shower curtain and nearly slipped out of the bath entirely. Vivian was standing in the bathroom with her jacket on and her bag on her shoulders, watching her silently.

'Viv! You nearly gave me a heart attack!' She reached past her and pulled a towel to her, wrapping it round herself. 'Funny girl,' she whispered, pressing her lips to Vivian's forehead.

Vivian pulled away, as she usually did. 'You're all wet, Mum. Hurry up, I want to go now.'

'I need to get ready first, babe. Give me ten minutes.'

Vivian followed her through to her bedroom, perching on the bed and watching as she got dressed, intently observing her putting on make-up. 'Why do people wear make-up?' she asked, picking up a lipstick and screwing it up and down, up and down.

'To look nice, I guess.'

'You already look nice.'

'Ah, thank you, sweetheart.'

'Does everyone wear it? Lexie has got some lip gloss, but I don't like it, it's sticky. Do I have to wear make-up?'

'Not if you don't want to. You're beautiful as you are.'

'I'm not,' said Vivian, matter-of-factly. 'I want to look like Lexie.'

'Vivian,' said Rachel, wracking her brain for the right words, 'everyone is different. They like different things, but that doesn't stop us being friends, or loving each other. You don't have to be like Lexie for her to like you.'

'No one else likes me, though. Everyone likes Lexie.'

'I don't think that's anything to do with how you look, though, darling. It can be difficult when you're eight, can't it? It will get better, I promise. Come on, let's go.'

—

The bar was crowded with Friday night customers, all jostling each other. Rachel was standing at the back wall by the steps that led down into the garden, waiting for Beth to come back with more drinks. She'd bumped into her at the tube station earlier in the week and despite trying to escape without notice, had been collared and strong-armed into handing over her number. Their catch-up had so far mainly consisted of Beth grilling her about exactly what she had been doing for the last ten years, no doubt in an effort to ascertain whether or not she was worth being friends with.

They'd briefly been close as teenagers, but Beth was the sort of person who could make you feel like you were their best friend but then drop you the second they found someone else interesting. Rachel was getting the distinct impression that this hadn't changed and was trying to think of an excuse to leave when her phone rang.

'Hello?'

'Hi, Rachel? It's Lucy.'

'Hi, is everything okay? Give me two secs to get outside – it's loud in here.' She pushed through the crowd, tapping Beth on the shoulder as she did and gesturing to her phone. 'Two secs,' she told her, before squeezing out through the people milling at the door.

'Lucy, hi, sorry, I'm at the Village – it's manic in there. What's up? Is Vivian okay?'

'Er, yes, Vivian's fine, it's just, I think you need to come and get her.' Rachel felt her stomach plunge, a looping sensation that made her feel drunker than she was.

'I'll come now. I'll literally be two minutes.' She tapped out an apology to Beth – who was bound to find someone to latch on to – and set off around the corner onto Eden Road and up to the little cottage. Knocking softly on the door she found herself biting her lip, nipping it hard enough to taste iron.

Lucy opened the door. 'Rachel, I'm so sorry, I tried to call your mum but she wasn't answering her mobile and I didn't like to try the landline in case she was in bed already...'

'It's fine, honestly, but what's wrong?'

'Come in.' She led Rachel into the little front room where Vivian was sitting on the sofa in her nightie. She didn't look up, staring down at the floor instead, her face blank. She was hugging her knees to her chest, chin on her knees. Lucy gestured with her head and Rachel followed her into the hallway.

'What happened?'

'It might be better if I show you. Come up.'

Rachel followed Lucy up the stairs and into a small bedroom, where Lexie lay sleeping. She looked around. 'I don't understand, did she hurt herself on something?'

'No,' said Lucy. 'Look.' She walked over to her daughter's sleeping form and ran her fingers over her head, and Rachel gasped, putting her hand to her mouth in shock. Lexie's hair had been cut off in ragged chunks, the edges rough in the dim light from the hallway.

'She brought the scissors with her, Rachel,' said Lucy. 'She waited until Lexie was asleep. I came in to check on them, and I found her cutting off her hair while she was asleep.' There were tears in her eyes. 'Why would she do that?'

# Rachel

I woke up to Alex kissing his way down my body again. I felt like the whole day had been a dream, so I didn't try to stop him; I encouraged him instead, lacing my fingers again through his hair. Maybe it wasn't even real. The way he was using his mouth and his fingers, I didn't think this was his first time, but it didn't make the guilt any less. I could feel it simmering beneath the pleasure. He moved over me, kissed me, and slid himself into me again and we rocked gently together, slowly and exquisitely building up a tension that made me shudder and moan into his mouth. I could feel him smile his sharp smile. I bit his lip.

It was becoming almost unbearably good when we both froze as the front door opened and closed. We heard Vivian take off her shoes and then she came up the stairs, quietly, every soft footstep hammering at me. Alex started to move his hips in small, agonising circles and resumed kissing me, nibbling at my neck, and I hated him with a sudden passion, paralysed by fear of discovery. Vivian went straight into the bathroom and I heard the shower hiss on, the sound of water hitting the floor muting when she got in. Alex heard it too and his slow hip movements turned into resounding, headboard banging thrusts and I orgasmed so intensely that I couldn't breathe. He finished, kissed me once more, firmly with promise, and then slipped silently out of the bed, into his clothes and out of the house like he was a part of the night.

I wanted to get up and check on Vivian; she spent an awfully long time in the shower and I wondered if she'd fallen asleep in there, but eventually the water stopped and she padded into her room and I didn't hear anything else. I didn't even know what the time was because I had left my phone out in the studio, and hadn't been out to get it.

I barely slept the rest of the night, imaging scenarios in which Vivian had come in to my room for some reason and caught me having sex with someone barely older than she was, or where Alex had bumped into her coming in the door, or any mixture of everything. I could feel my face burning with shame and the aftermath of a night of realising that all the needs and wants I'd suppressed for so long had never gone away; they were just waiting under the surface.

I got up when the dawn started to creep in, fingers of light reaching the bed, and I gave up on any pretence of sleep and went straight for coffee. I sat at the kitchen table drinking it as hot as I could bear it, scalding, and then I made another cup. I knew it would probably make me ill but I deserved to be ill. It felt like I sat there for hours, palms flat against the smooth wood. The table had come with the cottage and bore the marks of years. I loved it – I love all old things that are imbued with the past, which is funny considering how much I hate and fear my own. I traced for the thousandth time twin ruts in the wood that looked as if they had been made by a small child running an old metal toy car up and down, up and down. It had been sanded over and varnished again since then, but the scars remained. I'm not sure how long I sat there lost in that repetitive motion, in silence, thinking about scars.

Maybe it had been a mistake to close myself down to relationships for all those years, after Ciaran. It had been so intense with him, and now here I was with an equally unsuitable partner, having equally intense sex that I couldn't stop thinking about, reliving it in detail. Not that I could let it happen again, I tried to tell myself: I mustn't think any more of the slow drag of his fingers over flesh, the hidden promise of pleasure-pain in his gently biting teeth, his kiss.

I felt completely and utterly ashamed. I was aware of every place Alex had touched me, tender, used and even a little bruised on my shoulder where he must have nipped me. I pressed the sore spot, I dug my nail in. I deserved the pain.

I should have checked on Vivian.

# London

Carol felt sick with anger when she found about what Vivian had done to Lexie. Lucy had been very good about it, unbelievably, astoundingly gracious in fact, but things weren't the same any more. There hadn't been any invites for tea after school in the weeks since, or a Friday afternoon glass of wine. She missed her friend, and couldn't help a small part of her blaming her granddaughter. Why did she have to be so *odd*?

She found herself paying much closer attention to what Vivian was doing, and listing in her mind all the little things she had just dismissed over the years: that boy she had bitten, leaving a scar; the stolen phone (which had been found along with the missing handbag and sunglasses, stuffed behind Vivian's wardrobe); locking that other boy in the cupboard and refusing to apologise or even admit it was her, even now. It was always someone else's fault. It almost seemed like she didn't understand how to be a child. She had tried and tried to speak to Rachel about it, but she refused to listen. Claimed it was Vivian attention-seeking, promised to cut back on work, nothing was wrong. She just wasn't *seeing*.

There was no sign of Lucy in the playground at pick up. Vivian walked out of her classroom alone, her hands tucked behind the straps of her rucksack, head down. Carol felt a spurt of guilt at her earlier thoughts. She was just a little girl, and not a happy one. She needed support, not blame.

'How was your day today?' she asked, holding out the cereal bar she'd brought with her for a snack. Vivian looked at it and shook her head.

'I'm not hungry.' She was silent the rest of the way home, where she went straight up to her bedroom and shut the door.

Later Carol took a plate with a sandwich and some fruit up to her, moving lightly, and pushing open the door without knocking. Vivian, sitting at her mini writing desk, which was yet another guilt present from Rachel, startled. She pulled a book over onto the paper in front of her, the dark look on her face quickly smoothing away into its usual blankness.

'What are you up to?' said Carol, putting the plate down next to her. 'What's this—' She moved a hand towards the paper underneath the book.

Vivian smacked her hand away. 'Nothing! It's private. It's homework. It's for school.'

'Vivian! We do not hit! What's wrong with you today?'
'Nothing!'

Carol plonked down the plate next to the book and the hidden pages. 'Suit yourself! And get changed please, jammies on. Bring your school shirt down and put it in the wash.' As she came down the stairs the front door opened and Rachel came in, her phone pressed to her ear. Carol didn't understand what was so important that her daughter had to be available at all hours, glued to that damned lump of metal and plastic. It was nearly seven o'clock! She opened her mouth to speak to her, but Rachel just raised a palm and went past her into the kitchen, leaving her stranded and gaping like a fish. Two generations of her family who didn't think she was worth talking to.

The next morning after dropping Vivian at school – Rachel being long gone, as usual – Carol decided to spring clean. At least that was what she told herself. She ran a duster over all the furniture in Vivian's room. Everything was as it always was – neat. Her books were aligned on the shelf by height. All her clothes were neatly folded in her drawers – refolded, in fact. Carol hadn't put them in like that. Such an exacting child.

It was hard work, the cleaning. Tugging the drawers away from the walls to reach behind for anything that might have fallen. Nothing but a hair bobble and a lonely dust bunny. She changed the sheets, turning the mattress, even though it wasn't the season.

It was when she pulled out the bed to hoover down the side that she noticed the threads in the box frame, where the fabric had been cut to create a hiding place.

# Vivian

As soon as I get back I get straight in the shower. I want to wash tonight off me, rinse away the consuming anger that I'm still feeling – I can't get rid of it. But it doesn't work, it's still there. We went through this so much in therapy: ways to get rid of these vicious feelings. It isn't my fault, and what happened before wasn't my fault, either. Our group is broken, Tristan's stupid car crash didn't bring us back together. It's all broken apart and I can't bear it any more. I can't fix it now. It's done.

The shower eventually gets cold and I step out and head for my room. I decide to text Alex, even though he's probably dreaming. I tell him about what Molly did to me. He doesn't reply, and I fall asleep looking at the empty screen. My own dreams fall into each other, Alex and Molly, I don't know where one begins and the other ends. I feel pulled apart, like their hands have reached inside me. I hear the *snick* of the rat's ribs breaking, only it's my bones that break and my insides, thickly purple, meaty, that are exposed to their grasping, tugging fingers. I always dream of red hands, of bloody red hands. It wasn't my fault!

I wake up late, sweating. The weather is insane this summer, it feels like it's never going to be cool again. Memories from yesterday and last night crowd in like they do after that brief second of waking forgetfulness, and make me want to scratch at my skin, pull it right off, but I don't. I just get up and shower, again. My arms are sore and aching and I struggle to lift them to wash my hair. I feel so heavy and exhausted.

All the lightness and excitement that I felt after my afternoon with Alex has just ebbed away, and I want to get it back as soon as I can. I want to smother the awful nothing I'm feeling.

As I get dressed I look at myself in the mirror that hangs in my wardrobe. I don't look any different from yesterday morning, before Alex, before Molly. What is it that they see in me? Two people who could have anyone, not wanting each other, but me instead. I open my hand, look at it, at the lines on it. I make a fist, angry again that I didn't realise what was going on with Molly before. I could have stopped everything that went wrong, if I hadn't been so blind. She would have done anything for me, I could have made her do anything. I understand it now, the power that comes from being wanted, the control it gives you. How weak she must have felt, being the one wanting for once. But even now, in the bright morning, I can't see any way it could have been fixed. It's too late to use her wanting, everything's too broken. And besides, I have Alex now. I don't need Molly any more.

Mum is sitting at the kitchen table nursing a cup of coffee. I hate coffee. I get myself juice from the fridge instead. It's cold and sweet and I feel it sticking to my tongue. I sit opposite Mum but she doesn't look up.

'What's wrong?' I ask her, not actually caring but wanting a distraction from the pounding in my head.

'Nothing, babe,' she says, looking up but not at me, and plastering a weird smile on her face. 'Just a bit tired. Work not going very well this week, what with everything that's going on.'

As usual she's commandeering other people's drama and making it about her. She's got a little purple mark on her shoulder and it matches the circles under her eyes.

'Are you looking forward to Dorset next week?'

No. Our stupid annual painting holiday is the last thing I want to do; I want to stay here where Alex is, but then I think that getting away for a while could be a good thing, just in case.

'Yeah, sort of.'

'We can go straight from school on Friday if you get everything together. Have you got much washing that needs doing?'

'No.'

The inanity. How can it be like this after the explosion of everything in my life? I can't stand it. I can't stand her. I force out words, brambles in my throat.

'It will probably be cooler by the sea, if it's not raining by then. It always rains when we go on holiday.'

She smiles and I know she's thinking of the week we spent in Spain, near Valencia, when it rained so hard that everywhere flooded and people's cars floated off down the street. One man actually drowned. Imagine drowning in your car, rain filling it up drop by drop, slowly stealing the air. I think I know how he must have felt.

'Hopefully not as much as Spain, hey?' She croaks out a laugh, and I feel a flicker of hope that at least she's not going to be moody and annoying all day. She rubs at her shoulder and looks at me.

'How did you get that bruise?' she asks me, nodding her head at my shoulder. I reach up and realise I have a mark where Alex bit me yesterday, in the woods, when he came.

'I just banged it on something,' I lie, easily. Lies slip out so gracefully, so much softer than sharp truths. 'It doesn't hurt.' I don't ask her about hers as she tugs her T-shirt to cover it because, again, I don't really care. I want to get out of the house and find Alex but he hasn't texted me back yet. I'm pissed off, and starting to think he's ignoring my messages. Is he angry about what happened with Molly? He doesn't have to be, but boys are like that, I suppose. Jealous. I just want to see him and pick up where we left off. I want him to make me burn again.

# Rachel

I didn't leave the house on Sunday, except to go to the studio to retrieve my phone, which I found myself checking for messages from Alex, like a teenager. I claimed a migraine and hid in my room, not that Vivian cared. I knew I should ask her about why she had come home so late when she was supposed to be staying at Molly's, but I couldn't focus on anything. She slipped out of the house for school on Monday looking as exhausted as I felt, everything about her a little limp and jaded. I promised myself I would speak to her properly that night, thinking their petty drama would probably have resolved itself by then anyway.

I had been keeping such a close watch on her for so long that I had completely neglected myself, and I spent much of the morning trying to tell myself that what I had done was understandable in the circumstances. Who wouldn't have been flattered? I was vulnerable, a bit broken. Maybe I deserved some pleasure for once, however brief and potentially damaging. I wouldn't do it again, and I prayed he wouldn't tell anyone. He hadn't given me the impression he was the type, but that didn't stop my imagination.

Eventually, I went back to the studio to face my shame. I leafed through my work, trying to trace the point at which I had started using Alex's face as the inspiration for the faery prince. I had only known him for a week. A week, and I had fallen into bed with him like some idiot from a terrible movie, a Lolita in reverse. I couldn't get to the bottom of the feelings that I had for him. I wasn't sure I even had any; everything I was feeling was aimed at myself, arrows of guilt and disgust peppered with absolution. I hadn't done anything illegal, obviously, but surely it was immoral. I was embarrassed, and afraid that if people found out I wouldn't be able to live with it – not here. You couldn't be anonymous in the village: your business was everyone's business. Scandal was currency, and this would go a long way, especially at a time like this, when the whole place was swamped in grief for the Beaumont family, what was left of it. I tried to stop thinking.

The retro clock on the studio wall seemed to get louder and louder the more I tried to clear my head. The ticking turned into a whine of white noise in my ears and I thought I was going to pass out; I had to grip the desk as my vision swam in front of me. My focus came back as the hum passed, and I looked again at that picture, of Alex, of me, caught together and pulling away, the desperation, the struggle. I picked it up. It was good work, but I tore it slowly into strips and squares, ripping through our faces, dropping us like confetti into the waste bin.

–

I was making yet another cup of coffee when the doorbell went. My first worry was that it might be Alex, and I felt a fist of sudden anxiety worming up from my stomach to clutch at my throat. What would I say to him? What would he want, expect, from me now? I hadn't heard anything from him since Saturday and had tentatively begun to hope that he had got his older woman conquest and would just leave me alone. I crept through the hall and looked through the spy hole in the door.

It wasn't Alex, it was Abi, Molly's mum. I opened the door.

'Have the girls left yet?' she said, in a cheerful voice. 'Molly isn't answering her phone and she wanted me to write her a note for PE but I didn't get round to it so I thought I'd drop it in. I'll take it up to the school if I've missed her.'

I was confused, clouded. 'Molly hasn't been here, Abi,' I told her. 'Viv came home late Saturday night and she's been here on her own the rest of the weekend.'

Abi visibly paled at my words. I saw her swallow. 'She texted me, Rachel. She said they had decided to stay here instead and revise, and that she was going to stay last night, too. We were out on Saturday, most of yesterday too. I didn't think to check with you, as she's here such a lot. Are you sure Vivian was on her own?' I could see guilt slicing into her, lips pressed hard together, eyes widening and shining with worry. I remembered listening to Vivian coming up the stairs. I remembered Alex slowly moving inside me. She was alone.

'Yes, I was still awake but it was late, pitch dark. I didn't ask her why it was so late, why she came back, I just forgot. What are you going to do, do you want to come in? Shall we call the school and see if she's turned up? I'm sure she was just at one of the other girls' houses – shall we call Serena's mum?'

'I'm going to go home and call Gavin. I'll do a ring around,' Abi said. Her eyes were flicking between me and the path now, and I could see her fingers twisting in the loose, filmy material of her green skirt. I could almost feel the fear leaching from her skin like an oily mist, reaching for me, wrapping us both in its tendrils. Where the hell was Molly? Why didn't I ask Vivian what had happened and why she'd come home so late? I'd been so wrapped up in my own head I'd missed what was going on with my girl.

Abi turned and left me, almost running across the field and already on her phone, presumably trying Molly again, or Gavin. I had a sick feeling in my stomach and a writhing under my skin, like worms rooting to get out.

By the time Alex appeared at my door – like I knew, deep down, he would – I just pulled him inside, let him kiss me, while I tugged up handfuls of my dress; let him fuck me where we fell against the stairs, their edges digging into my back. The carpet was rough, burning on my skin, but I welcomed the pain.

It made me feel good. It made me forget.

# *London*

Vivian had been delighted to see the cake Carol had baked waiting for them at home. It was her favourite, a plain sponge with a jammy filling. Guilt chewed at her as she watched the little girl tuck into a slice, while she made them a special hot chocolate dotted with little marshmallows. It wasn't right to think so badly of your own flesh and blood, she told herself, as she watched them melt into the hot liquid, waiting for it to cool enough for Vivian.

'Nana, can I go and play in my room now?' asked her granddaughter, after she'd slurped the drink down loudly.

Carol swallowed painfully, and reached out to hold Vivian's hand. 'Actually, darling,' she said, wondering if she was doing the right thing without speaking to Rachel first, 'I wanted to speak to you about something.' She lifted the magazine that she'd placed on the table earlier, and slid out the piece of paper hidden beneath. It was a drawing of small, broken figures, all scribbled over in red, each one named as a classmate, with Lexie in the centre. It had made Carol cry when she found it, realising how bad Vivian must be feeling about the situation she was in, the falling out. The rage in it had actually frightened her. It wasn't normal.

Vivian's face fell as she looked at the paper, her eyes widening in a horror that would have been comical in any other situation. Her mouth fell open, but she didn't say anything.

'I found this in your room, sweetheart. It made me feel a bit worried about you, Vivian. About how you're feeling. This isn't very nice. I think that me and you and Mummy need to talk about how you're feeling.'

Carol reached out again for Vivian's hand, but the little girl snatched it away and suddenly sobbed. 'Please, don't tell Mummy! I won't do it any more, I promise.' She rubbed her eyes with her fists and her voice hitched. 'Please, Nana! Please! Don't make Mummy hate me even more.'

'Shh, love. Come here. Mummy doesn't hate you, why would you say that?' asked Carol, shocked by the unusual emotion in her granddaughter's voice.

'Because she's never here, she never wants to see me, and because I cutted Lexie's hair but I was just playing, I thought she would like it!'

'Mummy doesn't hate you,' said Carol, her guilt warping into shock and sadness as she pulled Vivian around and onto her lap. 'And I won't tell her if you don't want me to, but we need to have a proper talk about this, okay? Me and you. I didn't know you were feeling so bad.'

She held Vivian on her lap for a long time, rubbing the shaking little shoulders and feeling terrible about confronting her.

When Vivian finally pulled away, though, she couldn't help noticing that her eyes were dry.

# Vivian

I've just come out of science when Mrs Barker, who is hovering outside the lab, catches sight of me and beckons me over. She asks me to follow her to her office above the art block. It seems to take for ever to get there, like we are walking through glue. The air is thick and hazy and I wonder if I'm still dreaming. The noise of everyone else moving through the school to lunch is muted, like I'm listening underwater.

As I follow behind her I notice that she's wearing thick beige tights, despite the heat. There is a run in them that goes from her ankle right the way up to underneath her skirt. I imagine grey, bristly hairs sticking through the little holes; and grease from her skin, leaking through the gaps, hot and moist and sticky.

I've never been in Mrs Barker's office before. I look around. I thought it would be sparse, empty – she seems like such a sparse and empty sort of person. But the office is cluttered with photos and books and piles of paper and folders. There are wildflowers in a jar on the windowsill, starting to wilt. The colours sting my eyes and give me a headache. I wonder if someone gave them to her, or if she picked them for herself. I don't know who would want to pick flowers for Mrs Barker. We always joke that Mr Barker is her dog.

'Vivian, do you know where Molly is?' she asks me, as I stand there in front of her desk. There's no lead in – she doesn't ask me to sit down, and I wonder again about why she doesn't like me. Her mouth breathing is the only sound I can hear: it hisses in and out, in and out. She doesn't blink as she looks at me, and I see her dislike in the stiffness of her shoulders, the tilt of her face. What does she know about me? What is hiding in the grey filing cabinet under my initial? S for Sanders. S for secrets. There shouldn't be anything about me from my old school, but you never know. People have loose lips.

'No, miss.'

'You were at her house on Saturday night, though? For a sleepover?'

'Yes, miss.'

'Molly messaged her parents on Saturday night saying she was staying with you for the rest of the weekend. Where did you go?'

'I left her at her house, miss, she didn't come back to mine. I don't know why she said that. She was still asleep at her house when I left. I don't know where she is. She's probably just run off again.'

Mrs Barker's eyes are flinty and boring into mine. I hold them; I know she's trying to intimidate me and she can fuck off. Her and her nasty, muddy eyes. What business is this of hers, anyway?

'Did you have a falling out, Vivian?'

'No. I just wanted to go home.'

I can see that she doesn't believe me, but I don't care. The silence stretches between us until I break it, *snap*.

'Can I go now, miss?'

She nods reluctantly and I pick up my bag and leave her office, and I hear her pick up the phone, presumably to report back to whoever wanted to know what I knew about Molly. I want to go and find Serena and Tilly – assuming she's back – because I didn't see either of them this morning, and talk about where they think Molly might be.

I find both of them in the canteen at our table, poking at their lunches. Tilly looks thin and pasty, and I can see a rash of acne dancing across one cheek despite the layer of foundation that's plastered over it. I figure that grief must be a good diet, but not so great on the complexion. I'm surprised she even came back to school looking like that. Maybe her parents made her come. I wonder if Serena did the make-up. I picture her painting Tilly's face with gentle strokes of a brush, giving her a new mask to wear that is supposed to cover her sadness. It hasn't worked. I can still see it.

'Have you seen Molly?' I ask them, as I sit down. 'Barker just dragged me into her office to ask me. No one has seen her since Saturday, apparently.'

Serena just rolls her eyes.

'She's such an attention-seeker. I bet this is because I told her I knew about her and Matt. She's probably just off with some other boy somewhere.' She glances over to the corner where Matt is sitting and listening. He frowns and turns his head. I see him angle his body so he can hear what we are saying.

'It wouldn't be the first time,' adds Tilly. Her voice shocks me for a minute. It's corroded. It sounds like it's coming from somewhere far away: her light feathery voice has gone and been replaced with a dirty, grinding husk. 'She's always done it. She hates it when people are pissed off at her. She wants us to feel worried about her instead, so she runs off. She managed a whole night one time before you moved here and she wouldn't tell anyone where she had been, do you remember Serena? Her mum went *mental*.'

Even though Molly means nothing to me now, I feel an old tug of jealousy that their friendship, their group, predated me. They have all been friends since they were really small, they grew up here. I'm an interloper, an invasive species. These two never let me forget that, and the resentment bubbles up in me again. I try and squash it down, because I need them now. I still want everything to go back to how it was before. Everyone likes us. We are the popular girls.

'Well, I don't know where she is. She's been behaving really weirdly all summer, I don't know what's wrong with her. I hope she's not pregnant or something.' I deliberately pitch these words so blabbermouth Matt can hear them, and he goes a satisfying green. That will teach him to eavesdrop. Serena and Tilly don't react to this statement – obviously they know what Molly has been up to as well as I do, by now. We all leave our food to congeal on the plastic plates. We don't talk, or laugh like we usually do. They share heavy looks that I don't understand. It's all wrong.

After the break I go into the bathroom and I wash my hands over and over until after the bell is gone before I come out. I'm going to be late for registration but I want to walk past the college to see if I can see Alex anywhere. I don't, and I feel a burn of annoyance. Where is he? Why isn't he answering my messages?

–

There still aren't any messages from Alex when I get up, and it's Tuesday now. It's been fifty-six hours since I've seen him, or touched him, or even heard from him at all. I'm furious all over at the thought that he somehow might have tricked me into having sex, then ghosted me. I can feel the rage stabbing into my body, singing in my head, trying to provoke me into a storm. I'm lying on my bed trying to do a meditation exercise like the ones we had to do at the hospital, but it's not working. I'm breathing in through my nose and out through my mouth, but I can feel the air. It's like it's squirming into my body, hot and alive, and it's making me feel even worse. I grit my teeth until my jaw throbs with pain. I refuse to believe that he has just used me for sex. It's not happening to me.

I need to get ready for school. I shower, dress, and the routine takes the edge off. The walk through the woods will calm me down. I'm tempted to go to the stream first, it's still early enough, but I don't want to spoil all the memories I've made there this weekend, so I will just go to school as normal, as new normal anyway. I will try and make Serena and Tilly understand that I can be Molly now. She's left them, hasn't she? Left them to fend for themselves, but they don't need to if they have me. We can still be the popular girls. I can be Molly. Better than Molly, once Alex comes back.

They aren't waiting for me near reception like they should be. I wait on my own for ten minutes, like an idiot. They've already gone into class. They did this yesterday too, but I thought that maybe it was because it was Tilly's first day back since her stupid brother died. Why haven't they waited for me today? Serena always waits for me and Molly while Tilly gets a lift, or she used to. Things have changed, I have to expect that, but they still should have waited for me.

I walk in pretending that nothing's wrong. 'Hi, guys.'

'Hi,' says Serena, without a smile. She angles her body slightly away from me, facing Tilly like she's protecting her, blocking me out.

'Thanks for your messages by the way, Vivian. They really helped me last week,' Tilly murmurs in her rusty new voice.

I'm confused. 'What messages?'

They just look at each other, and then ignore me. It dawns on me that maybe I should have been messaging or calling Tilly to ask her how she was after Tristan's accident. I just didn't want to. I didn't know what to say. I should have asked Molly what to do, damn it. It's not just me, though, is it? There's a ring of silence around Tilly, like she's exerting this forcefield that no one wants to enter. I saw Chloe actually turn around and walk the other way when she caught sight of her yesterday after lunch. It's like she's diseased. I still can't believe her idiot brother actually managed to go and die. How fast was he going, anyway? It's his own fault he's dead, speeding in that crappy car. I almost tell Tilly this, just to see the look on her face, but I keep it in, tickling in my mouth. I imagine her reaction instead. Pale shock. The scar on her nose standing out in a silvery band, each freckle popping out. She hates them, her freckles. We used to tease her and say she sunbathed under a sieve, and she used to cry. It's harder to make them cry now, but I'm sure I could manage.

The end of registration saves any tears and the rest of the day is boring. I have two mock exams, which I didn't bother revising for. There's no point, really, as I already know all the answers – they're easy. I hope A levels are harder than these, or I'll be bored to death before I even get to leave school. Everyone else is moaning and groaning and saying they've definitely failed. They probably haven't.

I hate that you're meant to pretend you are stupid, like it's a thing, to want to be seen as not clever.

The bell whines for the end of the day and there's the usual mob stampede to leave. I see Serena and Tilly's shiny blonde heads make their way down the path. They didn't wait for me again. I can feel annoyance unfurling in my stomach, and I try and breathe it away. I don't understand why they are doing this. Are they not worried that Molly will come back and that they will have offended me, Molly's best friend? Or is this a planned break-up of the group? Do they think they are in charge now? It hurts my head thinking about it. I still don't have any messages from Alex.

I'm holding my phone when it goes off in my hand, and I almost drop it, and do an embarrassing slippy catch thing, but luckily no one is watching me.

I hope it's Alex, but it isn't – it's Abi. Molly must have given her my number for emergencies. She wants me to go over and talk to her about Molly running off. This is going to suck. I walk slowly through the woods and past the back of my house. I peer into the garden but Mum isn't in the studio, she must be out or in the house. I don't text her to tell her where I'm going. I can feel the threads that tie us together, that smother me, starting to fray and snap, slowly, slowly. I think she would like to keep me here for ever as a child under her watch, safe as she sees it in this tiny hole of a village. I don't want to be safe, it's stifling. I can't wait to get out and start again, and forget about everything that ever happened here, except for Alex. Who still hasn't called me. I will have to deal with him at some point too. I won't have it.

It's hot and hazy walking to Molly's house. All I can hear are crickets squeaking in the long grass of the verge.

Even the birds are too hot to fly; there is nothing in the sky except blue and the blazing sun. I've got another headache coming. I can feel it pulling then pressing behind my eyes, gathering itself up for a pounding assault in my skull. I don't want to do this but I know it will look odd if I refuse, so I walk straight up to Molly's green door and before I can even lift the brass knocker it opens and Abi almost falls out, falls onto me and grabs me in an unusual and most unwelcome sticky embrace. I can smell something on her, something sour, bitter. Despair, perhaps. Or wine.

'Vivian, thank you so much for coming over. Come in, please. Do you want a drink?'

She pulls me into the cooler interior of the house. I have always liked it here, with its plain walls and simple furniture. It's soothing. I know Molly hated it and preferred the exploding coloured chaos of my house, but I can't understand that. This house makes my headache abate somewhat. I think maybe Molly and I were born to the wrong mothers – I would have been happily neglected here, left to my own devices in a restful white box.

'Can I have a glass of water, please, Mrs Barnes?'

'Yes, of course – and I've told you, my name is Abi. Mrs Barnes is my mother-in-law!'

She clutches at this weak joke like she's been clutching at her neck. I can see the marks of her fingers on it, red welts that she probably isn't even aware of. I can see her hands shaking as she gets a glass from the tall cupboard and runs the tap for a moment before filling it for me. I'm glad of it, because my mouth and throat have gone papery and dry from the walk here, and perhaps from nerves as to what it is she wants from me.

She clears her throat and looks at me expectantly, hopefully. She thinks I know where Molly is, and that I'm going to tell her. I'm not.

'I don't know where Molly is, Mrs Barnes. I haven't heard from her since Saturday night, when I left.'

Her hopeful expression crumples. 'Why did you leave, Vivian? I don't understand why you left.'

'I was boiling hot. Molly wouldn't open the window – you know what she's like. I didn't want to wake her up so I just left. I figured she'd call me in the morning but she never did.' I let my own face fall, as if I'm worried and scared too, as if I miss her, though I'm none of these things: I'm still furious with her.

Her face pales at this and she closes her blue, Molly-like eyes and lifts a hand and runs it into her thick blonde hair, tangling her fingers up in it. It looks like she's pulling it, tight, at the scalp. Is she hurting herself on purpose? I lean in slightly to look. She rears back away from me and releases the fistful of hair, smoothing it down again.

'Vivian, why do you think Molly keeps doing this?' I know the answer to this. So does Abi. She just doesn't want to face up to what her benign neglect turned Molly into – a girl desperate for affection and attention from anyone who would give it to her. Even when it ruined everything else she had, that we had. I just shrug and look sad.

'Could you have a look in her room for me? You'd know better than me, I think, if anything else looked wrong, or was missing? All her perfume was smashed – I don't know why, she loves her perfume.' A lone, fat tear rolls down her cheek, cutting through her make-up. 'The police won't do anything, they just told me she'll turn up again, but something just doesn't feel right. They won't help, because of the other times she ran away.' She trails off, and the slick left by the first tear on her cheek pulses as another joins it. Rather than watch it, I leave her and go upstairs.

Molly's room looks like it usually does, but somehow it's different. Maybe it's the smell, but there's something stale about it. No one has been in here, breathing the air in and out; it's just been hanging, unused. I could do anything in here. I half-heartedly look down the side of the bed. There's a bundled-up pair of lacy knickers and a lot of dust. I wonder if they are there from the night with Matt. I lift the quilt and see if anything has been slipped between the frame and the mattress. I don't see anything at first, but then I spot a flash of something. It's a torn-off corner, a piece of blue foil from a condom wrapper by the look of it. She wasn't entirely stupid, then. I leave it there – there might be a fingerprint on it, or something useful.

I don't think Molly kept a diary or anything that sad. I never found one the times I poked around, and she never mentioned one. Most of her is out there in the world anyway, online, posed. Shiny hair, shiny teeth, shiny life. Except all those secret thoughts she had – she kept those to herself, locked up in her pretty yellow head. I wonder what secrets she had bubbling up out of her head on Saturday night, running away from her. I didn't ask her because I didn't care; it was too late to do anything about her wanting me. I think maybe she just wanted everyone, all of everyone, all the time. There was no room for anyone to want anything else but her.

I rummage through her drawers. Everything is just stuffed in, all jumbled and mixed up, trousers with pants and socks and tops. I have to stop myself from sorting it out into piles, tidying up as I search. But there's nothing here to tell Abi about, nothing embarrassing or shameful. Did Abi know what her daughter was up to, secretly? I bet she did. No one can be that blind, except maybe my mother, but that's taken a lot of work. I think Molly wanted her mum to notice what she was doing. Poor Molly-wolly.

Maybe she kept something on her laptop. Molly always kept her little laptop hidden away underneath things because she was paranoid about burglars. Like burglars would bother with the crappy houses in this poxy place. I can't see it anywhere and I try to remember if she brought it upstairs on Saturday. She usually would. I'm sure she did, under her arm, swaying up the stairs. She probably squirrelled it when I was in the bathroom, putting that stupid nightie on. Assuming Abi doesn't already have it, where would she have put it? Where would I hide something if I were Molly? Tall, slim Molly. My eyes go to the built-in wardrobe and the cupboards above it. I'm going to need the chair.

I spot the corner of the laptop, with its charger cord wrapped around it, underneath the winter clothes that are stuffed in the last cupboard I check. I can't believe Abi hasn't looked properly, frantically searching for every clue. Maybe she thinks Molly took it away with her. That would make sense, I suppose. Maybe she wasn't expecting it still to be here, and her room's such a tip it's impossible to see what Molly might have taken with her. I don't have a laptop; I have to share Mum's. I think Molly would want me to have her laptop, to look after it. Her secret keeper. There could be anything on here, now I think of it.

–

'Did you find anything, Vivian? Any notes or numbers or anything, anything at all?' Abi is where I left her, sitting on the tall stool at the kitchen island, hands wringing in her lap. Her eyes drop. 'What's that?'

'It's my hoody,' I tell her, even though it's actually one of Molly's that I've never seen her wear. It was stuffed down the back of her wardrobe with tags still on it. It's too big for me but it's wrapped around the little laptop and you can't see the edges, the way I'm holding it to me as if I'm hugging it for comfort. I don't need the charger as it's the same make as Mum's – I can use hers to charge it. I hid that inside the drawer unit, pulling the bottom one right out and dropping it in the space behind, underneath. No one will think to look for it there.

'I'm sorry, Abi, but it all looks normal. Her drawers are a mess – it looks like she's taken some stuff. I think she had a big rucksack, but I can't see it. You remember, the green one? From the school trip last year?'

'Yes, of course. Thank you, Vivian. I'm sorry I dragged you over like this. You think I'm an idiot, don't you?' Her wet eyes are cast down at the floor so she doesn't see me bite my lip to stop myself saying 'yes'. Instead I mumble a quick apology and I'm out of the door before she can try and hug me again.

# Rachel

I was in the shower leaning my head on the cool tiles when Alex slipped into the bathroom, and into the cubicle with me. I didn't even start in surprise; it was almost like I expected him to be there, like I had conjured him up as part of a fantasy. He must have just let himself in after Vivian left. I didn't care. His hands slid around my waist and up and over the edges of my ribs to briefly cup my breasts before sliding away again. He pressed himself against my back and a rush of goosebumps sprang up on my skin. I heard him squeeze a bottle and a floral scent mingled with the hiss of the water before his hands touched my head. I hadn't been to the hairdressers in years, preferring to snip at it myself, and I had forgotten the special intimacy of someone washing your hair, of their fingers slowly moving on your scalp. Mine tightened with pleasure, along with other parts of my body. I pushed back against him, against how much he wanted me. He ignored it, and kept gently circling his fingertips on my head, tilting it back and smoothing the water through it to rinse away the suds which pooled at our feet.

He kissed my neck, his hands returning to my body, slipping down the silky trails left by the rinsed shampoo, easily, smoothly. His clever fingers playing my body, moving from breasts to hips, between my legs too briefly, before skipping away again until I moaned with frustration, at which point he spun me to him and lifted me easily, kissing me with a fury that scorched my mouth and bruised my lips. He pressed me up against the tiles, easily holding me in place with one arm and the weight of his body while he used his other hand to guide himself into me. He stopped then, and held me, relishing the heat we made together and the cool water that slithered over us, slicked our skin. He rocked against me, hard, and the pleasure that built up between us was more intense than anything I'd ever felt before.

–

'Where did you learn that?' I asked him afterwards, as we lay on my bed, my eyes distracted by the long hand that was tracing the contours of my hips, the dips and peaks.

'Learn what?' he smiled, his voice gruff and almost shy.

'Come on. I'm pretty sure that sort of thing doesn't come naturally.'

'You seem to come naturally.' He laughed, easing his body over mine. Surely not again? He dipped his head to kiss slowly along my collarbone, propping himself on his arms which were either side of my chest, framing me.

'I don't know, really. I've had a few girlfriends. Women seem to like me for some reason.'

I couldn't think why.

'I just never thought it was always as nice for women, you know? My first girlfriend didn't seem to like anything, so I tried things until she did.'

'What happened to her?' I asked him, feeling suddenly short of breath as I felt his body start to stir again.

'She went to uni, miles away,' he murmured, mouth at my breasts, breath tickling. 'Were you worried you had deflowered me, Rachel?' He looked up at me with those wicked eyes and used his knee to move my legs apart, teasing me again. They were dark pools of colour in his face that I could have drowned in. Perhaps I did drown in them, the pleasure numbing everything else.

'Don't worry,' he said, thrusting suddenly, marvellously, gasping. 'I'm thoroughly despoiled.'

—

Later, I made my way to the studio, leaving Alex asleep on my bed, after he'd fucked me again. I want to say he made love to me, but how could it have been love, what I was doing? I was using him to hurt myself, and it was as delicious as it was painful. Self-harm without the razor blade. I knew that if it were found out, I would be a pariah in the small judgemental village; I was risking my carefully crafted small life. Vivian would be furious, disgusted. She would quite possibly never speak to me again, or worse.

Better now to remember it as somehow brutal, animal-istic. Better to forget the sweet trailing kisses that searched out every tender spot, the hands that stroked me as though I were clay to be moulded, perfected. The ocean eyes that held mine as my body shook, again and again, our hot breath fusing. It was a madness.

I had sat and watched him sleep for a while, traced him with my eyes, but it felt deeply wrong, like I didn't deserve that vulnerable part of him. He looked even younger when he was asleep, and I felt as old as I have ever felt. So I pulled on a dress and nothing else and I left him there, and retreated to the garden.

The air sang with light, it burst through the trees and sparkled on the glass doors of my studio. Such a bright, light day, despite the fear and the grief and the guilt that swamped me. Surely it should have been dark, cold, grey. Surely the colours should have been muted. I tried to work, but I couldn't find that place inside myself where it came from, that spark. Nothing came out right – how could I paint a prince who wasn't the boy sleeping in my bed? Much less pair him with the girl I had pictured as being my daughter, before I had replaced her face with my own. I didn't belong there any more, so I went back to the house.

Alex was sitting at the kitchen table, the kettle starting to boil. He looked up at me unsmilingly as I walked in, and pushed himself back on the chair. I took off my dress.

–

Abi called me on Wednesday, around lunchtime. She had finally convinced the police to take her seriously. Molly was a serial runaway – never longer than forty-eight hours – but there were records of it, and they'd done two full-scale searches, the whole village out in the woods, on the previous occasions, only for her to saunter home as if nothing had happened. The girl who cried wolf. But now they were listening, and they wanted to talk to Vivian.

I took the call from my bed, where Alex and I had ended up after he had appeared yet again, minutes after Vivian left for school. It was like her voice was in a bubble, and I was in another. Alex was kissing the insides of my thighs and running his hands up and down my stomach, down over my hips to my knees and back again. I wanted to grab his thick, silky hair and direct him to exactly where I wanted him, but there was this voice on the phone, telling me that the police wanted to speak to my daughter.

Through the haze I remembered another voice, long ago, telling me the same thing — *little red hands* — but I didn't want to think about that, either. I managed to tell her, to choke it out, that Vivian would be home around four and I hung up and I buried my fingers where I wanted them and roughly pulled Alex to where I wanted him, and everything dissolved around me.

—

'What was that call about?' Alex was nuzzling into my neck, brushing the tip of his nose through the hair above my ear, inhaling as he did. I cringed away, ticklish, but his arm was over me, holding me fast against him. He slung over a leg for good measure. 'Rach?'

I took a breath, reluctant to break the spell we had created together with such horrible news. 'One of my daughter's friends has gone missing,' I told him, watching his face change. 'The police want to speak to her about it.'

'Really? That sounds bad. Is Vivian worried?' He moved back and propped himself on an elbow, looking down at me.

'I... I haven't really spoken to her about it...'

'You haven't spoken to her about it?'

I could hear something in his voice, concern maybe. Or contempt. But it was true, I had barely seen Vivian, let alone spoken to her about it.

'Molly has a habit of pulling stunts like this.' I felt guilty for saying it, but it was true.

'Disappearing? Do you think Vivian knows what has happened to her?'

'I'm sure nothing has *happened* to her, Alex. But the police are coming later to speak to her. Vivian was the last person to see her, as far as we know.'

I felt Alex go still for a moment; he closed his eyes.

'Are they doing searches?'

'No, not yet, I don't think.'

'And they want to question Vivian? Do you think the police think she might have something to do with it?'

I sat up. 'What! Alex, no, of course not! What on earth would make you say that?' He looked at me sideways, pressed his lips together as if he wanted to say more. He reached up and pulled me back down beside him, pulling the sheet up to cover us.

'What is she like?' he asked, before pressing his lips to a sensitive spot on my neck.

'Who, Molly? She's lovely, I don't know why—'

'No, not Molly – Vivian. What is Vivian like? Are you close?' I wasn't sure I felt comfortable talking about Vivian with Alex – in fact, it felt horrible, like I was betraying her somehow – but he looked at me and I had a strange sense that it was somehow important to him, and it made me honest. 'Yes, we're close. It's only the two of us. She's very much her own person though, I guess. She's happy here, she has lovely friends – when they aren't running off, anyway. She's extraordinarily clever, but naïve at the same time. I wonder if she knows as much about the world as she thinks she does, sometimes.'

'When was she not happy? It sounds like she's happy now but wasn't before.'

I wriggled around to face him, to look at him. 'No, she wasn't. She had a very bad time at her old primary school. She never told me that she was being bullied, but my mother knew – she tried to tell me about it, but I was

216

so busy all the time, I let things slip. The other children didn't like her for some reason. I think when you're as smart as she is from a young age it can make you seem a bit odd to other kids, who aren't quite there yet. And she's always been very small for her age, easy to push around.'

'She didn't have any friends at all?'

'Only one, for a while. It became quite intense, and it didn't end well. We moved here to get a fresh start. Everything has been fine since we lived here, we've both been happy here.' Despite my words I could feel my throat tightening as I thought about everything that was happening, what I was doing that could ruin that happiness, the stupid, addictive affair we were having and what Vivian might do if she found out about it.

'Didn't *end well*?' The odd tone in his voice unnerved me, tipped me over the edge. 'What did your mother know? Did she… oh, shit, Rachel, please don't cry. I'm sorry, please…' I couldn't stop the tears, even as he tried to kiss them away. What would my mother think about what I was doing? Letting Vivian down again. I forced my reply out.

'No, I'm sorry, darling. She died, just before we had to leave London. It was an awful shock. We lived with her, Vivian and me. It broke me, then there was an accident at school, it was just too much. I can't…'

'Shh, it's fine, I'm so sorry, Rachel – I shouldn't have asked. I'm the first person to know you shouldn't ask about family, believe me.' He kissed me, kissed my cheeks until my tears stopped, and we were quiet after that, both lost in our own thoughts.

# *Vivian*

The police are at my house when I get home from school, two of them sitting in the front room. I'm not happy that Mum hasn't thought to warn me about this and I glare at her for a second. She looks like she's been taking antidepressants again: her face is almost slack, and vacant. She's in one of her weird moods, which is perfect bloody timing. She always goes to pieces when things aren't going exactly how she wants them to be. She's pathetic. I'm sick of her moping about Tristan – what even was he to her? He was my friend's brother. Now she's going to try to make people feel sorry for her about Molly when she has no right. She was my friend. It's always about her, and her secret scars and her dead parents. I hate her.

'Vivian?' The female police officer stands up from our sofa to shake my hand. She's tall, toweringly so, with frizzy blonde hair and rough red cheeks. She doesn't smile at me and I wonder for a stomach-looping second if they've found Molly. 'Would you like to sit down? We need to ask you a few questions about Molly's disappearance.' She sits back down, next to the man who is looking at me as he pulls out a notebook from his utility belt thing. I wonder if he's got a taser.

I sit down reluctantly. There's a gap that seems to take for ever between that and the police officer talking again. No doubt on purpose, trying to put me on edge. I assume that she must be in charge because the other officer with her doesn't say anything; he just makes notes in his little black notebook. I wonder if they are local police or if they've come down from the city especially.

'Vivian, what time did you last see Molly on Saturday night?'

'I don't know what time it was. I woke up and wanted to leave, so I came home.'

'And you didn't check the time?'

'No. I didn't have my phone.'

'And you didn't check it when you came in?'

'No. I just went straight to bed. I was tired.'

'What did Molly say when you left?'

'Nothing. She was asleep. I was too hot at her house. She would never open the window.'

'How has Molly been recently? Have you noticed anything unusual in her behaviour, or has she said anything to you about being unhappy?'

I think of her half-naked, grinding onto Matthew Grey. I think of her texting *my* Alex, trying to break us up, of her touching me. I think of the silver tear slick on her face.

'No.'

'Anything you can remember could be important, Vivian. She hasn't been seen by anyone since Saturday. Was she involved with anyone?'

'Yes.' I suddenly think of something I can actually tell them. 'Actually, yes, she was. She was having a thing with Tristan, Tilly Beaumont's brother who died. They'd been having sex.'

I see Mum rock slightly at this news – she had no idea Molly wasn't an angel. I wonder if she has any idea that I have had sex. I don't think so, she's been so out of it lately.

I'm sure I'm still innocent little Vivian in her stupid blind eyes.

'That's something we have been bearing in mind, Vivian,' says PC Red Cheeks. 'That she may have been upset by Tristan's murder.'

'Murder!' Mum suddenly pipes up, horror in her voice. 'He was in an accident, he wasn't murdered!'

'On the contrary, Miss Sanders,' says the male policeman in a rough, gravelled voice that doesn't suit his young face, 'we believe that Tristan's car may have been tampered with in some way prior to his accident. We are conducting enquiries as to that effect, and we also believe that Molly's disappearance could be connected. This is a small place, after all. If they were having some sort of relationship, it could be a lead.'

I'm not impressed about what they are saying about Tristan's death. I fidget, uneasy. No one actually wanted him to *die*, that's just ridiculous. If he's dead, it was his own fault that he couldn't control his car properly, surely? How is that murder?

'She wasn't just with Tristan, though,' I blurt out, disconcerted by this turn of events and wanting to get them under my control again. 'She was having sex with other boys, too. You should speak to Matthew Grey from school as well, and there are probably others. She was going off the rails, but no one knew why. I think she was drinking a lot too – cider and stuff, maybe vodka. She was drunk all the time. She always runs away, I'm sure she'll be back soon, pretending nothing has happened.' I deliberately cast my eyes down, bite my lip, hitch a breath. Should I tell them she was secretly in love with me too? No.

Both of them look at me for a long moment. They think I am a Judas, betraying Molly, but it's the truth. Everyone will find out eventually, anyway. They'll find out, and then they will forget, everything will blow over and everything can go back to normal. I can be popular again, everyone likes us. I just need to get Serena and Tilly back on my side, we don't need Molly. Molly went wrong.

PC Red Cheeks passes Mum a card with several phone numbers on it. Her fingernails are bitten right back to the quick, a red bead of blood glistening on one raw cuticle. She must have been chewing it on the way here. It holds my eye. There's nothing quite like the colour of fresh blood, but it's gone so quickly into a nasty, dark stain.

'My name is DS Henderson. Please call us straight away if you remember anything that might help us find Molly.'

They both stand up and I see that the policeman is even taller than PC Red Cheeks, Henderson, whatever. Mum is sitting like a statue on the sofa as I walk out with them, close the door behind them.

I stand for a second leaning against it – I need to take some deep breaths to settle my stomach. When I get back Mum is still there, frozen in the same position on the sofa, staring up at me all pale and wispy. The sudden lack of her substance, of her there-ness, is disquieting.

'Why didn't you tell me any of this, Vivian?' she whispers.

'Any of what?'

'Don't be evasive. What has been going on with Molly? You know where she is, don't you?'

'No! I don't know where she is – she's been a complete nightmare recently and I didn't tell you about any of it because it's not any of your business! I'm not nine! You can't expect me to tell you everything any more, you have to let it go. I'm not doing it.'

'Viv... you can't blame me for being concerned, not after what happened before...'

I can't believe she would bring that up. I lose it then. 'Just shut up! Shut! Up! Why didn't you tell me the police were here? Did you not think that it might upset me? I hate you!'

She rubs at her temples, then slowly pushes herself to her feet, moving like she aches everywhere. 'This weather is giving me an awful headache, Viv. I need to go and lie down. Are you okay to fix yourself some tea? There's still pasta in the fridge from yesterday.'

Did she not even hear any of that? Did I even say it? I feel like there is a vortex in my head, mixing everything around. I don't know where I am any more. I can only whisper. 'Mum, are we still going to Dorset on Friday?'

'Yes, darling, I don't see why not, unless you want to stay? I think we both need to get away from here for a while.'

'I don't want to stay, no.'

And then she goes upstairs, slowly, like an old person. I get my phone out of my school bag, but there's nothing on it. Nothing.

# Rachel

I woke up the next morning with a ringing head. I'd been drinking again after Vivian had gone to bed: I crept downstairs and drank a bottle of wine followed by gulps of vodka straight from the bottle I kept in the freezer for emergencies. The icy cold liquid had burned a trail from my throat to my stomach like acid, and there was still acid there when I got up. It didn't help me forget. Vivian's anger, the police visit. It frightened me to see her like that. It brought up bad memories of before. I kept picturing Lexie's mother, Lucy – how she'd looked when I'd seen her a few weeks before. I was so worried about how exhausted and worn she had looked. I had been so hopeful that Lexie would have recovered, learnt to cope with her injuries, that the scars had healed and could be masked, but there had to be a reason for Lucy to have looked so heartsick.

I'd managed to get as far as the kitchen table, wrapped in my dressing gown despite the stifling weather, and I was sitting wallowing, when there was a knock at the front door. I ignored it, but the knocking came again, insistent.

I edged my way along the hallway feeling like an old, worn-out husk. My head was light, my vision tunnelling, bile at my throat. I opened the door into the blinding light.

It was the police, again. DS Henderson and her henchman.

'Ms Sanders? May we come in?'

'Vivian isn't here. She's gone to school.'

'We wanted to speak to you, Ms Sanders.'

Feeling more than slightly confused I let them both bustle into my house and down into the kitchen. Not wanting to speak to them straight away, trying to gather my thoughts, I offered to make them tea. My hands shook as I picked teabags out of the little clay pot Vivian had made at school. It was an ugly little thing but I treasured it: one of my only clear memories of my father was his delight when I presented him with some small and lopsided object I had myself made at school. I made us all a cup and we sat at my small kitchen table in a stuffy, uncomfortable hush. DS Henderson broke it.

'Ms Sanders. Can you remember what time Vivian came home on Saturday night? We are still trying to establish a clearer timeline of Molly's disappearance.'

'So you're taking it seriously then? It's taken you long enough, she's been missing for four days!' I didn't want to answer the question. I had absolutely no idea what time Vivian had come home. I just knew it was dark – it had been pitch black in my room, everything I remember was touch, hands in the darkness and the taste of the salt on his skin.

'What time did Vivian come home, Ms Sanders?'

'I can't be sure. It must have been late, well after sundown anyway. I just remember it was dark and I had already gone to bed, and been asleep, but I don't know how long for.'

'Were you alone?'

'What! Yes, I was alone. I woke up when the front door opened. I heard her come up the stairs and into the shower.' The lies slipped out of my mouth easily, but my heart was pounding wildly, remembering the kisses on my body that had woken me, not Vivian.

'The shower?'

'Yes. She had a shower when she got in. She said yesterday, didn't she, that she'd left Molly's because she was hot. She probably wanted to cool down, rinse off. The weather's awful, isn't it?' I tried to laugh, but their faces remained stern.

'Are you aware of any issues Molly and Vivian may have been having recently?'

'With each other? None, as far as I know. They are very close – they have been for years. I think all the girls have been struggling with Tristan's accident, though. It's so awful.'

'Ms Sanders, we are fairly certain at this point that Tristan Beaumont's car had been tampered with before the accident.'

'I just can't believe it. Who would want to hurt him? I don't understand – surely it was something he did by accident? He was always tinkering with the stupid thing himself.'

The man was scribbling in his notepad. I could see his handwriting, a tiny illegible scrawl scattered across the page ignoring the lines. He pressed too hard with the pen; that must have made his hand ache, the grip.

'After we left you yesterday, we spoke to several of Molly's teachers. We were told that Vivian and Molly had a detention in the week before she disappeared. For fighting in the canteen. Did you know about this?' My eyes told them that I did not. Vivian's lies, coming to the surface. I could feel panic juddering in my chest – did they think Vivian was involved in Molly disappearing? Did I?

'Why are you even questioning me about this? Is this because of the accident? That's supposed to be sealed!' I blurted it out and then fear hit me with an almost physical shock. I felt like I was on a tightrope without a safety net, nothingness yawning beneath my feet.

'What accident, Ms Sanders?' The man spoke suddenly, looked up sharply, keen eyes piercing me. I couldn't answer, just shook my head, pressed my stupid lips together tightly. They didn't know, and I had told them. The scribbling went on again, question marks, the only noise in the room.

'I'm sorry to upset you. You're sure there wasn't any trouble brewing between Vivian and Molly?' DS Henderson took over again.

'No! Nothing, I told you! She didn't even mention the fight, and they were together same as always last week. It obviously wasn't anything serious.' I had to make an effort not to screech, and I put my shaking hands under the table. 'My daughter had nothing to do with Molly disappearing – she obviously has issues none of us knew about. Vivian adores Molly, she would never do anything to hurt her, or make her run away. This is ridiculous.'

They exchanged a cynical look, and then drained their cups at the same time. Standing up, looming over me, they thanked me for my time and then left, letting themselves out and leaving me nervous and worried.

No. There was no way she was involved in this, I refused to believe it. Before, in London, it had been an accident, the strain Vivian had been under that I had been too stupid to notice. It had been my fault, not hers. She

226

wasn't a bad person. She loved Molly. She wouldn't hurt Molly.

Almost as the front door closed, the back door opened, and Alex came in. My head was still spinning. I saw him looking at the empty wine bottle on the side, the vodka bottle beside it. A cool look at me. I realised the police had probably seen them too. They must have thought I was a lush who kept no track on her daughter, let her stay out to all hours. A small burn of real awareness started inside me, waking me up from the stupor I had let myself slip into. What was I doing?

Alex walked over to me and put his hands on my shoulders, ran them up to my neck, rubbing at the tension he found there. He always felt so cool to touch, cool and smooth and good. I put up one of my hands, held onto his. I knew it had to end, that foolish episode. But it was so hard; despite the difference in our ages, there was a genuine attraction and connection between us. I could feel it, and my head was full of constant, running justifications for my behaviour. But there was nothing healthy in it for either of us. It was a mistake.

'Alex. Alex, I'm so sorry, but this has to stop. We can't keep doing this, it isn't right. I'm old enough to be your mother. It's wrong. I can't do this any more.'

I looked up at him. I knew it might be the last time I got to see him, and I knew he would probably hate me. I wanted to punish myself by memorising the look on his beautiful face so I could remember it in the small hours of the night when I was alone, again.

It crumpled in shock. 'Please don't say that, Rach, please. I think you're amazing. This is the only good thing that's happened to me in years, you don't understand, please don't.' To my horror I saw tears beginning to gather in his beautiful eyes, threaten to spill, pooling onto his thick eyelashes. I'd had no idea there was any real emotional involvement, for either of us, really; I thought that it was just some awful physical addiction we had got caught up in. He got down onto his knees next to me as I sat there, shocked, put his hands to my face. 'Please, Rachel, please. Don't do this.'

I reached up, took his hands away and pushed them gently back towards him, traitorous fingers revelling one last time in how they felt on my skin. 'Alex, please – you must realise that this wasn't ever going to go anywhere? I thought you knew that, that it was just…'

'Just what? You were just using me?'

'No! Never! It's only been a week, it wasn't like that, it was never…' But I didn't know what to say to him, to that boy kneeling in front of me, beseeching me. I didn't understand what he wanted and it broke my heart. I didn't say anything else, I couldn't. His face lost all expression, closed up, his eyes a dark, pained green full of bitter tears that he brushed away, angrily. He shoved himself to his feet and stormed out of the kitchen, leaving me with his parting words.

'You know what? Fuck you. *Fuck* you. I should have known.'

By the time I understood what he should have known, it was too late.

# Vivian

I still haven't heard from Alex. It's like he's disappeared off the face of the earth. I even went into the reception in the college, made up some rubbish about him tutoring me and needing to find him. I don't think that the horrid woman there believed me, though; she just looked at me and laughed and said she couldn't tell me. Bitch.

After my failure with her I went to class and found that Tilly and Serena have moved tables. We all used to sit on the second row, but they have moved to the back, and there wasn't a space for me there. The rejection feels like a dagger under my ribs. I hold my hand briefly to my side, look at it, expecting blood. There's no blood, but there is the ever-present cold, simmering loathing. They've never liked me. They've always been jealous that Molly liked me the best. I'll show them.

I walk over to where they are sitting quietly, heads together over a magazine. Looking at some stupid make-up tutorial, vain little bitches. I hate them.

'Did you get an email from Molly?' I ask them, cool as you like.

'What?' says Serena, jerking toward me. 'No, what email? What did she say? Where is she, she's being fucking ridiculous now, her mum has rung me about eleventy billion times asking me if I know where she's gone!'

I smile at them. I've got the power now.

'She just said she was pissed off with her parents ignoring her and leaving her on her own all the time, so she's gone now and how do they like it. She probably emailed them the same thing, so hopefully Abi will stop giving you a hard time now. Like Molly would ever tell *you* anything, anyway.'

I take a second to enjoy the hurt look on her face – serves her right – and then I turn on my heel and go and sit in my usual seat as if everything is completely normal.

I don't have any lessons with Tilly and Serena because they are both thick, but I do find myself missing Molly a bit. She made me laugh in lessons, taking the piss out of everything and gossiping. I have maths first, and instead of sitting on my usual, now Molly-less table, I decide to sit next to Becky. She almost jumps out of her seat. Chloe isn't in this class either, also being a bit thick, but Becky can't hide her intelligence all the time. They moved her up a set a while ago. Maybe she is more interesting than she looks.

'Hi,' I say, as I get my books and stuff out.

'Err,' is the best she can manage. God, she really can't cope without her twin, can she?

'How is Chloe? I heard she was knocked up.'

Becky just gobbles like a turkey, mouth opening and closing, swallowing air. I half expect her to blow up like a balloon, or one of those puffer fish that are full of poison as well as being so spiky and expanding. 'No!' she manages, choking it out. 'Where did you hear that?'

'Tilly heard her crying in the loo about being late.'

'Oh. Well, no. She went to the doctor and he told her she missed her period because she wasn't eating enough and to stop starving herself.'

'Starving herself? I thought she was vegan?'

'It's just an excuse to not eat anything. I've seen her eating ham straight out of the fridge at her house when she thinks no one is watching.'

I burst out laughing; it takes me by surprise. I haven't laughed properly for weeks. Becky's pudding face breaks into a wicked grin. I didn't know she was capable of subterfuge against her beloved Chloe. I have misjudged her. Maybe I don't need Serena or Tilly after all, if I can get someone new. Becky isn't *that* ugly or fat or anything embarrassing, I suppose. Could she be moulded into something better than she is? Becky might be more biddable than Molly ever was.

–

We spend the rest of the lesson whispering and having a bit of a laugh: Becky has a vicious humour that I like, but then once the bell goes she shoots straight off and when I catch up I see her with Chloe. Well, I see her standing next to Chloe, who is snogging Dan's face off in the queue for the vending machine. I give her a cold look on my way past. She should have stuck with me.

I don't want it to look like I'm being shunned by sitting by myself at lunch so I take my sandwiches out to the field and sit under the oak tree. I know part of me is hoping that maybe Alex will be there. He isn't. I'm not going to message him any more; I'm not going to be some sad, desperate loser crying over wasting her virginity on some arsehole. It's not important. I feed most of my sandwiches to two fat wood pigeons, because each bite I take turns to sawdust in my mouth. I watch them bumbling around for a while bobbing for crumbs and making stupid cooing noises, shitting their purple shit all over the dead grass, and then I slowly walk back into school as if I don't care at all that I am alone.

I spend the rest of the afternoon lessons hardly focusing. I hate these last days of school at the end of the year that we waste on whatever the teacher deems to be a 'fun' end of term treat. They should just let us go. Finally, at the end of the day, I head back to my locker to get my stuff and find a piece of paper has been shoved through the gap. It's an amazing sketch of a girl lying beneath a tree, naked. At first I'm mortified in case anyone sees it, and press it quickly to my chest, but I glance furtively around me and see everyone is oblivious as usual.

It's a picture of me, from that afternoon. It's beautiful. Alex is back.

—

By the time I get home I'm so hacked off about his disappearing and reappearing act that I don't go into the house because Mum will be bound to notice how cross I am yet again, despite her pathetic depression. I pace around the garden instead, avoiding the heavy bees that stagger through the air around the lavender. I hate the smell of lavender. Nan always stank of it. I decide to poke around Mum's stuff instead – see how she likes her privacy being invaded for once. The studio is a glass box shining in the sun. It's hot in here, and messy. Her artist's desk is piled high with sketches, scraps of paper and ends of charcoal, littered with a dusting of rubber from a mass erasure of errant lines. There are finished paintings on the other work bench drying in the heat. I have to open all the doors to try and let some air in before I suffocate.

There is a large clock ticking on the wall, an unceasingly annoying noise that, once in your ears, refuses to leave. *Tick tock*, your life *tick tock*ing by.

Trying to ignore the clock I take a deep breath. I love the smell in here: paints and pastels, charcoal, even the paper itself, a smooth creamy smell, the end of trees. Underneath all that is the chemical kiss of white spirit cleaning the brushes that Mum leaves higgledy-piggledy in pots, ruining the bristles and distorting the points. You'd think she would have learnt to look after her things by now, but no.

Even the floor is untidy: half-empty packets and cellophane pieces, empty paint tubes and splatters of colour everywhere. A toddler would make less mess than my mother. There's no organisation here at all; this is a purely creative space and it itches at my mind, scurries in it, insistent. I don't know how she can work in here. It makes my head feel all fucked up. I don't know how she copes with it. I can't help it, I have to sort it out a bit – sorting has always calmed me down, everything should have a place, an order it belongs in.

Sketches and half-finished paintings from the *Prince of Dark Wings* are scattered everywhere so I sort them into piles. That pile is various versions of the prince from the back, wings arching, on the beach watching a boat disappearing over the waves. These ones are of the girl passing through the veil to his Fae world. There are loads and loads of paintings of creepy trees which I really like; I might ask if I can have one of these for my room. I keep making piles until I come to one that makes me freeze.

What the fuck? What the actual *fuck*? That's Alex. With wings.

# Rachel

The day before we went to Dorset, Vivian came running in from school like she was being chased. She bombed into the house without even pausing to speak to me, running right past my seat on the sofa where I had tucked myself with a book, trying vainly to read to distract myself.

I went up to Vivian's room to speak to her, to ask her why she had run in like the hounds of hell were after her. She was lying on her bed on her phone, tapping away, an intent, bristling look on her face.

'What on earth is wrong with you?'

She looked up and a blanket came down over her expression, smoothing away the fierce, pointed glare and replacing it with a stiff, calm mask. She looked straight at me. It was so rare that she would look directly at me, into my eyes. Usually hers would slide away, look to one side. I was almost chilled by the intensity in them.

'Nothing.'

I didn't believe her, but I didn't know how to press it without risking that look reappearing on her face. I stood there, voiceless.

'What?' she glanced up again, jaw tight.

'Do you know where Molly is?'

'No. Can you go now, please? I'm busy.' Eyes firmly back on the screen in her hands. I bit the inside of my cheek to keep the infuriated scream inside me, breathed out slowly. 'Darling, can you please get your packing done tonight so we can go straight to Dorset when you finish school tomorrow afternoon?'

She ignored me.

'Vivian! Are you listening to me?'

Her grey eyes flicked up to me for a scornful second before returning to her phone. She made one of her noncommittal grunts which I took to mean she had heard me. I decided that if there was no sign of any packing in the morning then I would pack for her, and she would not be impressed with what I chose. I was sick of her. I had spent the whole morning frantic with worry over how she was coping without Molly, and she was behaving like a shit. I was still sick over what I had done to Alex and I just didn't have the headspace to deal with a moody Vivian too.

I was walking past the phone in the hall when it rang, almost giving me a heart attack.

'Hello?'

'Rachel? It's Abi. Has Molly been in touch with Vivian? We've had an email from her!' Her voice was shaking.

'Oh, Abi, thank god. Is she okay?'

'It says she is. She says that she's punishing us for never being here, but we aren't away that much, Rachel, are we? I had no idea she felt this way, why wouldn't she tell me?'

The hurt and bewilderment in her tone was palpable, and I thought about the uncommunicative grouch in the bedroom upstairs. What wasn't *she* telling *me*? What secrets filled these girls, and stained their hidden lives?

'Abi, don't blame yourself. They're at such a difficult age. Did she say where she was? Is she okay? Is she coming back?'

'No, no, it didn't really say anything, I'm just so relieved to hear from her. Vivian didn't say anything on Tuesday. She came round to get one of her tops from Molly's room.'

'She didn't tell me she'd been to see you. I'll ask her if she's heard from her and I'll let you know, okay? I'll text you. I'm so happy she's got in touch, Abi. Speak soon.'

I carefully put the phone down, my head swimming with pure relief. It felt like wings unfolding inside me. I loved Molly almost as much as I loved Vivian, she was such a bright, shining girl. I can still remember the first time Vivian brought her home for tea after school. She had been so interested in everything, asked me a hundred questions about the cottage, the books, my pictures. Vivian had sat beside her, face glowing and enraptured with her clever new friend. I remember feeling a sharp dagger of concern – she was so like Lexie – but I had to give Vi the benefit of the doubt. All the therapists had told me that the accident had been just that – an accident. I couldn't blame a nine-year-old for those actions. She had been tormented by the other children and, unable to process her emotions, she had snapped and lashed out. It was my fault for not listening, letting it get that far: not hers. History wasn't repeating itself, and their friendship had seemed entirely normal. They'd been friends for years, and would be again I thought, once Molly came home. Again, I forced down the niggling doubts. Everything would be fine.

'Vivian! Viv!' I shouted up the stairs, transporting back to an utterly normal thing to be doing, a mother yelling to her teenager up the stairs. 'Have you heard from Molly?'

'Yeah.'

I barely heard the reply and stormed back up the stairs into her room. She was still on her phone, hair falling across her face.

'I just asked you if you knew where she was and you said no! Did you not think to tell me that you had actually heard from her? Did you not think I was worried sick about where she is? Anything could happen to her, Vivian! Where the hell is she?'

'I don't know,' said Vivian, still not looking at me. 'The email just said sorry for being a dick and she's not coming back.'

'What? Why is she not coming back? Where is she?'

'I just said. I. Don't. Know.'

'Do not speak to me like that, Vivian! I am not in the mood!'

I quickly texted Abi that Vivian had an email too and promised to get her to forward it to her so she could show the police.

My relief that Molly had been in touch curdled at the thought that she was saying she didn't want to come home. What was wrong with her? What had happened? Had Vivian done something to make her run away? Oh, I adored her, but she was flighty and impulsive. I was so afraid for her, thinking she was so grown up when she was still just a little girl; she was always that sweet little girl.

I rattled round the house, packing up things for Dorset, thinking about Molly and Vivian, all the quiet years I had lived through since we left London, how much Molly was a part of them, a healing part.

I finished my packing late, and couldn't hear anything from Vivian's room. I hadn't cooked any dinner, and she hadn't appeared to forage for herself. She was probably cross with me about something, but I really struggled to care. I managed to force some toast down, sitting again at the kitchen table where I had broken Alex's heart only a few hours before. I wanted so badly to text him, but I didn't want to lead him on or give him any false hope. I deleted his messages and his number so I couldn't. I was tempted to open more wine, but I didn't; I just went to bed instead, alone again.

I didn't sleep well that night either, snatches of rest broken with dreams of two golden girls and a dark, bleak boy.

–

The next day, with my concern over Molly having abated only slightly – she was still missing after all, and only fifteen despite her pretended maturity – my thoughts returned again to Alex. I hadn't heard from him since the morning before, but I could somehow sense a brooding hostility hanging over me, and a small part of me missed him badly. I checked my phone and the messages I'd gotten from Steve. Judging by all the pictures of cocktails, I could only imagine he was nursing a severe hangover by a pool. I sent him a message telling him I missed him. I was envious of his away-ness. I didn't want to be where I was any more.

I busied myself finishing packing for our trip, piling our travel easels and blank canvases into the back of the car, so we could leave after Vivian finished school that afternoon. We went every year to Lulworth Cove; it was one of my favourite places, I had holidayed there since I was a child myself and it was full of happy memories. Vivian's school finished a little earlier than most so we usually had a few days to ourselves by the sea before the hordes arrived.

I wasn't so unaware as to not have noticed that she had gradually disappeared into herself in the last few weeks. I told myself it was her age, hormones, teenage angst, Tristan's accident, and now missing her friend, but that small, niggling thought whispered in my head, *Remember.* I couldn't stop thinking about Lexie Coleman. I wondered if I should try and get in touch with Lucy, but I had even changed my number when we moved because I couldn't cope with bringing anything with us except memories, and they were heavy enough. Perhaps it really was best just to let it all lie. But it had proved surprisingly easy to disappear. I guess no one knew what to say to me: it was better to let me slip away unremarked. No one had ever looked for us.

Five minutes later, and I had changed my mind again. I didn't have any social media accounts except for my work website, which was just my name, Rachel Sanders Art, but I managed to find her easily enough. The account was private, but I could see her profile picture. It was of Lexie, aged five or six by the looks of it, an impish, gappy grin on her little face. It had been cropped down, but I could see the thin arm of another child around her shoulders. It hurt me to look at her face, her eyes. What did she look like now?

I still don't know how I let it all happen, that horror in London. Mum had warned me several times that Vivian wasn't behaving in a healthy way and that she was worried about her, but I didn't want to listen. I brushed it off as typical young girl behaviour – they do get obsessive at that age, and it's always about power games in girl groups. One day you were best friends, the next it was you-can't-sit-with-us. There was that incident at a sleepover with Lexie that I didn't like to remember, but I had been sure that it would all blow over. Lucy had been so good about it at the time. Mum didn't think it was normal, though. She thought that there must have been a deeper issue, and that there was a definite problem with how Vivian was coping with what I thought were normal childhood issues.

Apparently Vivian had had screaming rages about it, followed by hours of icy silence. I had tried to talk to her, about why she'd done it, but I'd never seen any of the tantrums. My mum was more a parent to her than I was, and I left her to deal with it like the coward I am. But then she died, and everything in my life blew up and I just ran away, like I ran away from Manchester and Ciaran. I just buried my head in the sand the way I always do.

I decided to stop moping and finish putting everything in to the car, cramming the small boot and backseat. I went upstairs to check if Vivian had actually listened to me and done her packing. Her room was almost spartan in its emptiness. Everything was hidden away in its own place. She always told me mess hurt her head. I hated the dull grey walls, which I had let her choose despite my own preference for rich colours: plums, currants, blues and deep elf-forest greens. But grey it was. Cold grey walls and a colder grey carpet, with white furniture.

There weren't any curtains at the window. She refused to have them, would never shut them even if I had hung some, preferring to be able to see the outside. There hadn't been any windows in the hospital, curtained or otherwise. I always wondered if that had something to do with the almost pathological desire she had developed to have a clear route out of anywhere whenever she wanted to.

Her little black suitcase was open on the bed. A quick sift through told me that she just needed to add in her many toiletries and chargers and we would be good to go. I turned to leave, and caught myself painfully on the edge of her desk. I stopped and rubbed my leg where I'd caught it, looking down at her stuff. Everything on it was arranged with military precision, angled just so, piled in size order. When a place is so irredeemably neat, it's easy to spot when something is out of place, and I noticed a piece of sketching paper: the familiar texture caught my eye. It was tucked into a copy of *Jane Eyre*. All I could see of it was a small part of the torn edge peeping out from between the pages, rumpling them slightly, and even as a needle of guilt stabbed at me for invading her privacy I slid it out from between them.

I breathed in, but no air reached my lungs, only shock. It was a nude sketch of a girl, laying prostrate on a blanket underneath a tree. She was on her back, slender arms raised above her head, knees up and apart, toes pointed like a dancer. A scribbling scratched nest of lines joined the top of her thighs, almost ripping the paper. It was chilling – the girl didn't have any features at all on her face, despite the careful details everywhere else. It gave her a blank, haunting appeal. I traced my finger over the collarbones, the slim shoulders. I knew the considered, precise lines of that body as well as I knew my own, as well as I knew who had drawn this.

It was Vivian.

## Vivian

I had such a bad headache on the way to school this morning. I couldn't sleep last night. My room was so hot I just sweated, trying to lie spread out on my bed so no bits of skin touched any other bits. The weather is heavy and almost crackling today, it lifts the little hairs on my arms and tickles the back of my neck. There's a storm coming.

Alex has been texting and calling me, but I've been ignoring him. He thinks he can have sex with me and then go missing for nearly a whole week? He said he had to go back to London to see his granddad and forgot his phone or some such bullshit, but I'm pretty sure the internet works up there just as well as it works here. He could have tracked me down. He thinks he can make it up to me with stupid gifts – a bloody drawing of all things. I didn't know he could draw, but he's nearly as good as my mum.

He doesn't know that I know that he knows her somehow. I haven't figured out what his game is yet, but I'm on to him. Finding that sketch of him in my mum's studio was so weird. It was definitely him as the faery prince with black raven wings. She always uses people she knows in her illustrations. Steve was on the last book cover she did, much to his eternal delight – he was showing off a copy to everyone that came in the pub for months.

Why would he have met her and not told me, though? And where? Unless she just saw him in the street and decided she liked his face. That's entirely possible here – it's a small place. And he is so ridiculously beautiful.

I decide to tell him I don't want to see him, and that we are going away after school, anyway. He replies straight away, and asks me to bunk off the afternoon and meet him at the gates in his car. He's never mentioned a car before. Another thing I didn't know about him – the things we could do with a car! More secrets. I know I shouldn't really fall for this, that if I go and see him now then he wins, but I am intrigued.

I also really want to have sex with him again. He needs to realise that he's *mine*. You don't just leave me; I'm the one who decides when things are over. Maybe sex is the way to teach him that, or maybe it isn't. Do I withhold it, or use more of it? We'll see. This isn't really something I've thought about before; the idea of it always repulsed me until I found out what it was like. Being wanted like that. When you're small and weedy you need all the power you can get, and he needs to be taught a lesson.

On the last day of term, there's always this restless, antsy feeling around, like everyone is holding their breath. It feels like we're all being squeezed in a fist. Serena and Tilly are still angry because I told them Molly had emailed me, when they haven't heard from her. I don't know what they expect, really. They haven't spoken to me all week since she's been gone, since they decided to act like six-year-olds and move fucking desks like I have leprosy or something. Did they ever even like me? Did they just pretend to because Molly did? I wonder what they would think if I told them what she did to me, how perverted she was. I don't need them, anyway; if I'm with Alex we won't need anyone. They're just lucky I have him to distract me. They can wait, anyway.

I'm thinking of how I can punish Alex for this week, but maybe I need to remember what he means to me, and what he knows. Alex knows what Molly did, because I told him. He knew about Tristan too, what he tried to do to me. I wouldn't tell Serena and Tilly anything about that but I trust him more than them, even if he did do a disappearing act on me. There's just something about him that makes me think he's like me. We're different, we're not like other people. Special.

Thinking of everything we've shared makes me change my mind – I will meet him – as I need to find out where he's been and how he got in my mum's pictures. Because they can't know each other. She tells me everything, doesn't she? She would have told me she had met someone who was at the college. And I can't even bear to think about them actually knowing each other – what if they talked about me? What would she tell him? The thought leaves a bad taste in my mouth so I push it away.

When everyone goes to lunch I gather up my things and I slip out of the door. As promised, Alex is waiting in a battered-looking car that's even more of a shit heap than Tristan's was. The doors have gone pink from the sun and there is a hub cap missing.

I have to fiddle with the handle of the door to get it to open before jumping in the passenger seat and just sitting there stiffly, giving Alex as cold a look as I can muster, even though my insides are tying themselves in knots about seeing him again. A low heat sparks in the bottom of my belly, a tight, stretching kind of feeling that makes me want to squeeze my legs together. He looks exhausted: he has dark rings under his eyes and his hair looks a bit funny, like it needs a wash, but he's still gorgeous. We don't say anything for a while. The car smells like him, slightly smoky, salted almost. Like the sea, even though we live so far away from it. He doesn't look like he knows what to say, so I talk, break the quiet.

'I have to be home soon. My mum wants to leave as soon as I get back to try and beat the traffic down to the coast.'

'Where are you going?'

'Dorset.'

'That's not very specific.'

'Why do you care?'

I'm completely mesmerised by his eyes, which are getting darker with every word we speak. I wonder if he's angry with me, but why would he be? I've not done anything to him; he's the one who buggered off to London and didn't even say goodbye. He puts a hand out – I notice he has bitten down his nails, they weren't like that before – and puts it on my shoulder, a thumb reaching into the gap between my neck and the collar of my shirt, scuffing up and down against the soft skin where I can feel my blood throbbing. His hand twitches, thumb still moving back and forth. Eyes even darker still, he bites his lip and I wish it was my lip.

'We're going to where those big rocks are in the sea. The arch. It's famous. A painting holiday, we go every year for a couple of days. We'll be back next week.'

'Durdle Door. I went there once, when I was a kid.'

'Isn't it so boring?' I reach out now myself and touch the skin of his knee. He has jean shorts on and the hairs on his leg tangle with the loose threads of the cut denim. I smooth them away, run the tip of my finger underneath the edge of the material and he shifts in his seat.

I have him, I know I do.

'No. It's beautiful. We had a lovely time. We were all happy then.'

His voice catches and he looks angry again when he says this; he flinches, and while part of me wonders why he was happy then but not now, another, bigger part of me doesn't really care. I have other things on my mind. I move my hand higher up. I don't want to quiz him about anything, I just want him. He shifts again, looks away out of the window.

'The police were at college this week, asking about Molly,' he tells me, and I bite my teeth together, try not to groan at her intrusion, again. 'Where do you think she is?' He's antsy, squirming, his thumb brushing back and forth, back and forth on my neck. I can feel tension in it.

'She's fine, she emailed me. She's just gone somewhere to hide for a few days because Serena was pissed at her for sleeping with Matt. She always runs off. She's probably embarrassed about last week too – you know, I told you. What she did to me.'

'I know what you told me.' He turns back to me, looks into my face, his hand moves to cup my cheek and I lean into it. 'She's okay? Honestly? Where is she?' I look back at him. I don't want to think about Molly or about where she is.

'Yes, she's fine. I promise. Now, do you want to drive this rust bucket somewhere more private?'

# Rachel

I was not sure what the parenting procedure was for finding a naked drawing of your fifteen-year-old daughter, which was quite possibly – well, definitely, if I'm honest – drawn by your erstwhile teenage lover. The shock of seeing it pulled me out of my dream state back to where I should have been. Awake. Observant. I had been so caught up in trying to forget what had happened years before that I took my eye off what was actually happening in front of me – how could I have been so unutterably stupid? That horrid, soulless boy – there were photos of Vivian all over my house and there was absolutely no way he couldn't have seen them. His eyes – damn them – were far too sharp.

I went into my bedroom and pulled out the bottom drawer of my bedside table, opening the notebook at the bottom and sliding out another sketch he had done, of me. An ink drawing of me looking down at him, my hair in shining Raphaelite curls around my face, an intent gleam in my eyes and a hard-bitten lip. He'd used just one wash of colour, high pink on the cheekbones. I could feel my face burning with that same colour. Oh, *god*, I couldn't bear it. How could he? What did he want? What was wrong with him that he would sleep with us both? Draw us both? I took the drawings down into the kitchen and I burnt them in the sink and rinsed away the black ashes, the bitter stench of smoke stinging my eyes.

I couldn't believe Vivian had just left it in her book. She was so secretive by nature that I couldn't understand why she hadn't squirrelled it away somewhere I wouldn't find it. I used to obsessively rifle through all her things, check her phone, insist on social media passwords, but I'd relented somewhat the past few years. Everything had been so normal. There were no odd antics, no uncontrolled raging and screaming. I had put her previous behaviour down to the trauma of going through an early puberty and losing her grandmother. The accident with Lexie had come so soon after my mother's death that it all seemed inextricably bound up together, and gave me a reason to excuse her horrific actions, her little red hands. She was only nine, a confused, emotionally conflicted little girl who had just lost her nan. She lashed out. It wasn't her fault.

And it had genuinely been fine since we moved to the village and started afresh: she'd made friends, clearly she'd been experimenting with her sexuality – she was growing up – just like I did. I felt sick suddenly at what I was doing. What was wrong with me? Why was I blaming Vivian? She'd done nothing at all to warrant this. Nothing. She was a victim in some sick game Alex was playing. She – like her idiot, idiot mother – had been taken in by a budding psychopath. I couldn't understand what his game plan was: did he get kicks out of hurting people like this? Trying to wreck families? I was an adult; I could step back and understand my own horrible behaviour – that's what six months of authorities-mandated family and solo therapy will do for you – but this would crush Vi. A boy she might think she was in love with, possibly sleeping with, carrying on with her own mother? *Fuck.*

A dark thought writhed in my head – was he involved in Molly's disappearance somehow, Tristan's accident? If betrayal as bad as this came so easily, what else might he be capable of?

I thought of all the strange questions he had asked me about Viv that I had blithely answered; the way he had turned up only when she was out. He must have been watching us, watching the house. Had I felt his eyes on us? Was he the reason I had felt a dark cloud of threat hanging over us in past days? Who was he? Where had he come from? He had fooled me so entirely that I felt ill.

I decided to head out into the garden for half an hour before Vivian got back; I needed the respite that the small industrious insect sounds and the scents of the flowers gave me. I was not overjoyed to realise that I'd been neglecting it like I'd been neglecting Vivian. The earth was scorched, almost powdery in its dryness. Leaves were coarse, parchment-like – they would crumble if I touched them. My flowers had drooped and the colours had faded like they do in old photographs, a garden in sepia tones. It was all turning to dust in front of me.

## Vivian

I'm not sure that was one of my better ideas. I don't think I have ever been so hot and sweaty in my life. Alex's hands are shaking as he does up his shorts, and we are both gasping for air. My knee hurts from banging it on the handbrake. I manage to clamber back into the passenger seat, tug my skirt back down, and we both sit for a while, breathing heavily. There was something missing this time – he was distracted, it wasn't as intense or good as the first time. He couldn't finish. He wasn't here, he was somewhere else, not with me.

I'm trying to think of something to say when I see Alex's wallet on the dashboard, and I reach out to grab it.

'What's your licence photo like, then? Does it make you look like a convict?'

Before I can pick it up he swipes it, rising up off the seat to stuff it in his back pocket. 'Don't.'

'What? Is it that bad?' I try to laugh it off, brushing away the discomfort I'm feeling at his behaviour.

'We should have gone back to the woods,' he says, sweeping his hair back off his forehead, craning his neck and back into a stretch. I watch the muscles in his arms tense and relax and tense again. 'I don't understand why you didn't want to.'

'I just didn't.'

'You don't have to be so weird about it. I just liked it there.'

'I'm not being weird about it! I just don't have time, and it's not an everyday sort of place, okay? Leave it alone!' My voice is too sharp, needle-like in the tight atmosphere we've created in the car. I bite my lip, hard.

He stares out into the trees and I don't know what he is thinking about. This is not going how I thought it would. He is supposed to be grovelling at my feet and begging for my forgiveness. I am not impressed. I attack.

'Alex, do you know my mother?'

The way he freezes, just for a split second, is enough to make all the suspicions I had come roaring back into my head. The picture of him I found in her studio, with great black raven wings. The eyes were all wrong, but I knew it was him.

'Who is your mother?' he asks, swallowing. Smooth neck, rippling.

'Rachel Sanders. Short, curly hair, stupid hippy clothes.' I can almost see his mind ticking, then he relaxes, shoulders leaning back against the seat.

'Does she teach the life drawing class in the village hall? I went a couple of weeks ago, but I never spoke to her. I thought she might have been your mum when I met you but I forgot to mention it. You look a bit like her, your bone structure maybe. Why are you asking?' He smiles and turns his attention back to me, lifting my hair away from my face and tucking it behind my ear. He strokes his thumb over my cheekbone before leaning in and kissing me gently at first, but then firmly, and I almost forget to answer him, swept up on the rush of his returning affection.

'She's stolen your face.' I tell him between kisses, laughing, relieved. 'She's a nightmare.'

He doesn't reply, but I feel him relax further, tension leaving.

'Stolen my face?'

'In her illustrations. I found a drawing of you with big raven wings; it freaked me out for a minute. But she always steals people's faces – it's not the first time I've recognised someone.'

'She sounds like a witch, stealing faces.'

'You have no idea. She's such a nightmare. What's your mum like?'

All the tension rushes back into his body and face, and he moves away from me, pretending to adjust the mirrors in the car, and reclipping his seatbelt.

'You okay to walk from here?'

'What?'

'Are you okay to walk home? I need to go the other way.' He leans past me to open the glove box and digs out a pair of knock-off aviators. Half the gilt is missing off the arms.

After a second of shock has passed, I don't reply to him; I just climb out of the car and slam the door, walking off without looking back, ignoring his wave as he drives past me down the road. He could have dropped me off a bit closer! Every bone in my body is telling me that something is very off about Alex's hot and cold behaviour.

There is something delicious about secrets that you can wheedle out of people, or just uncover through snooping, because then you have influence over them. Really good secrets mean they will do quite a lot for you, and I wonder if Alex has secrets like that. I wonder if he's just... bad. The thought of plucking them all out of him, using them, is delicious.

Mum is in the garden when I get home, looking miserable as usual and clipping the heads off all her manky-looking flowers, letting them fall to the ground. Everything is dead – the weather has murdered all her plants. She should have looked after them better.

'Is the car loaded?' I ask her. 'Have I got time for a quick shower?'

'Not really,' she replies. 'I only need to put your bag in and we're ready to go. Pack up your wires and washbag.'

I go into the house and run up the stairs. There's a weird smell in the air, like burning. God knows what she's been up to today; she's definitely losing it. I decide to have a very quick shower anyway, to wash Alex off me, and then I get everything together and drag my suitcase *bump, bump* down the stairs. The hollow noise reminds me of something and makes me smile.

Mum is already waiting in the car, tuning the radio as I lock the door. I hope I don't have to listen to her nineties crap all the way to bloody Dorset. I squeeze my suitcase in the boot and then get in the car.

I hate these road trips. Mum always tries to talk to me in the car. Apparently, it's easier to talk to people when they aren't directly looking at you. I don't like looking at anyone much, so maybe it's true. I don't really like talking to anyone either, unless I want something, so this is a losing situation for me. I can't wait until I'm old enough to leave home. I might never speak again.

She's fiddling with the sat nav, trying to get it to stick to the inside of the windscreen. Its electronic voice is already demanding we perform a u-turn when possible. I suspect it won't be the last time it asks us to do that.

'I meant to ask you – how are you getting on with your pill? Did you go back to the doctor? What did she say?'

*What? Oh, for god's sake.* 'The same as when we went. She asked me if my period was less painful. She said I can take them back to back if I want so I don't have to have any periods at all if I don't want to.'

'So, you're still using them?'

'Yeah, she gave me another three-month prescription and told me to look out for any weird hormonal stuff, headaches, DVT… you know.'

'Do you take them properly, Vi? You have to take them at the same time every day for them to be really effective.'

'Effective for what? Not having a period? I didn't know that, but I take one as soon as I wake up if you must know, not that it's any of your business. You should just be glad I'm not crippled in pain all the time, like I have been since I was ten!'

I'm pretty bitter about having inherited Mum's stupid early development. Puberty made me act on my worst feelings, do things nobody liked, have rages. Things have been better since then admittedly, because I know how to control myself now, but it was bad for a time. That thing with Lexie, it was too public. I just lost it. That's why they put me in the hospital and *therapy* afterwards. They thought I was mad, but it was just because of all my hormones and stuff. Ugh, that was even worse than fucking periods. The stuff I had to make up so they'd stop looking at me like I was an insect: the apologies, the crying. I didn't mean it. It wasn't my fault.

'You know the pill isn't as effective as condoms, Vi. It won't protect you from STDs. Remember we talked about that?'

This comment sideswipes me – was that what she was getting at all the time? I pretend to look for something in my bag and then sneak a look at her face. It looks like it usually does – she's concentrating on the road. Does she know about Alex? How would she know? She doesn't have any friends here except Steve because he feels sorry for her, the sad loser, so no one to have seen us and reported back, surely? I wonder if that bitch Molly said something to her when they were having one of their cosy little moments and I'm raging at her all over again.

'I was checking your packing earlier,' she says, and I get a sinking feeling in my stomach that I've slipped up somewhere. 'I found the drawing of the girl under the tree. It looks just like you.'

'What!' I say, trying to think on my feet, panicking. 'It hasn't even got a face. Why would you say it was me? I found it at school, I don't know who drew it. I was going to show you because it was good, but I forgot. Everything is going wrong recently, I keep forgetting to do things.' I look at her face, does she believe me? It's hard to tell. Maybe I should cry. That usually works.

'It was an odd thing to find, Viv. You know you can talk to me about anything, don't you? That you're supposed to talk to me?'

'Yes, Mum. You know I would, I promised I would.'

She doesn't look entirely convinced, but maybe I can work on that later. I don't want her interfering with things. As I'm thinking about how I can convince her it isn't me, my phone buzzes. It makes me jump as the girls' chat has gone dead since Molly isn't texting us, and Serena and Tilly aren't texting me, the bitches, but it's Alex. He asks if we're nearly there yet – very funny. Without really thinking about it I tell him Mum found the drawing he did of me, but that I told her it was of someone else and that she believed me because she's such an idiot, but he doesn't reply. I'll call him later and reassure him that she definitely believed me – why wouldn't she? She believes everything I tell her. She always has.

# Rachel

My daughter thought I was stupid. That drawing was quite clearly her, and I knew exactly who had drawn it. I didn't know how I could get her to admit it without revealing that I knew Alex too, knew his talents. I couldn't let her have a relationship with him. There was something wrong with the boy. I decided that when we got to Dorset and she was asleep I would research how to report underage sex to the police. Maybe I could text that policewoman who spoke to Vi about Molly running off? I had her card in my purse. I wanted so badly to call him, to scream my anger and frustration and betrayal down the line at him, let him know that I knew what he was up to, but that wasn't possible since I had deleted all his messages and his number in that misguided attempt to not be tempted to contact him in a weak moment. I wasn't weak any more. I was incandescent.

I didn't think it was worth pressing Vivian about what was going on; she clearly was not going to tell me the truth. I wondered what else she had been lying about. She used to lie before, so easily, with marvellous sincerity. I never heard about the other children bullying her, teasing her, hurting her; about even Lexie, finally, refusing to be friends with her. And then it was too late. Her lies were the veneer that stopped me from seeing the truth. The steering wheel was slick suddenly, my palms sweating with anxiety and gripping it too hard. I forced myself to relax – I didn't want my bad fingers to cramp up. We had another couple of hours' drive ahead of us.

We didn't talk as the scenery flashed past. Viv was engrossed in her phone and I had to concentrate on the stupid sat nav. I always got lost coming over the Downs and I didn't want to get stuck in Newbury again. Or Winchester, for that matter. I hated towns now, found them grey and toxic, suffocating. We passed by the potential urban pitfalls without a wrong turn and I made a mental note to thank Steve for convincing me to buy what was now my new favourite contraption. The dulcet tones of the woman in the little box on the windscreen were almost hypnotic. We were driving through the New Forest before I knew it. It is so beautiful there.

'You should look out for ponies, Viv.' She gave a cursory glance out the window and returned to tapping on her phone.

'I'm not eight, Mum. I don't really care about ponies.'

*You never have*, I thought to myself. When had Vivian ever been interested in animals? She'd never asked for a pet, never shown any interest in other people's. She hadn't even been upset when she found our neighbours' cat grotesquely dead in our garden, presumably killed by a fox. I'd always wanted to get a puppy, but I thought I'd wait until she left home.

We made Dorset in record time, both sweltering from the heat, limp with tiredness. The cottage we always stayed in was a miracle unto itself. It was beautifully tiny, with two shoebox bedrooms and an open plan downstairs, with old beams in the ceiling. I briefly thought that Alex would have to duck in that room, and then I was furious again. I distracted myself by deciding to properly unpack for once, rather than living out of a ramshackle suitcase for the next few days like I usually did. I knew that next door Vivian would have already put everything away neatly and was probably straightening the furniture.

I took out my clothes and turned to the ancient dresser. The drawers were lined with scented paper. I was immediately transported back to Walthamstow, to Mum's bedroom. The dusty, floral smell caught in my throat and my eyes stung. I wished she was there. I wished I'd listened to her. I hadn't listened, and then she died and the accident with Lexie happened and everything went so badly wrong, and it still hurt so much.

I remembered the last time I saw her. I was about to leave for work, looking for my house keys. Vivian was milling around upstairs, getting ready for school, and Mum was in the kitchen. She'd tried to speak to me – she'd almost been wringing her hands, clearly anxious about something, some drawings she said she'd found. But, as always, I'd already got half my mind in the office, on the storyboard I was working on for a huge commercial we were pitching for. I ignored her, told her to stop worrying about nothing. I just left. A negligent kiss, dropped on her soft cheek as I rushed past her and out of the door, smoothing Vivian's hair as she sat on the bottom stair putting her shoes on. You'd think I would have learnt to say goodbye properly to the people I loved.

I got a call from school to say that Vivian hadn't been picked up – I can still hear the phone ringing and ringing as I tried to call the house. I ended up texting and asking a neighbour to go in and check while I tried to get back as quickly as possible. I was too much a coward to just get there myself, to open the door.

The ambulance was already pulling away as I turned onto Maynard Road, a small crowd gathered on the pavement outside our house. Grief vultures, their pitying eyes leaching from me as I tried to run with heavy, stumbling dream legs.

I never did find those bloody drawings she was on about.

The present rushed back to me as I flinched back from the painful memory, spinning my head. I suddenly felt like I had hot lead in my stomach, burning, and there was a metallic taste in my mouth that made me nauseous. I barely made it to the bathroom.

# *London*

Sometimes when she was worried about something, truly worried, she felt it as an ache in her bones. A dragging weight she carried around, like when Rachel had been away at university with that awful man. Carol was sick with it again. There was something wrong, and she didn't know what to do. Despite talking to Vivian, despite Vivian saying what sounded like the right things, like healthy things, there was just something wrong. Maybe there had always been something wrong. She had tried to reassure the little girl that her mum didn't hate her, that she was busy because she needed to do much more work than a normal mum might because it was just her on her own, but she'd got the distinct impression that Vivian didn't actually care, but was just pretending to. It wasn't normal.

It was compounded by the way Rachel was behaving. She had retreated into herself and Carol didn't know how to reach her. Home late every night, out first thing. Exhausted. She had been like this after Vivian was born. Manic. Had to go to every baby group, had her weighed twice a week. Rocked her endlessly the nights she screamed incessantly, walking up and down the house fit to wear holes in the carpet, refusing help. Always prone to obsessing over everything: it all had to be perfect, all the time. Carol felt pulled between them, stretched to the point of breaking.

The kettle bubbled and clicked off, juddering on its stand. Carol picked up Rachel's travel mug and made her a coffee, the smell of it comforting somehow, reminding her of mornings she and Rachel's father David had sat in the kitchen drinking it together. He'd always made the best coffee. She could hear footsteps in the rooms above, doors opening and closing as her daughter and grand-daughter prepared themselves for another day. She felt tears start suddenly, the banality of the morning routine so at odds with the dread at her centre. Rachel bustled into the kitchen. 'Oh, thanks, Mum!' she said, spying her coffee. She picked up her handbag and rifled through it, rattling keys and putting in the phone that was always glued to her hand, before picking up the cup. 'Right, I need to run, I won't be late tonight, I promise.'

'Wait, please,' said Carol, her heart pounding, the words spilling out before she could think twice about them. 'We need to talk, love, it's important.'

'Right now? I really need to go, Mum, I've got a meeting first thing—'

But Carol couldn't hold it in. 'No, it can't wait. It's Vivian. I'm really worried about her – I found some drawings in her room, you need to look at them.'

'Drawings? Of what?'

'Rachel, please, will you just wait? I can get them, I've got them here—' But Rachel turned away.

'Mum, I can't – I'm sure it's nothing, okay? Just kid's stuff… you worry too much, Vivian is fine, I have to go – love you!' She pressed a quick kiss to Carol's cheek and then went down the hallway and out of the front door; it slammed behind her as the wind caught it. As she did,

Carol heard smaller footsteps going back up the stairs. She gasped, feeling short of breath. Had Vivian been listening again? She rubbed her face, pressing her fingers against her eyes. Guilt at betraying Vivian's trust joined the worry.

'Vivian!' she called. 'Are you ready, darling? Time to get your shoes on!' There was no reply. Gritting her teeth she went to the foot of the stairs and called again. 'Vivian?' No answer. She felt heavy footed as she walked up the steps, imagining the conversation she might be about to have, how to explain breaking her promise. She stopped at the top of the narrow staircase, hand to chest, her heart fluttering like a panicked bird in a cage.

Vivian was standing on the landing, her small face white, her breath hissing between clenched teeth as her hands came up. 'You said you wouldn't tell,' she whispered. 'You *promised*.'

Instinctively, Carol turned away from the hate she saw in Vivian's face. The uneven carpet never had been re-pinned. Small hands outstretched, and Carol's last feelings were of weightlessness, a flash of pain, darkness.

# *Vivian*

We've only been here five minutes and Mum is chucking up in the bathroom. I've just been in the car with her for the eternal afternoon hell drive; if I catch her stupid bug I'm going to kill her. I hate this cottage. It hasn't got any Wi-Fi. I'm not impressed at all. I can barely turn around in this bedroom, and I'm a bloody midget. Everything stinks like old people. I can't believe I'm stuck here for *days*.

I've already unpacked, and Mum's still in the bathroom puking so I shout to her that I'm going to go for a walk. I grab my rucksack and fill up my water bottle, then head out of the door. I think I hear her shouting something down to me, but I ignore her. The weather is still scorching, but it feels even heavier now. It's close, as Nana used to say. You can feel it touching you all the time with hot, slick fingers. I hope there will be a sea storm that we can watch from the windows. We're really near to the cliffs here.

The path to the top of Swyre Head is worn and pitted with pebbles; they are smooth and shine like glass. Thousands of feet have probably polished them on their way up here. I wonder how many of those feet never came down again. There is only a rickety, twisted wire-and-stake fence, broken in places, between me and the brink. I edge up as close as I can and look down at the waves smashing below, pounding against the beach again and again. I thought it would be calm with the day so bright but the sea attacks the shore relentlessly, it booms and crashes, and I think I can feel the vibrations underneath my feet, absorb its energy somehow. There's a line of purple on the horizon, and a hot breeze that smells of salt, reminding me of how Alex tastes, pushes at me, drying my lips. I can feel something in the air.

I amble along the path for the best view of the massive stone arch and the bay behind me. I take a couple of pictures and send one to Alex, then spend ages putting the same one online, using filters to enhance the shadows on the crevices in the cliffs. They look like an army of nightmare creatures, with long reaching arms and scratching fingers. Maybe they have come out of the arch, the gateway between the sea and sky, ready to rend and conquer. The creepy thoughts make my hairs rise on my neck and I laugh and the wind steals the sound away from my lips. Maybe I like it here after all.

# *Rachel*

Porcelain always feels so blissfully cold. It was the only pleasant thing about that particular moment. I wondered if I'd eaten something bad, but when had I last eaten, even? The days had been falling into each other, tumbling senselessly, like they had before. Maybe it was delayed motion sickness from the journey, or an overdose of rage to the system.

I heard Vivian leave, ignoring me when I asked her to get me a glass of water. I felt like I didn't know her any more. The daughter I'd had at the start of the summer had been usurped by the disconcerting, silent child of my memory, all the oddness, the otherness, resurfacing. I thought she had changed, but it was still there underneath. She had just hidden it from me.

My phone rang, an unknown mobile number. I didn't want to answer, but I had to. I had a suspicion of who it might be, and I was right.

'Rachel, it's me, I—'

'Stop. Just stop. I know what you've been doing, Alex. What the hell is wrong with you?'

'Nothing, you don't understand, please I need to tell you—' But I cut him off again, furious, furious with myself about how the sound of his voice made me feel, even then.

'No, *you* don't understand, Alex, you sick little bastard. I'm going to tell the police what you have been doing – my daughter is fifteen years old! Fifteen, she—'

'Please listen, Rachel – I'm sorry, it's not what you think, I promise, you just need to know...' He trailed off, sounding breathless, noises in the background fading away. Silence hung between us. What could he say? What could I?

'What do I need to know, Alex?'

'I didn't... I didn't plan any of this. I found you because I wanted to understand her, the truth about her, not you... I thought maybe you'd remember... I thought you would *recognise* me...' His conflicted voice trailed away again, but his words triggered something in the recesses of my mind.

Recognise? *Find* us? I had recognised him – he had reminded me of someone that very first night I saw him... I'd chosen to ignore it, though, thinking it didn't matter. Remember. *Remember.* Oh, god, no. I felt the blood drain from my face, a rushing sensation that rocked me.

Lexie's pretty eyes. He looked nothing like Lexie, but his eyes! Of course, they were the same as his mother's, his sister's. Those pretty eyes. I hadn't been able to place them in his grown, male face, so I had ignored my intuition that he reminded me of someone. His hair was so much darker than I remembered – the contrast had fooled me. He'd been so blonde as a child. All the revulsion I felt toward myself for the affair expanded inside me and it took every ounce of control I had not to be sick again.

'Liam,' I whispered, clutching my phone so hard I thought it might crack. 'Liam. Oh, god, Liam.'

'Finally she figures it out. Well done, Rachel.' Confliction gone, sarcasm bathed his voice instead, and it didn't suit him; it made him sound hard and uncaring. He *was* hard and uncaring. 'Is Vivian with you?' he demanded, brushing my realisation, my remembering, away, stoking again the blazing fury that he had sought to come between us like this, in such a vile way.

'I'm not telling you!' The line beeped as another call tried to connect; I couldn't hear anything else he was saying, so I shouted over him: 'Just leave us alone!'

I hung up, and I put my head in my hands. What had I done? Who had I let into my life? I should have realised who he was. I cast my mind back over those hours we spent together, his strange questions about Vivian: what she was like, our relationship. There was only one reason he would have tracked us down, ingratiated himself with us, entwined himself so thoroughly in both our lives.

Revenge. He was here to punish us, ruin us, for what happened to Lexie. An eye for an eye.

Shaking, brushing away useless tears, I picked up my phone to call Vivian, to find her, warn her, when I saw that I had a voice message from Abi. I dialled in, expecting it to tell me that Molly had come home, desperate for a small relief.

'Rachel?' I felt a peculiar shift deep in my chest as I listened, the fluttering hope I'd had that Molly was safe being shredded by terror. Her voice. 'Rachel... the police.' The words caught and tore in her throat, choking her. 'They found her, my baby, they found her body in the woods, and now they are at your house. Why are they at your house? What did you do? What did you *do?*' Then she broke, wrenching cries echoed down the crackling line, silenced abruptly by the end of the message.

I dropped the phone, fingers nerveless, ice cold. Molly hadn't run away. Molly was dead.

I had to find Vivian.

# Vivian

The wind has really picked up. My face is stinging, my hair thrashing at it, sharp strands getting in my mouth and eyes. The thin purple line on the horizon is topped now with billowing clouds, dirty yellow, grey and blackening. Swelling up like bruises. I should get back down to the cottage. All the other people who were on the path are gone; I could be the only person in the world up here, a queen on high. I struggle to turn away from the scene, but I do, pulling my feet and legs around to follow the smooth stones back to my mother.

My phone is ringing. It's Alex.

'Where are you?' he says, loudly.

'Er, hi, Alex. I'm fine, thanks. You know where I am. I just sent you a photo. I'm in Dorset, idiot.'

'So am I – are you still on the cliff path?'

'What? Why are you here?'

'Are you still on the path?' His voice is clipped, like he's running.

'Yes, but...' He hangs up on me. Why the hell has he followed us here? I stop at the top of the cliff path, to think. How will I explain him to my mother if she sees him with me? Why did he sound so weird? I am beginning to think that maybe Alex is more trouble than he is worth, that maybe it's time to just start all over again. I've done it before. And if someone like him is interested in me, not

Molly, then I don't have anything to worry about, do I? I can be whoever I want to be. I don't need either of them, any more.

I don't want Alex to find me until I have figured out what the hell is going on. I am debating trying to call him again from here, high on the cliff, where the reception is best, when suddenly Mum comes running up to me out of nowhere, making me jump. She grabs me with hard fingers, digging them into my arms.

'Ow, Mum, what are you doing? Get off!'

'Come back to the cottage, Vivian, quickly. We need to get back.'

'Why? What's going on?'

'Oh, god, darling, I don't know how to say this – Abi, she just called, she left a message…'

'What?'

'They found Molly. They found her, in the woods. She's dead.' Her face creases and reddens horribly. 'She said the police are at our house, Vivian. Why are the police at our house?'

*Shit.*

# Rachel

Vivian was silent, shocked, when I told her what Abi had told me. She collapsed, pulling me down beside her. She had gone painfully white, staring at nothing, hands clenching and unclenching in her lap, her lips moving soundlessly. I scanned the edges of her face, the face I loved. She was so beautiful, like a perfect line drawing, colourless. All the colour must have been on her inside.

I took one cold hand in mine, rubbed it. It was no use, mine were just as cold as hers. There was suddenly no warmth left, the cauldron heat of the summer had died away, cooling the sweat on my skin to make me shiver. Vivian was the same, trembling. Her eyes were flickering from side to side as if she were reading something on a page in front of her.

'How... how can she be dead? She emailed me... she emailed me yesterday... she can't be dead.'

I could barely make out her mumbles. I didn't know what to say to her; I just kept on massaging her cold, stiff hand between mine. 'Who would hurt her? She wouldn't hurt herself, I know she wouldn't.' Her voice sounded like it was coming from somewhere else, mechanical, forced. She began to rock, almost imperceptibly, back and forth. She pulled her hand away from mine and put both to her face. 'This isn't happening. This isn't happening. I'm dreaming.' She took her hands away from her face and stared at her delicate pink palms, rubbed one over the other, washing them in the air.

'Darling, I'm so sorry, you aren't dreaming. We need to get up – we can't stay here now.' Thoughts of a vengeful Alex – no, *Liam* – surged back into my mind. Did he know where we were? Vivian could have told him where we were staying. He could have been anywhere. 'Vivian, we need to get back to the cottage, my love, I have to tell you something, we need to talk about something…'

She ignored me, still staring at her hands.

The weather was about to explode, I could feel it juddering in the air, static. A low, aching rumble of thunder spread out over the sea and the wind dropped away to nothing. The water went still, like everything was being sucked into the storm clouds on the horizon. I felt like my mind was fracturing: misery, anger, fear; a maelstrom of emotion that matched the brewing storm, that I couldn't get a handle on. I had to warn Vivian about the danger we were in. I opened my mouth to try and catch the right words to tell her, I tried to put my arm around her, but she pushed me off.

And then it was too late and there was no time left for us.

'Rachel! Rachel! Get away from her!' The faint shout, the familiar voice, it rang in my ears, blending with the whine of shock. Then he was there, the mysterious boy who had so absorbed the last few weeks of our lives.

I was so angry at him. I jumped up, put myself between him and my daughter. 'What do you want, Liam? Haven't you already done enough? Go away!'

'Alex?' This from Vivian, eyes huge in her white face as she looked up at us both. 'Mum, how do you… what, wait… *Liam?*' Her incredulous words seemed to ring in the air. Alex – Liam, Alex, so many lies – stood in front of us, between us and the drop, and swung toward her, knuckles yellow on the clenched fists of his hands.

'You remember me, then? You fucking remember, now?' he hissed, raw and vicious.

'Please calm down, we can talk about this,' I said, trying so hard to be firm, calm.

'I don't understand. You aren't him. You aren't. You're Alex. You're my Alex.' Vivian's trembling voice as she used it sounded dry and afraid. Despite her denial, I could almost see her clever mind clicking everything together, so much faster than mine. I could still barely process the little blond boy of my memory and the dark almost-man before me. Lexie's brother. Lucy's son.

Here to hurt us.

'You ruined our lives!' he shouted, making small, jerky movements, shifting his weight from foot to foot. I had no idea what he was about to do, what he was capable of. Had he hurt Molly? Who else but him?

Vivian spoke again, more decisively than before. 'I didn't mean it, with Lexie. Is that why you're here? It was an accident, please, I'm so sorry!' Her face was crumpling, threatening tears, but her calculating eyes didn't move from his face.

'You are a fucking liar.' Frothing spit gathered at the corners of his mouth. 'You knew exactly what you were doing, you planned it, I know you did. You plan everything!' I put myself between them again, shielding Vivian. I had to protect her; I had failed her before, I couldn't again.

'Please come away from the edge, Liam.' I deliberately said his name again, forcing it past the fear in my throat. My mind was frantically trying to think of how to get us

273

both away from him. I could barely take my eyes off the sharp drop, not five feet away. Why wasn't there a fence? The waves had started again in earnest, smashing against the beach below, their power reverberating up the cliff to our feet.

He stepped toward me, and I saw some of the tension leave his body: his shoulders drooped. 'I just wanted the truth. Even if it was an accident, it ruined everything, *everything*. I don't know what I'm doing any more.' He was shaking his head, glancing between us, anguished now, unsure. He suddenly just looked young, lost. 'Rachel, it's not just that, there's more you don't know—'

I interrupted him, trying to calm him further, my hands spread out between us like fans. 'It *was* an accident, Liam. That *is* the truth. Vivian didn't mean to hurt Lexie. She was just a little girl.' I tried to inject a consoling note into my voice, talking down a panicked animal with soothing tones. It didn't work. He shook his head.

'No. You're wrong. It wasn't an accident, Rachel. She did it on purpose. I know that now.' I saw him take a deep breath, tears starting in his eyes. 'And I think you need to ask her about your mum. Do you honestly believe she just fell down the stairs? That she wasn't pushed? You told me, you told me that she knew there was a problem with Vivian, that you didn't listen. What did she know? What did she know about Vivian?'

The accusation hit me like a hammer, another piece of a horrific, bloodstained puzzle. No. *No.* I didn't want to believe him. He was a liar, a cheat. He had found us to do exactly this, to lie, to hurt us, to break us apart. But I couldn't block out the whispering, the voice in my subconscious that I had so firmly repressed for years.

Vivian just stared at him, eyes like coals. I could almost feel the wrath inside her, pulsating. Was it ever not there, that secret fury? *My mother, falling.*

'She's dead.' His voice cracked. I snapped back to him, my attention wrenched away from my daughter, who was still sitting on the ground, her arms wrapped around her knees, so tiny and frail, a doll.

'What? My mother? You know she is – I told you she was.'

'No. My sister. My sister is dead.' Tears spilling now, running down his face. 'She killed herself. She couldn't go outside, she wouldn't eat. She had panic attacks if we left her alone. Her face... how could you not know your own daughter was sick in the head?'

Hearing it from someone else, the painful idea that something was wrong with Vivian, churned everything up. It had never really gone away, however deeply I had tried to bury it, bury us, in a place where I thought I could watch her every move.

Her silence was deafening.

'Please, Liam, please don't do this to yourself.' I tried to touch him, but he reared back, so close now to the edge that it made me nauseous. The sky moaned as the wind picked up, the first droplets of rain spattering the hard soil underneath our feet, the smell of the earth filling my head.

'Rachel, you don't understand. I know you don't believe me.' The pain in his breaking voice lashed me. This wasn't happening. Then something in his face changed, and a small strange smile appeared through the tears. 'I have to make you see her.' He looked down. Another breath. 'I wasn't in London last week, Vivian. I was fucking your mother.'

He watched her, waiting.

'No!' she screamed.

I felt the colour of shame suffuse my cheeks as Vivian sprang up. There was no denying what had happened, she wasn't stupid. It was obvious he was telling the truth, and I knew my guilt was written all over my face. And her reaction was every bit as awful as I had feared it might be, from the second I found the drawing of her naked body.

# London

The days had been passing in an awful haze since the funeral. It was the first day that she'd come back to work, to stilted smiles and uncomfortable how-are-you's. No one ever seemed to know what to do with grief. It was too big.

Rachel had spent the morning ploughing through the emails that had accumulated in her absence, her thoughts straying constantly to Vivian on her own first day back in school. Even in all the time they had been together these past weeks, she had barely set eyes on her little girl except for when she remembered to feed her and put her to bed. She had tried to speak to her about her Nana, but her own heartbreak had got in the way, resulting in her sobbing and clutching at her daughter until the poor thing wriggled away and ran up to her room. She was too young to understand.

She was just thinking about getting herself a coffee to keep herself going when her phone began to vibrate in her handbag. It was the school number. Feeling nauseous – Vivian must have got upset, it was too soon to have gone back – she tapped the screen to answer. The word 'accident' wiped out every thought in her head; she couldn't hear what the person on the other end of the line was saying. *Accident. Hospital.*

Dropping everything, she grabbed her bag and ran from the office, not even stopping to explain where she was going. The journey seemed to take for ever, each stop on the tube an agony of waiting. All the other people, just sitting there, oblivious to the panic that was swamping her.

By the time she reached Whipps Cross hospital, shoving money at the taxi driver who had been outside the station, she was drenched in sweat. What had happened to Vivian? Where was she? She ran into the A&E, scanning the crowd. The man at the door tried to stop her, to speak to her, but she saw Miss Avon sitting on a chair at the back of the waiting room and brushed him aside, and ran to her.

'What's happened? Where's Vivian? Oh, my god!' As she reached her daughter's teacher she realised that the whey-faced woman was covered in blood, streaks of it down her skirt, a perfect, small bloody handprint above the waistband, glaring against the pale material of her shirt. 'Where is she?' She felt her stomach contract with terror. Not again, not her daughter. She'd just lost her mother, she couldn't lose Vivian too. *I promise, I promise,* she thought, *I'll do anything if she's okay, anything at all to keep her safe.*

Miss Avon looked up at her, her eyes glittering.

'It's not Vivian's,' she whispered, clenching her fists in her lap, looking down at the bloodstains.

'What? I don't understand, what's happened?'

'It's not Vivian's blood. It's Lexie Coleman's. Vivian attacked her. She stabbed her face with my scissors – she took them when I wasn't looking… her little face…' Her own face crumpled, and she looked like she was about to vomit. 'She stabbed her in her eye. She's blinded her, she could have *killed* her. What is *wrong* with her?'

The look of disgust on the teacher's face turned Rachel's world upside down. Her own blood was ringing in her ears, she was barely aware of a nurse appearing at her side and pulling her gently away, leading her down a gleaming corridor, light bouncing off the floor, into a curtained-off cubicle where her small daughter sat on a blue blanketed bed, looking down at her little red hands.

'Vivian,' she whispered, sitting beside her on the bed, not able to bring herself to touch her. 'Vivian, what did you do?'

Her daughter's blank face turned up to hers.

'It wasn't my fault, Mummy,' she said calmly, blood on her cheek, on her clothes, everywhere. 'It wasn't my fault. She deserved it.'

# Vivian

I can't process what I am seeing. His face, as he looks back at her. At *her*. And my mother, she's looking at me, somehow flushed and sick-yellow at the same time. All that time, when he was ignoring me, when I was wanting him, needing him, he was with her! My mother! I picture them writhing together, talking about me, laughing at me, and something snaps in my head.

'You are supposed to love *me*! *Me*, not her!' The words scream out of my throat, hurting, and before I realise it I am in front of him, hammering my useless fists against his chest. 'You liar! How could you do all those things with me and her too?'

He shoves me backwards easily, overpowering me with one hand. I nearly knock Mum over, feel her clutch at me, keep me upright.

'I just wanted to get the truth about what you are! You're a monster! Lexie knew you were evil, but no one believed her. Everyone said it was an accident, everyone. You don't care about anything, you're incapable.'

I cannot cope with the disgust in his voice. It's not true, what he's saying to me – I do care! Then my mother pushes in front of me again, trying to pull him away from the cliff edge, to talk him down, and every fibre of me screams, *How dare she touch what belongs to me!* Her focus is on him, and I see again the way he is looking at her as her hair whips around her face: he has never looked at me like that, never.

She isn't taking any notice of me at all, and I realise that if she believes him then I have nothing left to lose. I don't have to pretend any more. 'You whore! You disgusting, old *whore*. How could you? He was *mine*!'

She turns to me, looking so tragic that I almost smile, and then I throw out my arms, as hard as I can. The air whistles from her lungs as she staggers backwards toward the brink, and falls.

# Rachel

I stumbled and landed painfully on the rough, stony ground, winded by the shove, pain blooming in my chest. Vivian's eyes were wild, her teeth small and white and sharp in her screaming mouth. Her fingers clawed, and she went for my face, her nails scraping burning furrows in my cheeks.

Liam lunged. He grabbed her by her hair, making her shriek with anger and pain, and pulled her away from where I was curled, defenceless, on the ground. But they were too close to the edge; fear and vertigo spun my head and I couldn't catch my breath.

'You're blind, Rachel! Look at her! You're not safe, why can't you see that?' Liam had her by the neck, choking her.

I got to my knees and I tried to reach out and hold her and pull her away from him, but she kicked me, smashed at me with her feet, knocking me down yet again in her struggle, in her blind wrath.

'Tell her the truth, Vivian! Tell her the truth about why you hurt my sister! Tell her what you did to your own grandmother! Rachel, Lexie told me that Vivian was walking alone, the morning your mother died. She must have pushed her, then gone to school as if nothing had happened! No one listened, but it was true, I know it was.'

Trapped in Liam's brutal embrace, looking down at me, her familiar mask slipped back into place, but it was too late. I had seen her true face now and I could not unsee it.

Molly in the woods, my mother falling.

'I didn't do anything! I didn't hurt Nana! He's lying! He's trying to turn you against me! Mum, you have to believe me!' I could see her nails digging into his arm, scratching him like she had scratched me, and her eyes, her colourless eyes, caught mine as they so rarely did, and something broke apart inside me. I didn't believe her, not this time. Not again.

The world was black, roaring. A flash of lightening scored the sky and the rain beat down.

# Vivian

Everything is white hot: the pain of his fist in my hair, the hate. How could this have happened to me? How did I let myself be tricked, by that bitch's *brother* of all people! Liam Coleman, a background boy, a *nothing* boy! Fury in my mouth, searing and bitter as blood. I remember now what his sister's blood felt like rushing over my hand, that perfect colour. I fight the arm that is pinned across my neck. I want to hurt him.

'Stop lying!' He uses his arms to shake me like a dog. My mother is just collapsed on the grass, holding her hands to her cheeks, then looking at her bloody fingers. 'You're insane!' he shouts, making my ears ring.

'It's not true, it's not! I'm so sorry, please don't hurt me, I love you, please! I loved my Nana, I didn't hurt her. It wasn't me!' I spit out the lies like bullets, anything to get him off me.

'You don't love me, you want to control me and own me like you do with everyone you decide you want! *I found Molly, Vivian!* I wanted to go back, back to the woods to think, to the place *you* took me: it was special, and she was there. You left her there! I was actually beginning to think that maybe Lexie was wrong about you, but she wasn't, was she? You almost had me fooled too. I know everything now, what you're really like, you heartless bitch. I won't let you hurt anyone else. I know what you did. Just tell me the truth! You did it on purpose, you blinded my sister on purpose because she saw you for what you are! She was afraid of you.'

I cringe at his words as they fall about us. Molly's hair, black-blood drenched in the light from the moon, running and twisting in the stream. Lexie's eyes. My mother is gaping, looking from face to face – does she believe him? She can't. I need her to believe that I haven't done any of this. She always believes me! I scratch and writhe trying to get away. We're so close to the edge, but I don't think he even realises. I can hear the sea smashing the cliff beneath us. I pull, and kick, but I can't get him anywhere it will hurt him.

'Mum, help me!' She's just sitting there like a fucking idiot, her hair slick wet from the pouring rain, pasted in ribbons on her cheeks alongside the scarlet marks I shouldn't have made. I kick and twist again, waiting for a chance.

Then his grip loosens, slippery now, just for a heart-beat.

I get my chin down and I bite his arm as hard as I can, so hard it hurts, and now I really taste blood, iron in my mouth as his skin splits, tears beneath my teeth. I don't let go, and he cries out in pain. I love the sound.

He lets go of my hair to try and prise me off his arm, and as soon as I feel his hold on my neck slacken enough I let go and I wriggle down, and I'm free. I turn and I push him as hard as I can. I want to kill him. I want to see him fall. He has ruined everything, this is all his fault.

'Vivian!' My mother's voice above the shrieking wind reaches me, but doesn't. 'Vivian, stop!' I shove him again; he's hurt and off-balance, holding his injured arm, and it's my turn now. I put my shoulder into it. Admittedly, it's not as easy as pushing an interfering old bitch down the stairs, but maybe I'm stronger than I thought. He slips and falls to the wet ground, blood pumping through his fingers. I am the last one standing.

'You want the truth, Liam? Really? I *hated* your sister! She was as worthless as you are!' I kick him as hard as I can in the stomach – there's a satisfying grunt – then I stamp at his face with my foot, trying to push him over the edge. I'm vaguely aware of my mother getting to her feet behind us. I swear, if she touches me, she'll be the next one to go over.

The sky breaks, thunder cracking so loud – only it doesn't just come from the air, but the earth beneath us too, as the cliff begins to give way, to shake and shudder, and fall. He somehow scrambles away, but I'm too slow: I start to slide and I only just cling on to the dead grass, crumbling soil and stones slithering away, dragging at me.

'Mum! Mummy, help me!' I scream as my fingers dig into the earth, feel the dagger pain of my nails splitting, and she's there, oh, thank god, she's there, she believes me, she always believes me! She throws herself towards me, arms and hands reaching out for mine. Her fingers gripping, she has me, she'll save me. It's not too late.

'Did you hurt Molly?' she shouts, but I can barely hear her over the wind. 'Did you? *Did you hurt my mother?*'

I can't help it. I laugh.

# Rachel

I let her fall.

# Rachel

Her face, her bloody mouth, red teeth, screaming with laughter. I see it every night in my dreams. How could she laugh? She looked just like her father in that frozen moment. Conception and end. I let her fall. I watched her go. I hoped the cliff would take me too, but it didn't. It left me there, hollow and numb, staring, Liam beside me, weeping.

I watched my daughter die.

They uncovered her, down on the beach in the soil and the stones, her body as broken and twisted as her heart had been. I was afraid they wouldn't find her, that she would haunt me always, but she is dead and buried, nothing now but a drawing in a book, her face immortalised in print with her dark prince beside her.

Those endless hours in the police station: interviews, interrogations. Did you know? Did you know? Vivian. Tristan's car. Molly, skull crushed by a rock, found in a stream in the woods, a bloated horror. Those long showers she took. It was all her. Liam made a call to the police, when he found Molly among the watching trees, told them what he knew, who he suspected, then decided to take matters into his own hands. He wanted to save me, but I saved myself.

After finding Molly's body the police got a search warrant for our house. They broke the door down not an hour after we left, searched Vivian's room. They found a small pink laptop underneath a drawer, underneath the whole unit. I'd never have thought to look there. Molly's laptop, to send emails from Molly's account. An unutterable cruelty, making the people who loved her believe that she was still alive while she rotted, alone in the woods. Alone. We don't know how Vivian lured her there, in the dark. Maybe Molly thought it was an adventure, an excitement. The forest at night. Friends. A rock from a stream. Those long, long showers, washing away what she'd done. They found the search history on her phone too: mechanics, brake lines. You can find anything on the internet these days. It's how Alex – Liam – found me, through my work website. I should have changed my name when we left London, but it was my father's name, my mother's. I hadn't wanted to lose that link with them. I never thought something like this could happen – I refused to. I was blind.

He was at the inquest. Liam Coleman. He wanted to speak to me, to tell me he was sorry, but what does he have to be sorry for? If it hadn't been him, it would have been something or someone else, some other time. Vivian was unstable. She wasn't safe, and Molly paid the price. I only hope he can come back from this, make something of his life. I told him I'd look for his art, in the future. I made him promise to not stop drawing. I made him promise to forget about me.

All this pain. Maybe I should have listened to my mum at the very beginning when she'd told me to end the pregnancy. Vivian was a poison that Ciaran left in me, in my blood, in my womb. I'm so ashamed. I should have realised, I should have known. Maybe I did know. I didn't do enough to protect other people – I was only protecting myself with my lies. Now Tristan is dead, my sweet Molly is dead, and it's my fault.

I've put the cottage on the market, selling it cheaply in the hope someone will be able to put aside the fact that a teenage murderer and a murderer's mother used to live there. I've found a new town, far away, bigger, more anonymous. Somewhere I can remake myself, because I don't want to hide any more. I want to be free. I need to be free, for her.

I stroke the mound of my swelling belly. I won't make the same mistakes again, I promise.

I hope she has Lexie's pretty eyes.

# Acknowledgements

I'll admit that I never used to read the acknowledgements in books until I began to write myself, and I found it astounding just how many people it takes to produce a novel. I just hope I have managed to remember all mine.

Many thanks to my editor Louise Cullen for her vision and enthusiasm for my work, and to all the team at Canelo for their promotion and support and especially for the fantastic cover art by Lisa Brewster. Orange is the new everything.

Thanks to my agent Felicity Blunt and the team at Curtis Brown – especially ever-helpful Rosie Pierce, and Anna Davis, editing masterclass supremo.

To the great people at the Bath Novel Award, thank you for that incredible feeling of seeing my book on the longlist – I won't forget it.

I could not have written this book without the support of some incredible friends I made along the way. Marija Maher-Diffenthal, thank you for your cleverness, kindness, generosity and colourfulness. Liz Webb, thank you for always making me laugh and helping me nail the ending. Katherine Tansley, thank you for that final beta read that made me brave enough to click send. Jo McGrath, thank you for letting me read Hazel's burgeoning adventures, they are a joy. Each of you, our weekly lockdown Zooms kept me sane, and I can't wait to get back to the library with you all. All the rest of the Faber gang, thank you for making that six months so much fun – and especial thanks to Ips and Abbey for some early beta reads.

Thanks to the lovely Sophia-Marie Spiers, coffee friend, cheerleader and other-class-spy, co-conspirator and sweary WhatsApper. I can't wait to see your novel hit the shelves.

My various online course classmates too – Jennie Godfrey, Gautam Das, Jo Surridge, Jennifer Weller especially – much love and thanks for the support.

Frances Taylor, blogging buddy, thank you for your beta read. I hope you get out of Twitter jail soon #FreeFran.

Lottie Houghton, Kelly Houghton, Cliodhna Gillespie, Helen Etherington – you're the best friends a girl could ask for, thank you, I love you all.

The One Son Club, thank you for general enthusiasm and excitement and lovely cricket afternoons.

Josie, my favourite (only, but still favourite) sister – thank you for reading those endless first drafts. I hope you can bring yourself to read the polished version. Dad, same. Mum, thanks for being you. I wouldn't be me without you. Thanks as always and for ever to my long-suffering husband Mark and his exemplary question mark counting skills, and to my brilliant son Rian for giving the best hugs ever. Evie, you're a good girl too. Yes you are. Thanks for keeping my feet warm while I typed.

Finally, but definitely most importantly of all, thank you Ed Archer. One conversation with you sparked this entire journey and I can never thank you enough. Mate, you know it.